POWER AND FURY

EDEN CHRONICLES, 1 (2021 EDITION)

JAMES ERITH

POWER AND FURY
(aka THE POWER AND THE FURY)
First Published in 2013

2021 Edition
Jerico Press

Copyright © James Erith 2013

POWER AND FURY (2021) is written in UK English.
Paperback ISBN: 978-1-910134-50-4
Digital ISBN-13: 978-1-910134-28-3
(2021 edition is not compatible with Audiobook)

Original versions of The Power and The Fury:
Paperback ISBN-13: 978-1-910134-04-7
Hardback ISBN-13: 978-1-910134-05-4

AVAILABLE ON MOST DIGITAL PLATFORMS

www.JamesErith.com

To Florence

Eden Chronicles started out as a story for my Godchildren:
Isabella, Daisy, Archie, Iso and Ernest.

CONTENTS

ONE

A DREAM IS GIVEN

Archie tensed.

No, it was nothing, he thought, just a gust of wind rattling a loose tile on the roof, or the strange 'yessss!' sound that his twin, Daisy, shouted when scoring goals in her sleep. Then again, it could be Isabella sleep-talking about her science experiments. He took a deep breath as he recalled that her last sleep-talking dream was something to do with atmospheric pressure and barometers or some other weather-related thing.

Archie smiled and rolled over; who else but his sisters could dream of such odd and opposite things–football and weird scientific experiments.

He rubbed his eyes and yawned. His eyelids closed but, just before they locked tight, he noticed something above Daisy's head that forced them open.

A shudder ran through his body.

He closed his eyes, counted to three and opened them again, but the object was still there.

Archie gasped as he stared, his eyes unable to blink.

An angel?

But it couldn't be an angel... when had anyone truly seen an angel? His brain whirred. Then it had to be a ghost, or an alien. But ghosts weren't real either?

A cold sweat broke out over his forehead. He couldn't move a muscle. If it wasn't an angel or a ghost, he thought, then what was it?

As he concentrated, he saw a large, strange species of what appeared to be a spider with a covering like a thin, opaque jellyfish and spraying blue forks of electricity from its abdomen?

But what was it doing hovering over Daisy?

He exhaled as quietly as he could, desperate not to draw attention to himself. And now that his eyes were adjusting to the light, Archie could see delicate claw-like contraptions at the end of the thing's long slender legs moving in perfect time with Daisy's every breath.

As if the claws were somehow... feeding her.

Archie's heart pounded as a flurry of questions crowded his brain: Does it hurt? What if it's poison? What if it comes towards him–what then? Will it do the same to me, the same to Isabella, Old Man Wood, Mrs Pye–everyone in the house? His stomach churned. What if it's part of an alien invasion and hundreds more are about to drop out of the sky?

Shouldn't he *do* something?

And then another thought struck him and, absurd as it sounded, it felt... possible. Really possible. What if this creature– this 'spidery-angel'–had a connection with the strange dreams he'd been having?

Maybe it was giving Daisy a dream?

It felt so impossible but so right and, in a flash of clarity, it made total sense.

As if hearing his thoughts, the spidery-angel turned its head and stared at him with deep black eyes like cavernous empty holes. Archie froze as a chill rushed into his brain and in the very next moment the creature had vanished.

Gone. Just like that.

Archie stared out into the dark night air at nothing. His

heart thumped like a drum in his chest. Gradually, the iciness began to thaw but Archie remained as still as he could, terrified the thing might reappear directly on top of him. After what felt like a month, he sat up, shook out the arm he'd been lying on, and wiped the beads of sweat from his brow.

All he could see was the fabric of the large drape, perched like a tent above him, and the outline of the thick old wooden rafters beyond. And opposite lay Daisy, fast asleep, snoring as though nothing had happened.

Had the spidery creature been in his head, a figment of his imagination—part of another dream? He pinched himself and felt it.

And what was it doing to Daisy with those tiny claws on the end of its long legs? Sucking her brains out? Archie chuckled; no one in their right mind would steal those. Daisy's feet were wonderfully gifted for football and running, but her brains?

Archie replayed the scene in his mind again, as though searching through a film. He remembered the way the creature waited for her inhalations and then, as she drew air into her lungs, its tiny claws spun like crazy. Each time, he returned to the same conclusion; it wasn't *taking* anything from Daisy–more *giving* her something. And whatever it was, she had drawn it deep inside her.

Archie flicked on the bedside lamp and a gentle yellow glow filled the attic room just as Isabella yawned and rolled over. Archie waited until she had settled down then slipped out from under his duvet. He tiptoed silently towards Daisy's bed, a couple of wooden planks moaning in protest as he went.

He knelt down and surveyed her. She was silent and at peace, as pretty as anything with her golden hair tumbling wildly over the pillow, her mouth parted. He could detect her sleepy smell and leaned in until his face was just a few inches from hers. He inspected her nose, chin, lips, cheeks and ears. But there were no odd marks or stains, no bruises, no bleeding, nothing amiss.

Archie put his head in his hands. Perhaps he had imagined it.

He rubbed his face and readied himself to go back to bed when suddenly Daisy gasped as though she'd been stuck underwater and burst through to find air.

She groaned and tossed her head from side to side. Then, without warning, she sat bolt upright as though a massive electric current had smashed into her—her face missing his by a whisker, her wavy hair brushing his nose.

Archie's eyes nearly popped out of their sockets. He could feel her breath marking his cheek. He swayed to the side and noted that her eyes were shut tight. She was asleep!

Now she was mumbling, but he couldn't make out the words and he forced himself to listen harder.

What was it… "odd" followed by "wo-man?"

She repeated it, this time louder. This time the word "odd" sounded more like "blood" or "flood". And there was something else. Yes, a word like "a-shunt" before "woman" and then a word like… "bread". That was it.

But what did it mean? "Blood–a-shunt–woman–bread?"

Some sort of car accident?

Daisy repeated these words over and over, her voice growing louder and louder. And now it sounded like, "flood a shunt woman Fred".

'Flood a shunt woman Fred?' Archie whispered. What was she talking about?

In a flash, it came to him.

Archie reeled; he knew he wasn't mistaken. Now he said it with her. The first word was definitely "flood", followed by, "Ancient Woman… dead".

Blood drained from his face. He stood up and stared at his twin, his mouth open. It wasn't possible—it couldn't be. How could she have access to his very own nightmare, the exact same dream he'd had over the past few nights; flooding and a haggard old woman?

Was it a *twin thing*? No. Twin things never happened to them.

He noticed tears falling from Daisy's eyes, eyes which were now wide open and fixed on a point across the room.

Without warning, Daisy screamed.

Archie cowered, covering his ears.

She began to shake and her hands reached out as though clawing at an invisible figure. Words spilled out incoherently.

A moment later she stopped and, with a look of absolute dread and fear mixed upon her face, she spoke clearly, her words faint like whispers.

Archie leaned in but wished he hadn't, for her next words seem to stab him, as though a knife had been plunged into his heart.

'No, please Archie,' she said, 'don't do it.'

Soon, she was yelling, 'DON'T DO IT, ARCHIE ...

NO ... **PLEASE ...**

Then a scream.

... **NO-ooo!**'

TWO

THE WORST DECISION

John woke. He realised he was panting. He quickly figured that the wetness on his nightshirt was sweat. He rubbed his forehead with a sleeve and reached out in the dark for a glass of water and his spectacles.

Then he heard a long, agonising cry piercing the night.

He listened again, hearing only the distant moaning of floorboards and the scampering of mice scuttling from one hole to another.

There! The noise again. A groan, followed by a kind of high-pitched scream.

As quietly as he could, he stole out of bed, popped his feet in a pair of woolly slippers and sneaked towards the door.

On the landing, he stopped still. The sounds were coming from the attic room.

Daisy? As the other girls were further along in the airing cupboard, it had to be.

Treading on the outermost flank of the wooden steps to avoid excessive creaking, he crept up.

His wife, Charlotte, had earlier confided in him that Isabella had had a nightmare the previous night.

Were these related?

He hadn't given it too much thought. But now, something niggled the back of his mind.

He moved to the door, his ear attuned, and gently pushed it open.

'Archie,' he heard Daisy say. 'You have seriously funny hair.'

Funny hair, John thought.

There was another verbal outburst this time from Archie. 'Bella's going… over there. Watch out! Lightning… it's after us! GO!'

Lightning?

Now it was Daisy again, her voice urgent. 'You've got to do it, Archie,' he heard her say as if she was thrashing about. 'Find it! Find the clues, dur-brain.'

Clues?

'Rain!' Daisy suddenly yelled. '… another one. DIVE!'

Moments later, she screamed.

Outside, John's heart thumped. He scratched his head.

Rain? Not now. Surely… it couldn't be!

He scampered down the attic stairs. He needed to check his special file; the volume of his life's work.

As he passed the airing cupboard, he heard a groan.

'Umbrella? Rain… too hard,' followed quickly by a gasp. Sue or Isabella, he couldn't tell.

'I can't breathe… RUN…! Not there! No! Archie, help me.'

Them, as well.

Downstairs, John unlocked his safe and withdrew a thick, well-thumbed leather-bound notebook.

Flicking on the light, he fanned his way through, stopping now and then when a memory of an image came to him.

Then he found it.

"Vivid dreams of a storm and torrential rain are the starting points of the great prophecy."

He'd seen it on the stained-glass windows in the chapel at Upsall. And, now that he examined his old sketches that he'd made all those years ago in the second cavern in the desert area of Havilah in the Middle East, he remembered how it showed lightning bolts flashing out of the sky onto each one, *as they slept.*

The clues, the riddles.

'Goodness,' he whispered. 'The prophecy is finally here. It's starting. But why now?'

They're only teenage kids.

'Wake up! Charlotte, you've got to wake up!' He nudged her again.

'The dreams have come,' he whispered excitedly. 'They're all dreaming the same thing.'

She yawned and rubbed her eyes. 'Get back to bed you annoying man.'

'Seriously!' He turned on the light. 'Charlotte,' he began, his voice croaking between stern, serious, and delirious, 'you must listen.'

She sat up. 'What are you talking about?'

'The kids! They're all having nightmares about rain and lightning—'

'You're overreacting,' she said, sleepily. 'It's not going to happen yet. Not for years.'

John was animated. 'Listen. I woke up sweating. Then I heard Daisy, then Archie shouting about rain and lightning. On my way downstairs, Isabella mumbling about clues and umbrellas. *It is happening.*'

'It is not happening! They're far too young.' She rolled over. 'Go back to sleep. I'll talk to you in the morning.'

John regarded his wife with disbelief.

'You have to the count of five to sit up and pay attention, or—'

'Or what?' she slurred.

'I'll pour this glass of water over you.'

She laughed into her pillow, and closed her eyes.

'One.'

'Two.'

'Three.'

An eye opened. 'Seriously?'

'Four.' He picked up the glass, deliberately scraping it over the side-table.

She sat up, fast.

'Five,' he said, moving the glass towards her.

She ducked as he pulled the glass round to his lips and drank.

'You wouldn't dare.'

'At least I have your attention,' he said. 'The children are dreaming, Charlotte.'

'So—'

'They're dreaming about a flood, about rain, about lightning bolts, about clues. I've checked my book.'

'And you think…' she slipped out of bed and rubbed her eyes. 'OK, I get you. I need a cup of tea, or something stronger. Let's talk downstairs.'

As they passed the cupboard, a small voice crept out. Both parents looked at each other.

'Too much water… don't know where to find it…' a girl's muffled voice said. '…the house…the ruin. It's there isn't it? … RUN! RUN!' the voice yelled before, petering out.

John looked at his wife, whose eyes were hanging on stalks, her face suddenly pale and withdrawn.

They sipped a single malt whisky next to the metal range cooker.

'We cannot help them,' he said. 'You know this. If we breathe a word, it may have drastic repercussions, not just for us, but for everyone, and everything.'

Charlotte had been dreading this moment. 'I know, darling. I've left a few outfits and garments based on what we think they'll need. And I've hidden a postcard. That's all. They might not even find them, but I'll bet good money that Daisy will.'

'And I've concealed all the clues we've ever found,' he said. 'What about Sara?'

'Sara never told Sue anything, I'm sure of it. Right now, she's off on a romantic short-stay in Scotland.'

'Does Sue know about the arrangement…?'

'No, nothing. Sara never wanted to upset her. Like us, she kept it all a secret.' She sipped the Scotch, her nerves steeled by the alcohol. 'This whole situation is absolutely horrific. We must get away. As far—'

'And as quickly as possible,' he said, holding her hand firmly, controlling her shaking. 'Tomorrow we'll tell them something urgent has come up. We'll say our farewells the day after tomorrow as if we're off on just another trip without too much bluster and fuss. Agony though this is, it is imperative they work it out for themselves. We mustn't linger and we cannot interfere.'

Charlotte dropped her head, tears streaming out of her eyes.

'Painful as it is, my darling,' he continued, 'unless generations of our family have totally misinterpreted the writings, ancient scrolls, carvings and markings dotted about the planet, there is no other way but to leave them to it, to work it out with Old Man Wood as their mentor. Every time we've picked through the conditions, we find the same conclusion: we cannot aid them, and we cannot interfere. If they're to have any chance, our role is to lead those who've been watching us as far away from here as possible.'

She sighed. 'Any suggestions?'

'Caves in Afghanistan?'

She pursed her lips. 'Too remote. Too many land-mines, too many warlords. Not sure we'll get the friendliest welcome.' She raised her eyebrows as a thought popped in to her head. 'Remember that curious oasis close to Palmyra in Iraq—the one with the shallow tomb—and a two day journey from civilisation, now a burnt out hell-hole plundered by extremists?'

'How could I forget—'

'Well, it's difficult to get to, relatively unknown and bang in the middle of a conflict. But stuffed full of archaeological treasures. What do you think?'

'Sounds ideal,' he said, sitting up. 'But why don't we go to Hattusa in Turkey first and set a trail to send them on a wild goose chase, flinging out clues as we go. We've got friends there who'll be happy to help.'

'They'll makes a big difference,' she agreed. 'I'll contact the relevant agencies: the British museum, the Metropolitan in New York, our consulates plus the Turkish and Iraqi fixers for starters. We'll need a story, though. One that makes hairs tingle and pulses race.'

He paused in thought, his large hand stroking his chin.

'Let's leak that our years of research have led us to find important information in regards to…'

'Alexander the Great's gold?'

'Too obvious—flogged to death.'

'More Dead Sea scrolls? Egyptian stone tablets?' she said with a smile.

He shook his head again. 'Not sure it's got the wow factor we need. How about the Ark—'

'… of the Covenant?' she completed for him, grinning. 'Everyone's favourite religious artefact?'

'Why not?' he said. 'Sounds more interesting than the "Garden of Eden" whatever people want to make of it.' He sipped his tea blowing off the steam. 'Then we can watch the archaeological community and their billionaire sponsors drag their eyes—and their goons—off to various godforsaken parts of the middle east. And, while their attention is focused there, perhaps within the glare of the medias unforgiving eye, the Garden of Eden will be opened up right here under our very noses in good old Yorkshire.'

'That's what we hope,' she said, her voice wavering. '

'I'll make sure a postcard gets to the headmaster Solomon informing him we won't be back for half-term. And, once again we'll miss Daisy and Archie in their critical football matches,' he said, weariness in his voice.

'And the twins are in the final if they beat Easingwold, which they will,' she added, shaking her head. 'Daisy's going to be furious, though I'm sure Archie will be rather relieved. God, our parenting skills look dire—'

'What else do you suggest? You know we can't stay here a moment longer—too many people are on to us, sniffing around our research. Any slight interference and… well, I hardly dare think of the consequences.' He raised his eyebrows, his forehead crinkling.

'Our life's work is finally catching up with us.' He left the words hanging.

Charlotte squeezed his hand. 'All those messages we've found in crypts and burial chambers and religious writings and ancient tablets—'

'Lead to our biggest nightmare.'

She nodded, tears welling in her eyes as her tears restarted.

'Why us, darling?' she cried. 'Why so young?'

'Rotten timing. I suppose,' he said, handing her a tissue and using one himself. 'And because Old Man Wood's been here forever, so I suppose it was going to happen eventually. Our planet's been waiting for this time for an awfully long while and such things cannot be postponed, or bargained with. As my old friend Ahmed once said "the universe will know when it is ready".'

She sobbed freely. 'But they're only children! I thought it might be when they were stronger, in their thirties or forties, when we were old. Not while they're still kids. Do you think the old man will remember?'

'It might take something rather extraordinary to jog him back to an event that happened such a long time ago.'

A painful silence filled the room.

'They know nothing of real life, John. How can we expect them to save us without him?'

John shut his eyes. 'They have everything in front of them so try and think of it this way,' he said, trying to hold back his emotions. 'They wouldn't have been chosen if there wasn't a chance—'

'Oh really, John, seriously, what are their chances? Look at them. Isabella, stubborn and self-centred, Archie so laid back he's almost horizontal and Daisy, who doesn't care about anything apart from football. They're hardly representative of human endeavour and spirit, are they?'

'Thing is, maybe they are? Maybe they do have the qualities needed deep down? We can only hope, eh?'

'I wish you'd never met Ahmed.'

'Yes, I know what you mean. At least it's given us time to understand. Time to acquaint ourselves with this fate. And we've done everything we could…'

She snuggled into him, her body trembling. 'We'll probably never see them again.'

'I know. I have spent hours every day since they were born thinking about this moment.'

They held each other.

At length, John opened the book.

'*There will be a sequence of dream events,*' he read. '*From the first signs, there may be up to twelve days. A cloud will form, and the dreams will intensify.*'

'Twelve days.'

'Isabella had a nightmare the other night, so I suppose that makes it only ten, or eleven left.'

'It's a humbling thought,' he said, solemnly, 'to think that there may be less than twenty days left of our Earth. To give them any chance we too must be brave, darling.

The clock chimed three.

'What if the storm breaks after the game,' she said, barely controlling herself. 'They won't have the strength…'

'Sshhh. We can only pray that their path is not so tricky. Fate is a curious companion, but they are on their own now. Our little babies must take on a burden like no other.

Charlotte picked up her mobile and flicked at the screen but her mind wasn't on it.

'I tried,' she said softly as her eyes moistened. 'I've done all I can,' she said, her voice betraying her fear. 'I've left a few bits here and there—as much as I dare.' She wiped her nose with the back of her hand, as her shoulders shook with grief. 'Do you really think they'll come back to us?'

He smiled reassuringly and squeezed her arm. 'I just don't know,' he said. 'This great test of humankind will not be straightforward, nor without terrible danger. If they work together, if they talk to one another and understand what has been shown to them and exercise the freedom, the joys and innocence of youth, then perhaps they have a chance. If they don't, then I'm afraid we are all doomed. Each and every last one of us.'

THE ROUTE TO SCHOOL

Archie's cupped hands cascaded cold water onto his face, the shock waking him. First Daisy's mad dream, now this.

Wincing, he touched the mark, the nerve endings raw and sharp. Half an inch, as neat as a red underline.

The ghost! The blade!

Memories rushed in. Archie stared at the rouge on his fingers, mesmerised, and rubbed them till the stain cleared.

It can't be. His initial reaction.

How come? His next.

Archie crashed into the wall, then righted himself, before heading downstairs, his head spinning.

Why? Why me?

He heard the others in the kitchen, but their words died before his brain could register what they said. He tried to speak, but the sounds reverberated back, spiralling as if they were stuck in a vortex.

In the kitchen, the sink and table spun around the room, along with the outline of his sisters and Mrs Pye.

Tinkling glass? Raised voices?

So what.

He needed to breathe, clear his head. He needed to run.

Grabbing a jacket and his rucksack, he found the door, and sped across the courtyard to the track, which cut down towards the river. His head cleared as his speed picked up and soon he was hurtling along animal tracks, weaving through long grass, leaping over fallen branches, jumping foxholes, and untangling brambles from his clothes as he ducked, crashed, and bullied his way through thickets and bushes.

In a clearing, he approached a huge round boulder three times his height. In his mind's eye he measured the distance and set off at a sprint. At the last moment, he sprang up and grasped hold of a stony outcrop just high enough to haul him to the top. He reached into his bag, found his water bottle, and swirled the liquid around his mouth splashing a little on his face.

Breathing hard, his heart thumping in his chest, Archie watched the sun rise like red-hot coals burning under the base of the vast black cloud jettisoned above.

He'd dreamt that he had to do something horrific, something beyond imagination. And Daisy had had the same dream too. He was sure of it.

But why him?

And then, last night, he'd met a ghost.

And it really had happened.

He fingered the nick on his chin. How else could he have received such a neat cut?

He stared out over the valley, his eyes drawn to the candy shapes of the houses in the village of Upsall, perched just above the floodplain at the foot of the Yorkshire moors. He looked at the rugged, menacing, dark forest and jagged rocks that jutted out of the steep slopes like gnarled, angry faces and noticed how in contrast were the manicured, cartoon-coloured stripes of light and dark green which highlighted the school playing fields on the valley floor.

Man's doing down below, he thought, *God's above.*

More questions crowded his brain.

What if he didn't survive? What if he couldn't find the stupid cave? Who was this ancient woman?

And the ghost said it would return. It hadn't mentioned a time, or a place, only that it would be back. And soon.

But why?

Archie cast his eye over the large old oaks that marked the position of the meandering river. To him they guarded the village like sentries positioned at perfect intervals. Upsall looked stronger and more important than the old, monastic-looking school buildings whose distinctive, high, square tower rose up into the heavens. It felt like a perfect contrast to the river curving elegantly in front.

In the distance, the soaring cliffs protected the village like a shield. He saw how Upsall had fostered a sense of security with its toffee-coloured chunks of masonry and loophole arrow-slit holes dotted on the older buildings. Balancing this were subtle lines of symmetry; the intricate round, rose window pixelated with stained glass resting above a meaty, carved oak door.

Right now, he needed a shield of his own. But where would that come from?

He looked to his right towards the sheer rock face that climbed high above him, dwarfing all things below.

He listened.

Strange.

No eagles. No hawks or harriers circling or soaring like model aircraft.

In fact, he noticed an almost intolerable silence.

He flicked his wrist, glanced at the dial and sighed. If he didn't get a move on, he'd be late again.

Standing up, he extended his arms wide before sliding down the stone curvature and tumbling over and over until he collided with the thick trunk of a larch.

Archie brushed himself down, feeling a multitude of soon-to-be bruises birthing in the tissue under his skin.

Then he heard the noise, a rustling of leaves close by. A mild thrashing sound followed by a soft thump, just beneath him down the slope.

Archie readied himself to run when he heard a yelp.

He reached in to the brambles and looked over the bank into the bushes below.

'What are you doing here?' he said. 'Little leverets shouldn't be here in the forest,' Archie fixed his eyes on the scared animal as the baby hare thrashed harder, rearing up and trying to get away only tying itself up more.

Archie held onto a branch, lowering himself into the brambles.

He spoke evenly, hoping it was soothing enough not to frighten the creature even more.

'If I don't get you out, you're going to be the easiest meal old Mr Fox ever had. Don't go crazy. Understand?'

Even if the leveret had no idea what he was talking about, speaking to it felt like the right thing to do and Archie never took his eyes away even as it tried to break free. Exhausted, the baby hare soon fell to the ground, its chest pounding from the exertion.

Unpicking several brambles caught in his clothes, Archie sneaked closer, the leveret's large brown eyes studying his every move. Archie reached down to find both hind-legs bound by thorny tendrils.

'You poor thing,' he said. 'I'll cut you out… if you let me.' He hoped the animal understood.

With great care, Archie reached down and stroked the leveret behind its ears which were tucked flat into the animals head. Archie pulled out his penknife and, keeping the blade out of sight, moved it towards the leveret's snared legs knowing full well that a sharp kick would almost certainly damage both of them.

When the barbs were free instead of dashing off at high speed the leveret lay still.

'You can't stay here, little hare. You and your family belong up on the ruin or on the playing fields. Go on, run off to your nest or wherever you want.'

Archie sensed the hare was somehow waiting for him. He leaned down and petted it again. 'I think I'll call you Rocky. I might have to carry you.'

Archie gathered the leveret into his arms carefully tucking-in its legs but cradling the animal's body all the same.

He fought his way onto the makeshift path, ripping his jumper and shirt on every conceivable variety of thorn, and from here he weaved through the undergrowth towards the silver band of the river that cut through the red and yellow apron of autumn leaves towards school.

Walking as fast as he dared along the towpath, over the bridge and onto the playing fields, Archie caught his breath as he neared the chapel steps. His heart sank when he saw his elder sister, Isabella, rushing over to intercept.

'Where the hell have you been?' she demanded

'In the forest.'

'That's an understatement, most of it is on you.' Her face twisted. 'And what is that?'

'Oh. This is Rocky,' he said with a smile, looking down at the leveret. 'I found him trapped in the bushes on the way down—'

'Archie! Not another animal. You've got to stop this insane wildlife rescue-mission-crusade. It's becoming a joke.' She gave him a once over. 'You look a total wreck.'

Archie shrugged. 'It wasn't my fault. I fell over a couple of times and I couldn't leave Rocky, he's hurt—'

'I don't care,' she stormed. 'Put that fluffy thing down and get inside!' She stopped and crinkled her nose. 'Oh my Lord! You stink, and you're covered in blood,' she said. 'Actually, you can't go in there.'

Archie scratched Rocky's head, and set the leveret down watching it limp away over the playing fields. Archie stared at it with a grin on his face. 'I hope he's going to be all right.'

'It's a hare, Arch.'

'Actually, technically it's a leveret.'

'And the smell?'

'I dunno, Bells. It could be Rocky, or I might have landed in something.'

'Archie. Go home and change. You're an embarrassment and you'll only run into trouble—'

'No way,' he replied defiantly. 'I want to know if Daisy made the team. It's unmissable.'

He pulled a sock up for her benefit and wiped his brow with a cuff while lamely brushing himself down. Then he sprinted towards the chapel door, Isabella chasing behind, slipping in moments before her.

He ran, head down, almost bent over double, across the flagstones until he found his row, squeezed in to his class position, and sat, conscious that others were staring at him.

Further along, he noticed Daisy chatting animatedly to her friends, while others were turning off their phones. He caught her eye.

She frowned back, and mouthed something at him.

Was it about the team?

She jabbed a finger.

Or about him? Was she having a dig at him as well?

He smiled back weakly, and folded his head into his hands.

For a brief moment, he experienced the intrusion of being watched, similar to the sensation he'd felt the previous night with the ghost. His instinct was right. On the platform at the far end of the hall stood Mr Solomon, the headmaster, whose eyes bore into him like lasers.

Archie's heart sank. Those who had even the tiniest scuffs, or tears, or missing buttons, were being entered into his dreaded red book. Maybe Isabella's warning wasn't so misdirected after all.

He gave himself a quick once-over. Utterly appalling. He reckoned he had about three-seconds to get up and sneak through the side entrance.

Instead, he grappled with his tie, drew up his socks, and dragged a hand roughly through his hair, removing the tendrils of a creeper, several strands of grass and a piece of bark. Then, before he could tidy himself further, a familiar voice boomed through the hall.

'Good morning, school,' it said. 'Please rise.'

FOUR

THE FATE OF WORLDS

With a tiny flash, the same spider-like dreamspinner Archie had seen perched over Daisy uncurled from her fiery, electric blue midriff known as an "maghole".

Genesis stood on six long, thread-like, spidery legs and looked out over a desolate landscape through ovate black eyes. A soft wind brushed through her and she sniffed the stale air remembering how, long ago, grasses, trees, and beasts filled the pink, green, and ochre-coloured landscapes of the planet of the Garden of Eden.

Filled with insects and spiders, this area of the Garden of Eden was known as the "Arachnid Patch" and it was here where the dreamspinners harvested spider webs from millions of spider silks for fashioning dream powders, or dusts, to create dreams of love, kindness, and inventiveness for all living entities.

These lands, though hostile to most and rarely visited by other species, had been bountiful to dreamspinners and thereby beneficial to all living creatures, notably human beings.

On this exact spot, she remembered, an area had been cleared and a tall, open-roofed structure hastily constructed. Its outer perimeter was like a giant wooden palisade, and from afar it looked like a fortress with outer walls high enough and thick enough to shield it from the lurking eyes and ears of the tallest and craftiest of beasts who dared to enter into the "Patch".

Genesis remembered how the Council of One Hundred had debated the fate of the worlds around a huge circular table made from one slice of the trunk of a pink mammoth tree. Here, humans, animals and trees had argued and raged before finally putting their differences to rest.

Invisible to all except other dreamspinners, Genesis had bathed in the warm blue energy currents that splayed over her from her mother's electrical maghole while watching the drama unfold below. She recalled the desperate faces of the Founders of the Garden of Eden as they listened the charges against them. These five, four men and a woman, moulded by the irresistible energies of the universe, forged in birth from the collisions of sand, waters and gases at the very beginning, were found to be guilty of corrupting all life.

The Founders had yearned for forgiveness, demanding an end to magic, begging them to find a way of destroying their immortality. They did not seek pity, just atonement for their part in the destruction, and Genesis remembered how tears had rolled down their cheeks as they accepted their punishment; all bar one.

That man was Cain, from the planet of Havilah. Cain, who threatened to freeze every human being on Havilah if he burned. Cain, whose light blue eyes exuded a dark, menacing power beyond that of others, felt his fate did not in any way justify his actions.

Genesis uncurled a long leg, turning the tip into a needle and then a pincer before dipping it into her fizzling maghole, feeling the soothing mass of energy swirling within. The old memories were returning.

Cain had delivered on his promise.

The moment flames had licked at his flesh, his spell had cast all Havilarian people into domed, crystal-like puddles exactly where they stood.

And now, devoid of form and starved of magic, Cain—to this day—hadn't figured out how to turn the Havilarian people back.

Genesis had often watched the Frozen Lord, as he was known, roam his palace with a hope that burned from within his spirit-shell, always looking, never giving up the search to find and restore his power. But as the millennia wore on, she'd noted how his vibration had moved to frustration, and from here to anger.

Genesis glided like a ghost, her limbs floating on particles of air until she reached the top of the great stone. From here she stared over the wastelands of the desolate planet.

Strange how events had turned out.

The world of the Garden of Eden in front of her devoid of life, while Havilah, not even visible as a pinprick in the night sky, was starved of people. All the while, Earth had trudged on, oblivious to the planets they had yet to discover, oblivious to the destructive wars and machinations of the other worlds.

For this reason, dreamspinners were deeply associated with Earth. Nothing thrilled Genesis more than to sneak away and watch a human dream. It thrilled her to see how they twisted and reacted, and how the dusts filled them with hope and creativity to give their world meaning.

And, now, as if out of the blue, the mysterious energies of the universe had reawakened.

The inscription on the huge rock beside her held the instructions.

Genesis pushed her old, wiry legs out into the sky, scanning for vibrations and for *answers*. There was no point in denying these forces, these changes. They just were.

The fate of dreamspinners, the destiny of animals, plant life, and every living being on Earth was about to rest in the hands and minds of three humans under the protection of Adam, once the eldest of the Founders, exiled to Earth so, so long ago. His role was to assist with this exact moment just as they had agreed.

When the time came to give the final part of the Tripodean Dream, known as the "Gifts of Eden", these three humans would be named as the Heirs of Eden and they would have seven days to fulfil their tasks to demonstrate all the qualities of the current human race.

Fail, and all life on Earth would perish, hailing in a new epoch.

Now, only two parts of this dream remained to be given.

FIVE

GOOD AND BAD NEWS

Mr Solomon patted the breast pocket of his coarse tweed suit and raised his thick eyebrows. Twenty-five years he'd been at the school, almost to the day. Twenty years as headmaster, and his performance every morning was the same now as it was then.

'Quiet... please,' he said.

Wasn't it strange, he thought, how noise levels always seemed to rise as conversations rushed to a conclusion?

He removed his glasses from his round, ruddy nose and inspected the students.

'Thank you. Please sit.'

Two hundred and seventy-two pupils parked on the hard, wooden benches lined up row upon row, the noise whispering into the huge, vaulted ceiling above.

From weighty cross-beams, large chandelier lights dangled from thick, black metal chains, illuminating those below with a dim, church-like glow.

From their tall portraits on the sides, former headmasters eyed this generation of children sternly, while etched onto dark wooden panels running around the perimeter of the hall, the names of former scholars, captains, and musicians reminded the children of past glories.

Solomon stared out over the throng and cleared his throat.

'School dress!'

Archie audibly groaned. He had a strong urge to disappear.

'I see some of you shaking,' Solomon said, smiling and staring around the room. 'And rightly so,' he continued. 'Standards have deteriorated since the beginning of term. After leave, those who fail to comply with every part of the school uniform code will discover the joys of additional detention. Now, to show you what I'm talking about, no one is quivering more this morning than our school goalkeeping hero, Archie de Lowe.'

A cheer went up.

'de Lowe, please be upstanding.'

Archie sat stone-still in disbelief.

Not again.

He felt a jab in his back and another from the side.

'Come on, Archie. Up you get.'

Archie regarded his worn shoes, and, taking a deep breath, rose from behind the significant frame of his friend Gus Williams. Every single pair of eyes stared at him and Archie heard a group of girls giggling. His face reddened, the heat of his blush growing by the second. He didn't dare look up.

'Archie, I really do hate to make an example of you,' Solomon continued, 'but this morning you have beaten your spectacular record of being a total and utter shambles.'

Cautious laughter flittered around the hall.

'It is almost as if you fail to realise that a dress-code actually exists. In fact, you are almost the perfect example of how not to appear in school.'

The head addressed the assembly.

'Let us examine our specimen. His shoes are filthy; he has no belt and, as a result, we can see rather colourful underwear. His socks are around his ankles because there are no elastic garters holding them up, and even these are torn to bits—like everything else.'

Solomon paused as laughter pealed into the rafters. 'His shirt has a button missing, his tie is halfway across his chest and, I'm not sure how this happened, but he appears to be wearing the wrong coloured jersey! Please turn around, de Lowe.'

Archie shifted.

'Yes, just as I suspected,' Solomon continued. 'Blazer ripped and, of course, his hair is not only too long, but a decent imitation of a filthy mop head.'

Archie feigned a smile while others pointed and grinned.

On Solomon's instruction, while hopelessly attempting to pull his attire together, Archie sat down and glanced up towards his sister, Isabella.

Her hard, cold stare drilled into him as she ground her jaw, which, from experience, was never a good sign.

Solomon's tone softened as he smiled, showing his small, tea-stained teeth.

'Is there a reason for this mornings astonishing mess, Archie?'

Archie ran a hand through his hair, removing a burr. 'I, er, well, yes, sir.'

'And?'

'I found an injured leveret, sir, in the forest. Its legs were trapped. I carried it down—'

'A baby hare, trapped in the woods? An unlikely tale, de Lowe, as hares live in open land. Furthermore, they are not creatures one ordinarily carries about.' He paused for effect. 'You do come up with the most hare-brained schemes.'

The other teachers laughed politely. Students groaned.

Archie bowed his head.

'Hare or no hare,' Solomon continued, 'let this be a lesson to you all, not just you, Archie. Today, and today only, because you are a key part of our famous football team, you are excused.

And this, of course, leads me on to the main item of this morning's agenda.'

With these words, the mood in the hall lightened as if a gust of fresher, happier air had blown in. The noise level increased.

Along the row, nibbling her nails, Daisy stared at the floor.

The headmaster raised an arm for quiet.

'Most of you are aware of the situation. As a small school, our selection for teams is limited and I regrettably endorsed that a girl could play in our boys team. As you know, this team has gone on to great things to the tremendous credit of our school. However, we… were found out.'

The headmaster pulled a letter from his breast pocket and waved it in the air.

'Let me interpret the relevant parts of this communication I received yesterday from the president of our Football Association.'

He nudged his glasses onto the bridge of his nose and thumbed his way down the page.

'What they are saying, is this: if Daisy de Lowe has played in ten matches in a row this season, they are willing to be lenient. Well, anyone, has she?'

He spied a hand from the back.

'Yes. Sue Lowden. Do you have the answer?'

'Daisy's played in twelve, sir. Thirteen if you add the German touring side.'

'Thank you, Miss Lowden.'

A buzz moved around the room.

'*It is our opinion,*' he read, '*that Upsall School has taken advantage of the goodwill of our league. However, until we received an anonymous letter highlighting the anomaly, not one opposition team reported or noticed Miss de Lowe's disguise.*'

A hissing noise developed and several heads turned to the right.

Mr Solomon continued, this time up a gear.

'*Our decision is this,*' he read. '*Should Upsall School win, then, with the full backing of the Football Association, Miss de Lowe will be allowed to continue playing for Upsall School boys and the regulations across the county will be changed with immediate effect—'*

Cheers filled the air.

'*However,*' Solomon said, and he raised his hand for quiet, '*should Upsall lose,*' and here, his voice went so quiet, '*then it will be Miss de Lowe's last game for the Upsall School's boys eleven.*'

Solomon picked Daisy out of the assembly and spoke directly to her.

'So, there we have it, Daisy. I have spoken with the authorities to make sure we completely understand this ruling. You will play in tomorrow's boys final against Sutton. But lose, and it will be your last game for the school until we have enough girls willing to play in a girls team. I hope that moment is not too far away.'

Daisy nodded back.

'Very good,' he said. 'Regardless of the outcome, this doesn't mean your sporting career is temporarily over here at Upsall,' the headmaster continued, as a smile slipped onto his round face.

'No, no, no! Not by any means. It would appear that your exploits on the soccer field have been "talent-spotted".' Solomon's eyes sparkled. 'After half term,' and here he slowed, using every ounce of his experience to engage the assembly, 'you have been invited to join the England ladies national training squad.'

Gasps shot out from the assembly floor.

'Yes, yes, I'll repeat it again. The England squad. It is a terrific honour that you've been picked to train with your fellow country-women, the youngest player ever to be invited. Daisy,' he said sincerely, 'we are all extremely proud of you.'

Applause rallied and Solomon let it continue for its deserved time.

'There we have it, Daisy. There's plenty for you to look forward to after half term.'

Solomon then crashed his hand down on the lectern, making the juniors at the front jump.

'But let's make sure that we jolly well win so we can change these silly rules forever!'

Kemp watched as Daisy headed down the assembly row. As she approached he thrust out a leg stopping her in her tracks. Shrugging, Daisy promptly kicked his shin hard enough to hear him whimper.

'I only wanted to say congratulations,' he said, rubbing his leg.

'Yeah, right.' Daisy sneered, looking up at him. 'You've never congratulated anyone on anything, have you Kemp?'

'I meant it,' he said, hurt.

'Sure. If you really meant it,' she whispered, leaning down, 'give me a little kiss.'

Kemp almost toppled over the back of his chair. 'Jeez Daisy, you're even weirder than both of the other two put together—'

'You're referring to my brother and sister, Kemp?'

He flushed and blustered. 'Yeah. I mean, no. Oh heck—'

Daisy tousled her hair and pouted. 'Don't be a shy boy, Kemp. I'm waiting.'

Kemp tried to pull himself together. 'No way. I wouldn't kiss you if you paid me—'

She smiled at his deep discomfort and whispered. 'Know what, bad boy, I sooo think you're on to me.'

Kemp reddened and his nose expanded sideways, incredulity sketched on his face.

A bellow of laughter came from big Gus Williams who had been listening to every word from the row in front. 'Daisy,' he said. 'You are totally hilarious. Forget this loser, if it's any consolation,' and he flashed his friendly, toothy smile at her. 'I'll give you a kiss!'

'Yes, I know you would, Gus,' she said, as an entourage of fans approached. 'Thing is, you like everyone don't you… hey girls,' Daisy said, pointing at Kemp's red face. 'Take a gander at that visage! All I wanted was a little kiss!'

Daisy winked at both the boys before being whisked away by the giggling, chatty crowd.

Gus turned to Kemp, his large eyes bulging with excitement.

'Kicked by a girl, but not kissed by a girl, Kemp. That's not right for a tough boy like you?'

'You're asking for it, Williams,' Kemp spat. 'I'll have you.'

'Anytime,' Gus replied, his voice levelling. 'Happy to oblige, whenever you've got a minute. Just you and me, Kemp.'

SIX

ASGARD UNDERSTANDS

Asgard the dreamspinner sat alone, floating, watching planet Earth spinning, as it always did.

Every so often a tiny burst of light, invisible to other creatures, flashed for a nano-second. He mused that he was not the only dreamspinner taking time from dream-giving to reflect upon Genesis's extraordinary news.

Asgard noted Earth's moon rising in the near distance against the endless expanse of space.

Twisting, as if his legs were made of rubber, he dabbled several slender legs in his maghole, enjoying how the warmth from the blue electrical field bathed them.

Was there still a need for inspirational, magical dreams? Dreams that offered insight or inspired change or for dreams that prompted love and joy?

Asgard cranked his small, round head, and stared at a distant star, as he replaced one leg in his maghole with another.

Their purpose as dream-givers would not end simply because no *joyful* dreams remained. So long as *any dream* were given, he reasoned, from *any* powder blended from *any* spider's web, surely the dreamspinners would continue to have a purpose? If dreams were nightmares, at least the dreamspinners would exist to knit and spin them?

This, he realised was the choice.

He thought of the boy. The boy who knew nothing.

What did fate have in mind for him and his sisters? Immediate death?

It was now perfectly clear that Adam had failed in his task to nurture and train the Heirs of Eden, if indeed these three children *were* the Heirs of Eden. Even Genesis could tell Adam was no longer the man he once was. The old man's sharp mind was but a shadow. Earth had drowned him in a pool of denial, and apathy.

Asgard had tried to explain to Genesis that it must be a mistake. But the elder dreamspinner would not listen. Genesis had swept aside the doubters and told them that the words on the great stone could not be twisted.

He'd visited the monolith to see them for himself. And it was exactly as Genesis said:

The three Heirs of Eden of the human race are those who live under the protection of Adam on Earth.

They alone must receive the Tripodean Dream.

But the Heirs of Eden were children!

If they didn't die at the very first hurdle it would take them seven years, not seven days. If these children were the measure of life on Earth, then perhaps the planet deserved its outcome.

Or maybe Adam was in the wrong place, caring for the wrong people.

Asgard noticed a pinprick of yellow light coming from a spot on a nearby star's dark surface. The birthing of dreamspinners, he realised, hatching from cocoons in caverns dotted around the universe. More dreamspinners, to nurture, guide, and instruct in the art of dream-giving for the booming populations on planets around the universe.

Asgard reached into his maghole with one hand and weighed up his last dream dusts from the planet of the Garden of Eden. Forty dreams, he estimated; more if he thinned them out. But did he really want to dilute such precious cargo?

Asgard flashed out of his maghole, landing in a huge cavern. He hovered in mid-air, extended his legs wide and switched, by thought alone, out of his invisible mode.

Suddenly, a flurry of activity appeared like magic in front of him. Dreamspinners dashed here and there across the sky, blue flashes denoting the arrival of some, and the departure of others.

He turned his wiry neck upward towards the roof of the cave, and found it packed with yellowy-brown cocoons stacked in layer upon layer like the neat chambers of a beehive.

Walking across the air, he passed younger dreamspinners, who turned or bowed their heads in a sign of respect for their Elders.

He noted a flash next to him and turned.

'Gaia,' Asgard said, his legs vibrating together so fast as to form words. 'I see you.'

'And I you, Asgard,' she replied, her vibrations softer. 'You have come to see the birthing?'

'By their movement, the time is close,' he said, indicating lines of dreamspinners perched in the air. 'Many crowd the chamber.'

'It has always been so,' Gaia replied. 'They are our future. But what kind of future do we leave them?' her vibrations dimmed. 'Have you heard who the Heirs of Eden are?' she said.

'I am aware that they are young. But, of course, this is nature's will—'

'There!' cried a voice. 'See! The sun is nearly in line with the entrance.'

A sudden flurry of activity began, with blue lights flashing everywhere. Asgard and Gaia were almost blinded as dreamspinners flashed into the chamber, unfurling from their magholes and into their visible forms as they did so.

The entire cavern buzzed with excitement.

From the cocoons high above, one chamber wriggled and shook more violently than before. Then another, and, before long, multiple cocoons along the length of the huge ceiling rattled, cracked, and split, exposing tiny dreamspinners.

Then, the entire ceiling seemed to open up like popcorn and before long, the tiny, spider-like creatures flapped about like new-born chicks, clawing at the air as if swimming in a thick soup.

The onlookers, dreamspinners of all shapes and sizes, vibrated words of love and encouragement.

'Fall! Jump into the light!' said a youth nearby, as cocoon sections spiralled to the ground like loose strands of straw.

To the mock-horror of the crowd of dreamspinners, the first tiny creatures plummeted towards the rocky ground beneath them. A collective gasp shot out.

Asgard noticed how Gaia covered her black eyes.

As they fell from the dark roof into the bright sunlight, a sudden bolt of bright golden light flashed in, enveloping the first hatchlings in circles of iridescent light, stopping them exactly where they were.

Then, as if a firework display had gone into overload, the remaining hatchlings tumbled through the air and, as the energy bathed them, these fledglings were now dreamspinners; borne of light and energy, ready for a life of giving dreams.

Asgard too, vibrated his feelings, offering the newcomers strength, love, and a long life.

The energies of creation, he mused, were always beautiful.

He was about to flip into his maghole when an idea of immense magnitude slipped neatly into his mind. Picking his way across the sky, he leaned into the jagged rock-edges of the huge cavern, out of sight.

This last Earth night, he'd taken Cain, the Frozen Lord, to see the boy. Initially, he'd gone to ask the spirit what he thought about having children as Heirs of Eden. After all, if anyone could remember and comprehend the tasks ahead, it was, he suspected, Cain.

Asgard recalled how he had flipped out of his maghole into the main chamber of Cain's sprawling palace which stretched above the face of the canyon overlooking the ruddy, sandy-coloured rocks of the city below.

He'd looked over the once bustling rock city of Havilaria, capital of Havilah, and its renowned stone formations and, even for a dreamspinner, the dramatic cityscape, with its huge craggy buttes that soared into the air like icebergs, and the deep canyon that circumnavigated it, filled him with wonder. He remembered how the cacophony of noise had once risen up from the narrow streets, and how the rock faces above were perforated with neat, square holes of ancient dwellings that had once sparkled with a million candles in the moonlight.

Now, the only sounds were echoes of squawks from the large birds, redundant from their past lives of flying people from one great rock to the next, who now inhabited roof tops, their wide, messy nests formed from debris and branches plucked from the river. The city's once celebrated house-caves were overrun with creepers, and the diamond, ruby and emerald stones—found naturally in the rock—were now covered over by dust; forgotten and unloved.

Asgard had picked out Cain's low vibrations and talked to the ghost who'd answered in a brusque, hostile, and bitter manner. Later, in return for information on the forthcoming trials of the Heirs of Eden, Asgard revealed the dreamspinner's secret of the maghole, and when Cain realised how the maghole might transport him, the former Founder's mood lifted.

Asgard told Cain that three children were the Heirs of Eden and the ghost thundered that this was impossible. He demanded to go directly to the Heirs of Eden to see the boy for himself—through his maghole.

Not long after this, Cain, the blind spirit, had faced the Heirs of Eden and stood in front of the Heir the humans called Archie.

The entire episode had been extraordinarily risky. Now, Asgard needed to think.

Turning invisible, he inverted through his maghole, sending him in an instant to his favourite place several miles above the Earth's orbit.

As he hovered in space, he remembered how he'd watched the ghost, Cain, produce a knife and flick the boy's chin. He watched how the ghost marvelled at the spot of blood.

And all the while, the boy's eyes bulged. Disbelieving.

Cain had a kind strength ordinary ghosts did not possess. The way he could carry objects for a certain length of time, pull things, lacerate with a small blade.

But an idea had nestled into his mind and it had refused to budge. And now, as he floated alone above the blue and white orb below him, he considered it deeply.

What if one of the Heirs of Eden might somehow ally with Cain? Perhaps this boy Archie?

Why did this sound so right and yet feel so horribly wrong? The more he dwelled on this idea, the more excited and more fearful he became. Asgard sensed his maghole expanding as the enormity of his mission dawned upon him.

After eons, the dreamspinners, the most lasting species created at the dawn of time, would no longer be neutral in the ways of the universes.

But it must be done, he reasoned, *for the benefit of all.*

SEVEN

KEMP'S STORY

Archie draped an arm around his twin Daisy. 'What was Kemp going on about?'

Daisy ran her hands through her hair. 'Oh, nothing. I was teasing him about being a pillock.' She smiled cheekily at her brother and sighed. 'Why does Kemp hate me so much?'

Archie rubbed his freckled nose and laughed. 'Because he's jealous of you. And because you booted him off the team, and because I don't think he knows how to talk to girls.' Archie pondered this for a second. 'Or boys either, for that matter.'

Daisy shook her head. 'He was always giving away fouls and kicking people... and that was last year—'

'He's like an elephant who never forgets—'

'Well, he's ridiculous,' she complained, 'elephant or not.'

Archie grabbed his sister playfully by the waist. 'Strange thing though, you know, the way he looks at you,' he said, smirking.

'Never! Although I did ask him for a kiss—as a joke! Gus thought it was hilarious.'

Archie grinned and glanced over to the far end of the hall, where Kemp was talking to his friends. They locked eyes for a moment, then Kemp reached into his pocket for his mobile.

Archie turned back to his twin sister, concerned. 'Big mistake to kick him. You know, other people do actually feel pain in their legs, even if you don't—'

'I wonder,' Daisy said, staring airily into the distance, 'would Kemp even know me if I didn't play football? I mean, is there another side to him? How did he end up being such a knob?'

Archie shrugged. 'Kemp's actually okay. He's got problems—'

'Yeah, right. Tell me about it.'

'I'm serious, Daisy. He told me about it in a session of detention.'

'I don't believe you.'

'It's true. He made me swear never to tell anyone.'

'Well, go on, then,' Daisy urged, nudging him. 'Tell me.'

'I can't, Daisy, it's a secret.'

'Don't be silly,' she implored. 'He told me his friends are going to kick the life out of me—'

'It's still a no,' Archie said. 'Do you understand what having a "secret" means?'

'Of course.'

'So, that's why I can't tell you.'

'*Yes*, you can,' Daisy insisted. 'For curiosity's sake, and because it's sometimes wiser to know your enemy better than you know your friends.'

Archie wavered for a second and shook his head, even if Daisy did have a point. 'Sorry.'

'*Pleeease*,' Daisy begged.

'No.'

'*Pleeease*, Winkle.'

'God. All right,' he sighed. 'As long as you swear you absolutely won't tell anyone. And never call me that name.'

Daisy wobbled her head inconclusively.

'I mean it,' Archie said, 'don't breathe a word.' He eyed her carefully. 'If he finds out he'll rip off my arms, suck my eyes out and give them to Isabella on a stick.'

'Yeah, yeah. Sure. Not a soul. I promise.'

'Okay,' he began, reluctantly, wondering how he'd given in quite so easily. 'The thing is, Kemp's parents died very suddenly when he was little. He never talks about it. And now he lives with his aunt, who he can't stand. There—'

'That's awful,' Daisy said, her eyes wide. 'How?'

'What do you mean... how?'

'Did they die?'

'Oh, I see,' he said. 'One night, driving along in an open-top car way up on the edge of the moors, they hit something, a deer, a fox—no one really knows.' Archie's voice turned to a whisper. 'The rest is properly grim.'

'Go on,' Daisy said, her eyes bulging with excitement.

Archie looked over his shoulder to see Kemp exiting at the far end of the hall. 'Apparently, the car skidded off the road, smashed into rocks and plummeted into a ravine where it blew up. Charred, disjointed remains were found scattered much later.'

Daisy whistled. 'Jeeeeez! I can see why he doesn't want anyone to know.'

'There's more.'

'Is it worse?'

'Yeah. I suppose,' Archie said. 'It took days before the car was found. And when they did, they discovered the bones of only one body. They reckoned the other one was eaten by something.'

'God no! That's terrible,' Daisy said, staring at the floor. 'You like him a bit, don't you?'

'Yeah, apart from when he's a jerk to you two.'

'Well then, Archie, come on, tell me more, I mean let's face it, he's probably organising my death right now.'

Archie ran a hand through his hair. 'Beneath all that macho

stuff he's quite soft—it's a barrier he puts up to protect himself, well, that's what his shrink says—'

'*Shrink?*' Daisy blurted. 'He has a shrink?'

A few heads turned their way. 'Yes, shrink, psychiatrist, whatever—keep your voice down.'

'They're not doing a particularly good job.'

Archie shot his twin a look. 'Tell me about it. He seems to snap in and out. I mean, in detention, when he said all this, he cried buckets and went on and on about wanting a normal life with a normal family. And then he thumped me really hard on the shoulder and ordered me not to tell anyone. Remember that massive bruise I had when I said I'd fallen out of a tree?'

'Oh yeah, I thought that was a bit odd.'

'I couldn't move my arm for a week,' he said, rolling his shoulder in its socket. 'He's sad, bored, and to be honest, lonely. Everyone hates him, and he knows it.'

'Even his sidekicks, Jackson and Pulse?'

'Those freaks pretend they're best mates, but it's fear that glues them together. Ever seen how they jump to attention when he's around or their heads get cracked? One moment he's charming and funny, the next he's pure evil. It's like a switch flicks in his head—and he's strong for his age—the only boy who can match him is Williams—'

'Yeah, I noticed sparks flying between them earlier,' she said. 'But, Arch, why does Kemp like you?'

'Because,' Archie said, raising his eyebrows, 'I'm probably not worth beating up. And because I don't deliberately *piss him off.*'

Daisy thumped him playfully on the arm. 'He's a loser, Arch. Why doesn't he try being nice for a change?'

'Apparently it's something to do with offloading emotional pain. That's why Solomon and the teachers leave him alone so he can do what he likes; they're terrified he'll go even further off the rails. I mean, think about it, if our parents got killed we'd probably go a bit nuts, although to be fair,' and he pinched Daisy on the cheek, 'you're almost there.'

She smiled, sarcastically. 'Our parents are never around, so it's almost the same thing,' she said, a frown slipping onto the corners of her mouth. 'I can't believe they've gone away again right before the game.'

Archie was glad that he wasn't the only one who missed them but he didn't want to dwell on it. 'Are you sure you're all right, you know, about the match?'

'Yeah,' she said. 'Thanks, Arch.'

'It's great news about the England call up. Nothing less than you deserve,' he said, smiling earnestly at her. His voice croaked. 'There is another thing,' he said. 'Do you remember,' he began cautiously, sensing his moment, 'anything about your nightmare last night?'

'Which one?' she said, way too quickly.

'Put it this way, you woke me up again.'

She looked confused, and blushed. 'Did I? Was it loud?'

'Yeah! The entire Vale of York are probably queuing up outside ready to beat you up. You screamed your head off—I thought you might remember, that's all. Wondered if you were okay?'

She shook her head. 'Now you mention it, I did have a nightmare about being in the middle of a storm.'

'And that's it?'

'And then finding three tablets in a cave lined with totally random pictures.' She pulled a face and laughed. 'Crazy, huh? If I'm honest, it's all a bit of a blur. You know, dreams…'

Archie's face dropped. Eventually, he spoke. 'But nothing about me and, perhaps, the small matter of a murder?'

'Seriously, Arch? A murder?'

'Sure.' Archie reddened.

'Nah, Don't think so. Why?' she thumped him playfully. 'Was that scene this morning something to do with this? Mrs

Pye's furious with you. And as for Isabella... So, tell me, who've you been bumping off?'

'It's not like that,' he replied, struggling to think about how to explain it. 'You see, I've had this recurring nightmare...' Archie petered out as if was too painful to broach.

'Actually—' she started, tentatively.

But Daisy was interrupted by the figure of Mr Solomon blocking out the light.

'Daisy, Archie, there you are. Now, where is that sister of yours?'

'Over here,' Isabella said, rushing towards them. 'Been showing my project to Mrs Douglas. Tuns out she doesn't know the slightest thing about paleomagnatism.' Her eyes rolled up as if reaching for the correct term.

'Her grasp of the matter is remarkably *loose*, to say the least.'

EIGHT

ASGARD'S PLAN

Asgard flipped into his maghole, arriving in the next moment on the planet of Havilah.

Wasn't it strange how the inhabited planets had once been so similar, but so utterly different? How Assyria and Cush had been vibrant worlds bathed in a richness of plants and sparkling seas, with living, moving mountains and wonderful, colourful animals. And how Earth had embodied a range of more static options like their trees whose roots remained fastened to the soil, and mountains who moved like sleepy tortoises, and sands which lay flat and lifeless on the ground.

Then there was Havilah. In every corner there were marvels of nature: towering rock formations in vivid blues, reds, and sparkly whites. Moving forests with colour-co-ordinated trees, and luminescent sea waters. Not to mention the rivers that defied gravity and ran, like snakes, above the land, or the snow and rain that covered the rock cities in multi-coloured droplets like confetti.

Asgard remembered the golden ceiling and the glittering chandeliers that sparkled so brightly that people dared not stare long at them. He remembered the windows cut from jewels and the polished floors made from intricate patterns of coloured gemstones and shaded timbers, and the great wall of rock that made up one entire length of the palace, with clear, sparkling waters washing down one side like a waterfall.

Now, a veil of grey dust and grime smothered it all like a thick blanket.

The dreamspinner walked through the air feeling for Cain's vibration. Soon, Asgard found himself facing a huge piece of furniture with hundreds upon hundreds of drawers lined up row after row in neat columns.

A drawer opened nearby, its contents spilling through the air and spreading over the ground. Cain, Asgard realised, was searching through his vast stores of precious stones and jewellery, looking for his branchwand.

'Who's there?' Cain called out. 'Which rapscallion of a rascal is it? I'll have you. I'll have you right and proper when I find it.' Another drawer dived through the air, splintering on impact, diamonds splaying into the dust. 'Because, thief, when I get my branchwand back, I'll have just enough magic to turn you into a vile piece of slime.'

With his opaque outline shimmering and his blue maghole spraying electrically from his maghole, Asgard materialised above Cain's head.

Cain sensed the strong vibrations. 'Who are you and what do you want? I may be blind, but I see things. Do not underestimate me.'

'It is I, Asgard, the dreamspinner.'

'The dreamspinner, again?' Cain said at length. 'Well, well, well. You have returned. It is lucky I am blind so I cannot see your ugly body.' He floated a little further down. 'All this exertion exhausts me.'

'You talked with the Heir,' Asgard said. 'What do you think?'

Cain sniffed the air. 'I do not believe those weak humans on earth are the Heirs of Eden. They are children. They have no magic, nor do they possess a sense of nature. IT IS WRONG!' he yelled.

'It is true,' Asgard replied.

'You jest, dreamspinner! Tell me, foul sorcerer of dreams, who are the real Heirs? Where are these men who are blessed with power and incantations? Huh, tell me.'

Asgard plucked his way across the air in silence and then spoke. 'Those protected by Adam become the Heirs of Eden, even if the old wizard has forgotten it. It has always been so. I have seen the writing.'

'That's as may be, but it was a foolish idea,' Cain snorted. 'You wish to tell me something else though, don't you?'

'On Earth, the clouds are building, Cain. The sky is darkening—'

Cain went quiet. 'Then you do not lie,' he said, his voice barely above a whisper. 'While I am stuck here alone in this empty, dying land, the planet of the Garden of Eden may be reborn and inflict more useless creations on the worlds. It is diabolical—'

'I come with a suggestion,' Asgard cut in. 'The final part of the Tripodean Dream will soon be given—'

Cain roared as two drawers flew out at the same time, sailed through the air and joined the heap of smashed wood on the floor. Cain floated down and peered through the debris in silence.

'They will not succeed,' he said, softly. 'They require wisdom, strength and cunning—decades of learning and years of understanding charms. The must have attained physical training to the highest degree. But these infants are less than twenty years old. They do not even understand what is shown to them in their dreams. Is that right, dreamspinner?'

'Yes.'

'Then they will never make it past the storm.'

'It is my conclusion, also,' Asgard said.

'And what of Adam?'

'He has grown old. He remembers nothing,' the dream-spinner said. 'Earth has mellowed him. He may be more of a hindrance to the Heirs, than a help.'

Cain groaned. 'So, ugly creature, why have you returned?'

'I can aid you,' Asgard answered, his fingers vibrating the sound. 'The time for change is now.'

'You have my ear, dreamspinner.'

Asgard took his time. 'The supply of dream-powders from the Garden of Eden stored in the great Atrium have ended. Now, we knit and spin from powders made from spider webs on Earth and Havilah.'

Cain sounded genuinely surprised. 'Dreamspinners have stored dream-powders from the Garden of Eden for all this time?'

'Yes,' Asgard replied. 'These are the dream-powders that nourish us and the creatures we give them to.'

'You gamble that they will fail and you have an alternative…?'

'I do,' Asgard replied. 'To me, their failure is as clear as the air.'

Cain sighed. 'What can I do? I was cut down from being a warrior, an artist, a lover, and a ruler, to a restless spirit with the strength of a faun,' Cain moaned. 'Yes, I have way more sway than those vile ghosts I see from time to time, but I have neither eyes for magic nor enough physical strength for a fight. You have a plan for all that?'

Asgard paused. 'I will tell you more of dreamspinners—'

'Oh why not!' the ghost replied, his voice laced with sarcasm.

'If a solid being,' Asgard continued, 'of flesh and blood travels through our maghole we may suffer to the point of death.'

'What is your point?' Cain shot back.

'You are not a solid being,' Asgard responded. 'You are a spirit.'

'Yes, yes. Why repeat yourself? It is how you took me to the boy.'

Asgard paused and then signed again rapidly, his slender claws flashing in the air, humming.

'What if you were to absorb into a human body?'

Cain paused for a beat. 'Ugly dreamspinner, how would this be in any way possible?'

'Dreamspinners know that if a human was to freely and willingly offer its body to a spirit, there is not a law in the universe that says they cannot both be connected.'

'Ha! You talk piffle of a bygone age.'

'I do not jest,' Asgard replied. 'A merger would give you substance. You would move with purpose. You would have strength. You would be able to see.'

'Intriguing,' Cain mused. 'Get a human to absorb into me? I have never considered it. Why have I not known about it?'

'Because, Cain, this feat is not easy to accomplish—'

'Why so?'

'For many humans, ghosts do not exist. Furthermore, apart from you, spirits are weak, and unlike you, they have no desire for life. They move quickly to other places, or stagnate.'

Cain let out a frustrated groan. 'But, dreamspinner, in a physical sense, how might this actually happen?'

'A union cannot be forced,' Asgard said. 'It must be the true will of the person of flesh.'

'I see,' Cain said. 'It isn't exactly an ideal negotiating platform, is it?'

Asgard dipped a long almost icicle-like leg into the blue, radiating hole of his abdomen.

'As the storm approaches, you might try and form an alliance with one who realises that there is no further hope. One who might dream of a future elsewhere.'

'That would be possible?'

'Yes. For humans, life on Earth is cherished,' Asgard said, his vibrations softening. 'Better still would be an alliance with a child.'

'A human child?' Cain spat.

'Indeed. But you would have to offer something great in return. Something almost as good as life.'

Cain circled the dreamspinner. 'Your words are clever, you strange, vile-looking, dream-giving creature,' he crowed. 'But if I was to merge with human flesh, wouldn't it curtail my movements to travel through a dreamspinner? And then what?'

'I am unsure. It has never been tried. Yoking with a large human may cause great harm,' Asgard said. 'A child might only wear us down, over time.'

'You're thinking of the boy you took me to?'

'That boy, exactly.'

'An Heir of Eden?' Cain chuckled. 'Well, well.'

'He is one of the three.'

'Oh, but can you imagine it?' Cain said. 'Stuck on that dead-end planet of Earth, harnessed to a revolting child.' He sighed. 'But then again, an Heir with me... in harmony. Do other dreamspinners know?'

'I am alone, for now,' Asgard said. 'But dreamspinners will rally to me when they learn the path I wish to take. Dreams must always be given.'

'Indeed, I imagine they will flock to you,' Cain said, clapping his hands together, although being a ghost it made absolutely no noise whatsoever. 'For you, dreams are all you have.'

NINE

A WORD FROM THE HEADMASTER

'A quick word, if I may,' Mr Solomon said, his voice kind and his manner fatherly but firm. He looked them over sympathetically. 'It pains me to say this, but this morning I received a communiqué from your parents who are now somewhere deep in the Middle East. They will not be back for the football or indeed for the whole of half term.' He scanned their sad faces. 'It appears they have discovered something of great interest.'

Archie and Daisy exchanged glances, remembering their teary farewell.

'They left yesterday,' Archie said, 'in a bit of a hurry. Didn't really say where they were going.'

'What does it say—what are they doing?' Isabella asked, as she attempted to read the headmaster's notepad upside down.

The principal folded the pad into his midriff. 'Well, it's light on actual detail, which, given the circumstances is the very least you deserve. To be honest, I'm not at all happy about it—'

'But we have—' Isabella started.

'Yes, I know you're fortunate to have your caretakers at Eden Cottage,' the headmaster said, 'but this is the third time I've had to reprimand you in the last two terms. Your parents have an obligation to you and to this school beyond the callings of their work, regardless of their fame and regardless of their accomplishments in archaeology. What if your caretakers should suffer a heart attack or a seizure or a fall?' he continued. 'Then what would you do?'

The children stared at the floor.

Isabella finally broke the silence. 'Sir, Mrs Lowden's brilliant at helping out. We'll use her as back-up.'

Mr Solomon nodded. 'Very well, but before you go, Isabella, I'm going to entrust you as the eldest to take a letter back to your parents. Collect it from my office before you go.'

He cleared his throat and turned to the twins. 'I have given you some simple homework over the break. Please, at least, give it some effort, especially you, Daisy. Your academic record is nigh on appalling, so I'd like you to do some reading on this topic and then reflect carefully on it—preferably before you dream up some hare-brained scheme,' he smiled badly at Archie, 'that gets our animal lover here battered into little pieces.

'In Chapter Four of your textbook there is a particularly valuable resource for your essay after half term entitled "*Did God create the universe, or did the universe create God?*"'

Then, in one movement, as though suddenly aware of the time, Solomon straightened, and looked over the top of his half-moon spectacles. 'Now, for goodness' sake, over this half term, behave yourselves, children; I cannot and will not have the police and Social Services chasing us around with your parents nowhere in sight. Please do not run into trouble. Understood?'

'Yes, sir,' the children said in unison.

'Excellent. Very best of luck with the football tomorrow morning,' he said in a softer voice, and a twinkle in his eye. 'There will be a big crowd cheering you on and several members of the press. The circumstances surrounding this game, and the fact that the final involves our rivals has caught the imagination of the entire region.' He darted a look at Isabella. 'Best behaviour, please. Now run along.'

Archie and Daisy scampered off down the corridor, the noise of their footsteps echoing off the old sandstone walls. Mr Solomon mumbled something about the time and, as he turned, he noticed Isabella lingering.

'Excuse me, sir,' she said.

'Yes, Isabella,' the headmaster said, impatiently. 'What is it now?'

'Well, it's the weather, sir.'

Solomon sighed. 'Yes, what about it?'

Isabella hesitated. For the first time in her life, her brain had jammed. 'I've made a weather barometer,' she finally spat out.

'Yes, congratulations on your skilful endeavour,' he replied. 'Mrs Douglas notified me. And, atmospheric pressure isn't even on your syllabus—'

'From my readings,' she began, 'there's going to be a simply massive—'

'Storm?' Solomon interrupted with a wry smile. He bent down a little. 'Well, I'm pleased that your readings match up with the area forecast, but I don't believe there's anything to fear. A bit of rain and some thunder perhaps. As a precaution, please remind your class to take their umbrellas and water-proofs as I mentioned in assembly.'

The headmaster scratched his chin and smiled at her. 'While you're here, let me remind you that it would be a terrible idea to race on to the pitch again. Please leave events on the pitch to the referee and other officials—whatever the circumstances.'

Solomon smiled in his false, head-masterly way and straightened.

'I expect nothing less than immaculate conduct, Isabella. There will be drastic repercussions if you brandish that temper of yours again.' He paused for effect. 'Do I make myself perfectly clear?'

Isabella nodded.

'Good. Now, I really must fly.'

That girl was one of Upsall's finest ever pupils, Solomon thought. Making barometers in her spare time, for fun. He'd never have dreamt of doing such a thing, nor would ninety-nine per cent of pupils they'd ever had at the school. He liked that. And he rather liked the fact that she wasn't afraid to confront anyone who laid a finger on her brother and sister. And now that he thought about it, there were a surprisingly large number of incidents.

Well, it was perfectly sweet of her to try and warn him, but he had a leaving party and other pressing matters to attend to. Nothing would stop his celebrations, certainly not a little storm and a warning from a pupil with a homemade air-pressure contraption.

Sue looked up as Isabella opened the door.

She noted how, when Isabella's straight brown hair with a tiny twist hung like a curtain over her forehead, it made her look slightly older than her.

They were alike in so many ways: top of the academic pile, both of them enjoying intellectual challenges rather than sporting endeavour, and their features were remarkably similar: fine, mousy hair, narrow faces, straight noses and brown eyes, although Sue's lips were fuller and her eyebrows finer. But she was frequently told how similar they were and the joke went round that they were more twins than Archie and Daisy.

The obvious difference was that Sue's appearance turned heads—she exuded sex appeal—and she looked after herself; her clothes and hair had a sense of style, whereas Isabella had a nerdy, more academic air and her clothes often sat on her like cloth sacks. Isabella regarded boy's general infatuation with Sue as a complete waste of time.

'What's up now?' Sue said.

Isabella's scowl had pulled her brow over her nose as though it were held by an invisible clip. She slumped into a chair.

'You won't believe what I did,' she began. 'I told Solomon there was going to be a massive storm.'

Sue gasped. 'You did what?'

'I told him about the barometer.'

'Are you insane?' Sue said, turning a little red. 'I hope you didn't tell him it stemmed from my dream?'

'Of course I didn't!' Isabella said, holding her head in her hands. 'It was so embarrassing—he said he'd seen news of the storm on the forecast. I mean, what was I thinking?'

'I can't believe you did that,' Sue said, draping an arm around her and trying hard not to smile. 'But at least you tried.' Sue ran her hand over the scientific instrument her friend had made. 'Maybe your barometer's faulty—perhaps the calibration's wrong?'

'It's not possible,' Isabella said, frowning. 'Every time I reset it, exactly the same thing happens.'

'Well, please don't spend too long fiddling with it,' Sue said. 'You've got to watch the football tomorrow. It might be Daisy's final game. In any case, I'm required to keep you under control after last week.'

Isabella felt a burning sensation filling her cheeks. 'I know, I know. Solomon reminded me of that too. I just don't seem able to help myself—'

'Well, you must. You can't verbally abuse the referee and get yourself manhandled off the pitch, screaming like a loon. And you've done it twice.' Her eyes flashed at Isabella. 'You'll be expelled if you're stupid enough to do it again.'

'But Daisy gets kicked and flattened more than anyone—'

'I know,' Sue said, 'but she doesn't make a squeak. It's a mystery she makes it through week after week and continues to smile as if nothing's happened. It's half the attraction—what makes her unique. You need to do the same, Isabella, and start controlling that nasty temper of yours.'

TEN

CAIN WONDERS

Cain realised the dreamspinner had disappeared by the instant lack of the strange, intense energy they emitted. He made a mental note to remember how the buzz tickled his aura.

For the first time in an age, Cain had a sense of urgency and energy about him. But he worried that he might have confused this sensation with frustration, or, perhaps, trepidation?

The dreamspinner understood how incredibly difficult it would be to succour a child to join with him because, to the common eye, he was nothing more than a sad old ghost, and he knew it. So why would an Heir of Eden agree to such a thing? In fact, why would *any* human child willingly give themselves over to *him*?

Cain hovered to the floor and lay back. He marvelled at the idea of being a little bit whole, a fraction human and to have just enough flesh, blood, and bone so that he might walk, dance, and maybe even see?

Was it truly possible?

His thoughts returned to the boy.

What had made him nick his cheeks with the knife? Was it the thrill of leaving Havilah or the desire to see if he could use his sixth-sense with the human form? Or was it a tiny piece of revenge?

It was a stupid thing to do, though. How would the boy trust him again, willingly, when he'd already been violated?

Cain threw himself at the door, flying straight through. He arrived in the old walled courtyard, scanned the area and hovered through it, dust puffing meekly to the side as he went. Cain located his thin cane and tapped it over the ground moving in a straight line across the yard. Soon he touched on a lump, like a large, overturned saucer stuck down with glue.

Cain sighed and knelt down.

'Hello, young one,' he said. 'One day soon, you, and all my people will once again see the beautiful world of Havilah all for yourselves. The moons, the sky, and the court of the castle. You will breathe the air and taste the honey of our bees. And, one day, when you are bigger, you'll drink the wines from our vines and press the flesh of others.' Cain grinned as his mood changed. 'And you will sing and dance and fight and love. Just as I once did.'

'But, alas, as I have told you a million times, you will never see me,' he sighed deeply. 'And I, regrettably, will never see your dear, sweet face with my eyes, unless I can fathom a way to join with a human.'

Cain allowed himself a smile.

'And, on this score, my dear little fellow,' he said, 'I have news.'

Cain had no idea if the small boy stuck in the puddle beneath him could hear. But he liked to talk, nonetheless, for there was no one else; aside from his man-servant, Schmerger, and Schmerger's mysterious, elven-like kind.

'So, child, if I am not able to use force, how shall a union with a human be done?' he said. 'In another time, I would have snapped off a finger or two, or pressed hot oil into orifices, and, yes, they would beg to do my bidding. But, now, if I am to find a person to join me, they must wish to do it with their whole heart.'

Cain tapped his cane on a cobble, thinking out loud. 'If these children are indeed the Heirs of Eden, as Asgard claims, then how must they feel? Afraid? Fearful? Confused?'

Cain jumped up.

'The prophecy! The Tripodean Dream! I must recall every detail,' he said. 'How did it go? If my memory still serves me, the dream states that they must solve three riddles in order to find three tablets. And these stone tablets hold the clues to the one key of the Garden of Eden.' Cain floated onto his back. 'They have one chance and all must survive. If they fail, Earth is destroyed and,' Cain smiled, 'Havilah awakens.'

Cain shot into the air startling a bird which shrilled noisily.

'Infants such as these Heirs could never do it. Never!'

Cain clasped his hands and floated down to the ground.

I suspect that that boy has an overwhelming desire to put the images he's seen in his dreams as far out of his mind as he possibly can.

'It is simple,' he said out loud. 'To secure the boy, I must take away his greatest fear.'

Cain grinned.

Love and fear, he thought, as the idea formed. *The two greatest weapons of manipulation known to mankind. And the thing is, I do believe I know where his fears lie.*

ELEVEN

STORM WARNING

'The thing is,' Isabella said, 'I don't know if I'm overly tired or not thinking straight, but I've done some calculations and I'm beginning to think that you might be right!'

'You really think so?' Sue said.

'Yes!' Isabella whispered. 'Going on what you've told me, I think it's going to be absolutely massive. Look, here's some data showing severe weather depression models exactly like—'

'Where did you get this?'

'I pulled it off the web,' Isabella replied. 'Hacked into the Met Office databank and downloaded all their flood sequences and weather system models from around the world.' She ran her finger down the page. 'Look, here's the flooding data from Pakistan a couple of years ago, and this one's from Queensland, Australia; and here, this one's from that super-storm in Eastern USA; and this one's from Eastern Europe. Can you see the similarities in humidity and cloud density; it's unbelievable—inches of rain—a proper deluge; potential for devastation on a huge scale.'

Sue sat down and whistled. 'You're predicting rainwater at a couple of inches every twenty minutes covering a surface area of say ten square miles—based on what I saw in my sleep! We'll be white water rafting in less than two hours—'

'I know! Scary, huh. You told me that the rain was so hard and heavy you felt you could hardly breathe—that it was weighing you down, right? So I've tried to figure out how much rain that would be and then multiplied it by the area involved, the potential volume the land can absorb and the capacity of the river to drain it away. Then I've added in the tidal flow of the river at York, and the increased effects of a full moon—'

Sue was astonished. 'Look, Isabella,' she began hesitantly. 'Let's get this straight. I had a really bad nightmare about you and the twins and a flood here at school. It was very real, sure, but it was only a dream.' She looked straight into her eyes. 'All of this,' she waved a hand at the barometer, 'it's great—really amazing, but it's pretty mad too.'

'I mentioned the storm to Solomon because I believe you, Sue.'

'You do?'

Isabella drummed on the desk. 'Yes, of course I do,' she said, her breathing shallower. 'You see, I know it sounds crazy, but I think I had the same dream. A couple of times.'

Sue nearly fell off her chair. 'You... as well? Why didn't you say something? How similar?'

'Well, most of it was to do with extreme precipitation, like yours, but at the end, it goes a bit crazy. I just can't remember.'

'Didn't you write it down?' Sue said. 'If you don't scribble dreams the moment you wake up, there's no way—'

'Well, I never do,' Isabella replied. 'It's where we differ.'

Sue tapped the spreadsheet. 'But if this evidence stacks up, shouldn't we say something?'

Isabella shook her head. 'Forecasters screwed up years ago before they knew what they were doing, before satellites and computer modelling,' she said. 'All we have is a homemade, slightly random experiment and a couple of freaky dreams. No one will believe us, look how Solomon reacted.'

'We'll be laughed out of school—'

'Yes, yes. I know,' Isabella said, rubbing her brow. 'I'm keeping my mouth zipped, for now.'

'Me, same,' Sue said. She paused. 'Isabella, I really need to talk to you about something else—'

'Aha!' boomed the voice they least wanted to hear.

Kemp strode in, turned a chair around and sat down slowly.

Isabella straightened. 'What can I do for you, Kemp, boys?' she said.

'Chief nerd, Mrs Douglas, wants to see you right away' he said. 'And seriously, it's a real request. I'm just being super-friendly.'

Isabella smiled, but her eyes were narrow and icy. 'Thank you, Kemp. You've delivered your message so now you can leave; we're busy.'

Kemp opened a book. 'I'm gonna stay here for a while,' he replied putting his feet up on the desk. 'I believe I'm allowed to and, furthermore, he smiled and ran a hand through his hair. 'You don't by any chance fancy a date, Sue—'

Sue stared back at his happy face open-mouthed. 'With a jerk like you?'

'There's no need to be like that,' Kemp said, standing up and grasping his heart. He turned to his mates and winked.

'One day, Sue, it'll be you and me? I can feel it in my bones.'

He extended his arm and gave Sue's bottom a playful tap.

Quick as a flash, she rounded on him, slapping his face, the sound like a snapping twig.

'Don't you dare touch me, you animal.' Sue chided. 'You're fourteen, and your hormones are clearly entering ignition phases, Kemp. Touch me again and I'll report you for assault.'

Kemp's happy face vanished and a look of anger flashed in his dark eyes. 'You'll do what? Tell on me? Tell on me... again,' Kemp fumed. 'Yeah, well big deal! Do you have any idea the number of hours I've spent in detention because of you two—?'

'You deserve everything you get,' Isabella said calmly.

'Forty-two,' he said, ignoring her. 'That's how many. Forty-two wasted hours.' He thumped the table. 'The teachers must think you're making it up, the way you pick on me—'

'Pick on *you*. Get lost, loser,' Isabella said, 'you make me want to vomit.'

Kemp smiled. 'Well now, speaking of vomit, a little bird tells me you've made a ba-rom-eter?' He said the word very slowly and as he did he felt under the desk and pulled away some sticky tape. He held up a small recording device. 'Hello little birdie.'

Isabella shrieked.

'Brilliant isn't it?' Kemp said, turning the black box around in his hands. 'Superb reception for such a tiny thing. I'll tell you what I'll do,' he continued, rubbing home his advantage, 'just before the football starts I'll announce—perhaps with Coach's megaphone—that there's a big storm on its way which will devastate the whole area. What was it, boys?' he turned to the sniggering pair. 'Ah, that's it... white water rafting in two hours ...' He looked triumphant. 'And all because you dreamt about it. Isn't that lovely.'

The boys laughed, thickly.

Isabella's face was like thunder. 'That's immoral... and illegal, Kemp!'

He waved her protest away. 'Now, pray tell where this clever barometer thing is.' He took a couple of paces to their desk. 'Christ, is this it?' he picked it up.

'Don't you dare—'

'A glass jar filled with liquid and a straw.' Kemp seemed genuinely disappointed. 'What a pathetic, terrible, useless piece of sh—'

'Put it down!' Isabella demanded.

'Why? If anyone saw this you'd be laughed out of school.' He turned it around in his hands.

'Put it down—'

'Give me one good reason?'

'Because I asked you to, that's why.'

'Not good enough—'

'Because it's an important part of my module—'

Kemp sneered. 'No it isn't. It's not even on your syllabus.'

'Please—'

'What will you do if I don't?'

'Put it down!' Isabella roared.

The door swung open.

'Archie,' Isabella gasped, relieved, 'what are you doing here?'

'Oh!' he looked at their faces. 'I'm dropping off a book... what's going on?'

Kemp held the barometer in the air. 'Archie, my friend. Your sister thinks she should tell the world about a huge storm that's coming based on this hilarious scientific instrument. What do you think?' Kemp placed the barometer on the edge of the desk where it swayed for a moment and then righted itself.

Archie frowned. 'Er, I don't know.'

'Well if you don't know, Archie, then I really should break it —to save these girls showing it to anyone and making complete idiots of themselves—'

'No!' Isabella cried.

Kemp ignored her and raised an eyebrow, 'and of course, to protect the great academic reputation of Upsall School.' Kemp laughed and slapped the desk with his free hand.

'I don't think that's a good idea,' Archie said, trying to read his sister's face. 'Why don't you give it back?'

'What!' exclaimed Kemp, turning on him. 'Don't get me wrong, but I'm the one who's going to decide whether they can or can't have it back. Tell you what,' said Kemp, addressing the girls again, 'if Sue goes out with me, I'll give it back.'

'Never!' Both girls instinctively replied. Sue slid her chair back so fast it fell backwards and clattered on the floor.

'There are rules for a reason, Kemp,' Isabella said, regaining her composure, 'so listen up. Here's what happens; you put the barometer down and leave it exactly as it is, while we go and get Mr Steele. Do you understand?'

Kemp scratched his fat nose. 'Steele will never believe you— and I've done nothing wrong. Nothing. Your little brother can prove that, can't you Archie?'

Archie shrugged his shoulders.

The girls began to gather up their things and headed towards the door.

Kemp wasn't finished. He winked at Sue and blew a kiss to Isabella.

'Remember, Mrs Douglas wants to see you both in the science labs. I'm just the messenger.'

'You'll pay for this,' Isabella yelled, as she closed the door, 'if it's the last thing I do.'

Sue turned and she spoke slowly with typical clarity.

'Let's get this straight once and for all, Kemp. I will never, ever go out with you, even if we're the last two people alive on this planet. Do you completely understand?'

TWELVE

SWEAR ON YOUR LIFE

'Christ alive, Kemp,' Mason said, 'you're asking for it, didn't you hear her? She's gone off to get Steele. He'll go mental.'

Kemp smiled. 'You really think so? Well, I don't know how it got there—do you?'

Mason suddenly realised what he meant. 'Me, neither,' he said, his voice as thick as dough.

'Nor me,' said Wilcox shrugging his shoulders.

'That leaves only one other person who could have witnessed it.' Kemp turned to Archie. 'So Archie, tell me, did you by any chance see who dropped the barometer out of the window?'

'Well, I'm not blind,' Archie replied.

Kemp rolled his eyes. 'I don't think he gets it, lads. I don't think he quite grasps the seriousness of the situation. Look, Archie, I like you, and if you want me to continue liking you, all you have to say is that you didn't see anything. Get it?'

'Right,' Archie said, wondering why it was that Kemp was such a massive jerk when Mason and Wilcox were around. 'I won't say a word,' he said mechanically.

Kemp hesitated. 'I'm not sure that's really acceptable. Swear on your life that you won't tell anyone.'

'Oh come on,' Archie replied, 'I'm not a kid and I'm not a sneak. You know that.'

'Archie, I need you to promise—on your life—that you're not going to tell anyone, that's all,' Kemp insisted. 'I mean, unlike your sister, you can keep your mouth shut, can't you?'

'If you didn't want anyone to know,' Archie argued, 'why did you throw it out of the window in the first place?'

Kemp smiled. Wasn't it funny how threatening words seemed to cause Archie no pain and physical beating seemed to cause Daisy, his twin, no pain either?

He stepped in front of Archie and pulled himself up.

'Your big sister doesn't like me and you know that very well. You also know she's responsible for putting me in detention pretty much every week for the last two years. You'll have to promise me you won't tell anyone,' he demanded.

'Give me a break,' Archie replied.

'Archie, promise, on your life, that you won't tell anyone, that's all I'm asking. I mean, you can keep cool, can't you?'

'If you didn't want anyone to know,' Archie replied, 'why did you do it in the first place?'

'To protect the excellent academic reputation of Upsall School,' he said. 'And, anyway, your sister hates me and cannot be trusted. Prove you're different.'

'Bog off, Kemp. My sister doesn't like you because you do idiotic things like throw barometers out of windows and sneak dead rats into sports bags.'

Kemp chuckled. Two years ago, he'd found a dead rodent by the river and hid it in Isabella's games bag. He waited. And every day he waited, getting more and more excited about the slowly decomposing rat. For the best part of a week, while everyone wondered what the terrible smell was, he waited. Then, on the afternoon of the school cross-country run, as Isabella put on her tracksuit bottoms, out plopped the remains, maggots spraying over her things like discarded rice.

Dynamite.

Archie sighed. 'Look, Kemp, if it means that much to you, I'll do it, but only if *you* swear, on your life that you won't do any more harmful, stupid things to Isabella, Sue, or Daisy.'

Kemp stuck out his jaw and moved it from side to side contemplating Archie's request. At last, he nodded and said, 'Okay, I agree. But it ends when she gets me into detention again.'

Archie nodded.

'Come on then,' Kemp said. 'You say it first.'

'Do I really have to?'

'Yeah, course you do—if you want me to do the same.'

Archie rolled his eyes. 'I swear, on my life, that I won't tell anyone that you dropped the stupid barometer out of the window. Satisfied.'

Kemp nodded. 'Easy, wasn't it?'

'Now you do it!'

Kemp looked him in the eye. 'I swear on my life not to harm your sisters, and not to play any more silly tricks on them. There, that good enough?'

'I suppose.'

Kemp's tone changed and he ushered Archie aside.

'Hey, sorry, Arch. You don't have to say it... I know, I know,' he said putting his hands in the air. 'I've been a massive dick.'

'You're telling me!' Archie replied. 'Why, Kemp? Why do you do it?'

Kemp shrugged. 'Dunno. Boredom. Can't seem to help myself when I see your sisters—'

'Look out!' Jackson said, as he ran back into the classroom. 'Steele's on his way.'

'Come on!' Kemp said. 'Out of the window!'

They ran to the window and pulled up the blind.

Isabella, Sue and Mrs Pike stared up at them.

'Drat,' Kemp said, under his breath. He smiled pleasantly back at them.

'Kemp, and Archie de Lowe,' the old teacher hollered. 'Who

would have guessed? What can you tell me about the mess down here?'

Kemp opened the window. 'Hello, Miss. Is there a problem?'

'You know perfectly well there is!'

'Sorry. I don't what you're talking about, Miss?'

'This debris, here,' Mrs Pike shrieked, pointing at the concrete.

Kemp peered like a sailor looking down from deck, a quizzical expression etched on his brow. 'I have no idea what you're talking about,' he replied. 'Window's been closed all along, hasn't it, boys?' He shrugged. 'What is it?'

Isabella shrieked. 'Kemp, you know perfectly well what it is!'

'Glass?' he offered.

'Yes!'

'A smashed Coke bottle perhaps?'

'No, Kemp, it was Isabella's barometer.'

'A bar-hom-tier,' Kemp repeated, thickly. 'What on earth is that?'

'Archie, did you see Kemp with it earlier?' the teacher hollered.

Archie stared at the floor.

'Tell me, what happened?'

'Dunno,' Archie said, running a hand through his hair.

'Archie, what do you mean, you "dunno"?'

'Dunno,' Archie said again, reddening.

Kemp looked straight into Mrs Pike's eyes. 'Honestly, there's been no one around. We've been chatting about animals, life, and situation comedy—'

'Great!' Isabella stormed, addressing Archie. 'Kemp's made you swear not to tell or something childish like that, hasn't he? You, Kemp,' she said pointing at him, 'you were the last person to have it. It must have been you.'

'Then prove it,' Kemp said, thrusting out his jaw.

'I shouldn't have to,' she pleaded. 'Archie, all you have to do is tell us what happened—'

Archie shook his head.

'Expel him!' Isabella shouted pointing at Kemp.

'But I haven't done anything—'

Isabella stamped her foot. 'Yes, you have!'

'Prove it!' he yelled back.

'You had it last! I saw it in your hands, admit it—'

'NO! Innocent until proven guilty—'

'You are guilty!'

'In whose court?'

'*I DID IT!*' Archie yelled, his voice cutting above theirs.

The school bell chimed, the echo circling around their heads.

'It was me.'

'*You*?' Isabella quizzed.

'*Archie*?' Mr Steele said.

'de Lowe?' said Mrs Pike.

'Yes,' Archie sighed. 'I was fed up with you two always getting at each other, so I thought I'd, you know…toss it out.' He bowed his head. 'I'm sorry.'

Isabella looked confused. This wasn't the sort of thing Archie would do, so why was he taking sides with Kemp?

'What did you say to Archie, Kemp? It smells like you've done a pathetic deal or something—'

Kemp bit his lip and stared hard at her, his eyes cold and narrow. Then he spun and marched out of the room.

THIRTEEN

GUS TALKS TO SUE

'Are those real tears, or are you just pleased to see me,' Gus said on finding Sue later, as he pulled a folded red and white polka-dot handkerchief out of his pocket.

Sue shot him a look but her face broke into a smile. 'Oh! I don't know. It's that oaf, again. He's got hold of Isabella's experiment, smashed it, and she's gone nuts.' She dabbed her eyes and offered it back.

'Ah. No, keep it,' he said. 'I've got a drawer full. Dad has a thing about them—'

'Thanks, Gus.'

'Want to talk about it?'

She shook her head.

'You sure? I'm all ears, and teeth,' he said grinning. 'Don't worry about Kemp—I've got a plan where he's concerned. Right now, there are disturbing rumours leaking about these corridors concerning our headmaster.'

'Solomon?'

'Aye,' he said in mock way with an eyebrow raised. He paused.

'Well—'

He shook his head. 'Can't tell you,' he said.

'Why not?'

'It might cheer you up.'

The corners of her mouth turned up and she hit him playfully in the chest.

'Well,' Gus continued, 'I just happened to be in the old school—'

'Just happened?'

'Yes. Taking an arbitrary stroll down the passageways leading to his study—'

'Gus!'

'Do you want me to tell you, or not?' he said, stealing a glance over her shoulder.

She nodded.

'As you probably know, Solomon's having a massive party tomorrow night after the football. I happened to be standing outside when I heard this extraordinary noise.'

'What noise?'

'Well, singing, I think. Terrible sort of opera, like baritone cat-wails.'

Sue tittered. 'So?'

'That's not the best bit,' Gus said. 'You see, he then started talking but I'm sure there wasn't anyone in there.'

'How do you know?'

'He hadn't shut the door—'

'You didn't—?'

Gus pulled a face. 'Only quickly. I couldn't help it. Bet you'd have done the same?'

'No way!'

'Well, anyway, there he was, wearing a dress—'

'You're kidding!'

'Yeah. Okay, so it was a kilt… I hope. Green and blue crisscrosses, and, on his top, a white string vest.'

'A singlet? What was he doing?'

'Introducing himself.'

'What?'

'Practicing his how-do-you-doo's, his voice getting posher and posher. *"Oh, how do you do, Mayor, how do you do Your Eminence, that sort of thing".*'

Sue laughed as Gus raised his eyebrows.

'Then what?'

'I sneaked off. Told you it would cheer you up. Now, important stuff. I need some advice.'

Sue cocked her head. 'Go on.'

Gus's face contorted. 'I need a date. Got a party over half-term.'

'You're asking me for a date.'

Gus coughed and blushed. 'Er. No. Not really. Just advice, or a bit of guidance as to whom I might approach.'

'Oh,' she said. 'Right.'

Gus couldn't tell if her tone betrayed a hint of disappointment.

'Anyone spring to mind?'

'Daisy?' he squeaked.

'Which one? Daisy Martin or Daisy de Lowe.'

'Either.'

She rolled her eyes. 'Really?'

Gus looked taken aback. 'Why not?'

'Daisy Martin is pretty, but she's, you know, a bit soppy, forever sweeping back her hair and sighing. You'd be bored senseless. On the other hand, de Lowe will probably tear the place up, and, if there's dancing, you'd better have your dancing shoes on.'

Gus's forehead rolled. 'I hate dancing.'

Footsteps made them turn.

Sue squeezed his arm. 'I've got to go. I'll come up with something, don't you worry. I'll let you know before half term, okay?' She looked him in the eye.

Gus smiled. 'Thanks, Sue. Discretion, please. Don't want it leaked around or everyone will think I'm desperate.'

'No problem. Hey, and thanks for cheering me up, Gus. Love the hanky.'

FOURTEEN

STORM GLASS

'You must think I'm a fool, Arch. It's perfectly clear that Kemp put you up to this.' Her tone softened. 'Didn't he?'

Archie kept his eyes down.

She sighed. 'Have it your own way, Archie. I just don't understand how you can be friends with him. I just wish you'd been honest with me, Arch. That's what really hurts.'

'I'm sorry about your experiment,' he said, raising his eyes.

Isabella pressed her lips together. 'Don't be. It kept bottoming out. Actually, I've researched a better idea. I'm going to make a Fitzroy storm glass.'

'A Fitz glass?'

'No, a Fitz-ROY storm glass. It's a brilliant bit of kit, a kind of old-fashioned weather gauge, and, as a punishment for your behaviour, you can help me make it.'

Archie smiled. 'Why the craze about weather stuff?'

'Well, if you must know,' she said, 'there's a curious weather system developing.' She hesitated a little. 'This may sound a bit mental, but Sue and I have had a premonition; a dream about torrential rain, flooding, that kind of thing.'

Archie reeled, and put a hand out to steady himself.

'But you're always saying how unscientific things like dreams are and that they're irrelevant—'

'Nevertheless, Archie,' she said, curtly, 'dreams are viable mechanisms of the brain.'

Archie cleared his throat. 'Bells, do you dream a lot?'

'No,' she said. 'I never dream, well, not until recently. But I've got an intensely strong feeling about this one. So, I reckon there's no harm in trying to find out if there's any scientific substance to it.'

Archie scratched his head and wondered if he should mention *his* appalling dreams, and Daisy's shouting in the middle of the night. Instead, he heard himself asking, 'How does this Fitzglass-thing work?'

'It shows what's happening with the weather through the liquid in the glass which, I believe, mirrors what's going on outside… I think. For example, if the liquid is clear, the weather will be clear. If small crystals form, then snow is on its way—'

'And what if there's a storm…?' Archie asked.

'When a thunderstorm's coming, the liquid should be cloudy with small star-like crystals in it, and so on.'

'Nice.'

'First, I'll need a few ingredients—and this, bro, is where you come in.'

Archie rubbed his hands. He loved projects like this where he didn't quite know where it was going.

'First, go and bat your eyelids at Mrs Culver. Ask for ten grams of camphor; she'll have some for food flavouring. Tell her you need some in Chemistry to show how a compound can burn without leaving an ash residue. If she starts asking questions, mention oxygen in a scientifically related question. For some reason, Mrs Culver can't bear the word "oxygen".

'Then, go and find Mr Pike in the Maintenance Department. Ask him for distilled water. Fill a large, plastic bottle if you can; he keeps some for his forklift batteries.'

Isabella scratched her forehead thoughtfully, making sure

she hadn't forgotten anything. 'Have you got that? Camphor and distilled water. I'll find some ethanol and the other bits from Chemistry later on. Shouldn't be too difficult,' she added, almost as a reminder to herself.

'Where shall we meet?' he asked.

Isabella smiled. 'The science labs are free straight after lunch. One-thirty. I'll see you there.'

'Gotta look like you mean it, Archie,' Sue said, as she threw a lab-coat at Archie.

Archie handed over the camphor while Sue began to heat a beaker of distilled water.

In silence, as Archie and Sue looked on, Isabella added each component until the beaker was half full. The ethanol and camphor were poured in last. When these had dissolved, Isabella asked Archie to find a large test tube sealed with a stopper. She exchanged the liquid into the test tube and filled it a couple of centimetres from the top, and capped it off.

Archie put the experiment in a holding device on the desk.

'Archie,' Isabella said, 'please wash those beakers while we put everything away.'

He headed to the far corner of the laboratory, but, just as he was about to place the beaker in the sink, the door swung open.

Instinctively, Archie ducked under the table.

'Aha! *There* you are,' Kemp said, with big smile. 'Been looking all over for you girls.'

'GO AWAY!' they shouted.

'Whoa! Calm down. I've come to apologise.' He looked down at the desk. 'What's all this then? Doing some illegal experiments, are we? That's terribly exciting. Creating a bomb or some poisons or a wee bit of chemical warfare—'

'It's none of your business, Kemp. Leave us alone.'

'Biological warfare?'

'No, Kemp it's—'

'Mustard gas, radiation? Come on, I'm offering an olive branch and I'm sorry about earlier. Got a little out of hand, didn't it? Actually, have either of you seen Archie?'

Isabella caught Archie staring at her from behind one of the desks, out of Kemp's eye line, shaking his head vigorously.

'Er, no. Sorry. No idea,' she said, brushing an imaginary speck off her lab coat.

Kemp regarded her suspiciously before his eyes moved to the test tube on the desk.

'This is your experiment, is it? A test-tube full of cloudy potions. Cor. Brilliant.'

'Thanks for your interest, Kemp,' Sue said, in her most condescending manner. 'But, to be honest, this is a very dull investigation we're doing, dealing with the creation of crystals using camphor, ethanol, distilled water, and a couple of other things you probably wouldn't understand.'

But Kemp was like a dog chasing a scent, and his tone changed. 'If it's so boring, why are you doing it in lunch break?'

'For fun!' Isabella tried.

Kemp looked at her and cringed.

'Really?'

'As I said, Kemp, it's a simple experiment—'

'I don't believe you.' He stepped closer. 'It doesn't add up.'

'Please, go away, and leave us alone,' Isabella said, as sweetly as she could, remembering Archie's advice.

Her words fell on deaf ears. 'Why won't you tell me what you're doing?' Kemp quizzed. 'I'm quite keen on the old chemistry.'

'Why should we?' Isabella snapped.

Kemp smiled back. 'Cos, otherwise I'll smash it—'

'You wouldn't dare.' Isabella lunged for the test tube, but Kemp was too quick.

'Give it back, immediately!'

'No way. Come on, what's in it?' he said, inspecting it. 'A lethal poison, a nerve agent, a deadly virus—'

'Don't be stupid.'

'From where I'm standing, I'm not the one being stupid,' he said.

Isabella huffed. 'If you must know, it's a Fitzroy storm glass—'

'Well, well, well,' Kemp said, slowly. 'You're not still going on about this bleeding storm? When will you two grow up and do what everyone else does?' He looked at one, then the other. 'Watch the weather forecast on this thing called the telly. Oh, hang on, don't tell me; you haven't got one!'

'Of course we do,' Isabella raged.

Kemp raised an eyebrow. 'I'm not sure I believe you. Thing is, you de Lowes are so backwards I wouldn't be surprised if your mum has to shave Neolithic hair off her body. We'd never know, though, because she seems to have disowned you.' He cocked an eye at Isabella's puce face. 'And that old woman who looks after you, with whiskers coming out of her face like a cat…' he opened his eyes wide theatrically as if stunned by an idea. 'I know what you should make,' he paused, holding the test-tube in front of his eyes, 'a potion for hair removal! You've got customers in your very own home!'

Kemp brushed aside Isabella's howls. 'Now, clever clogs, let me fill you in. Last night the man on the TELLY,' he said this in a deliberately loud voice, 'said that there might be a storm over the next couple of days, but not a big one, and certainly not one with white-water rafting.'

Kemp marched to the corner of the room, near to where Archie was hiding under the table.

Isabella gasped lightly.

'I tell you what,' Kemp continued, 'I'm going to do you a favour and put you out of this ridiculous weather preoccupation once and for all. I'm going to spin this tube thing like a spinning top. You do know what that is, don't you? By the time you get over here, it'll either be in bits on the floor, or, by some miracle, you may have grabbed it. But, if and when this happens, I'll be long gone out of the door. Then you can go and do what everyone else does and watch the weather forecast on the box.' He grinned. 'You'll find it comes after the news.'

Kemp, with the test-tube in the palms of his hands, drew them quickly apart. The tube spun fast and straight, and, while the girls fixated upon it, Kemp strode through the door, turning the lights off after him.

The sound of the latch clicking seemed to accentuate the wobbling of the glass. In an instant, the girls rushed over in near darkness, but, in their haste, they careered into the lab furniture creating a din of scraping chairs and upturned tables.

As the crashing sounds receded, the test tube wobbled to its conclusion, followed, moments later, by the tinkling sound of breaking glass.

In the following silence, all they could hear was a huge roar of laughter coming from outside the classroom.

FIFTEEN

GENESIS CONSIDERS THE TASK AHEAD

The large dreamspinner studied each of her delicate, long, slender legs one by one, as if paying homage to them for their service. For the first time she noted the wear and tear; the way so many had turned grey when once they were bright white and how her slender slithers of knuckles and joints were now worn thin.

As Genesis seamlessly morphed each leg from a pincer, to a needle, then back to a long leg again, a deep sense of foreboding filled her.

What if these Heirs of Eden do not understand?

She shivered at the possibility. Putting the thought aside, she sent vibrations from her rapidly moving legs to the waiting dreamspinners, the Elders of the dreamspinners: Gaia, Juno, and Asgard.

'The Tripodean Dream comes with a gift for each Heir of Eden,' Genesis said, as she dipped three long legs into her maghole and withdrew some microscopic granules, studying the ends. 'These gifts are physical talents designed to assist each one to whom the prophecy has been given. They are known as the Gifts of the Garden of Eden.'

'Then the stories are true,' Gaia vibrated.

'Yes. These crystals were passed to me by my mother, as once they were handed to her. If the Heirs of Eden succeed in the tasks set before them they will open the planet of the Garden of Eden to life once more,' she said. 'Dream powders will be replenished. Wondrous times may begin afresh for all life.'

A strong vibration cut through the air.

'Why do we meddle?' Asgard said, his fingers moving quickly. 'If you had not spun the Tripodean Dream, who is to say that life would not have continued just as before. Besides, the Tripodean Dream has been given to Heirs of Eden who are but *children* of man. They are not equipped to tackle what lies ahead; the storm alone will tear them to pieces—'

'The riddles and tests were prepared by Adam the Great when he was a wizard at the height of his powers in the Garden of Eden. It is ancient magic—'

'But these children do not seek it. They do not even know of the consequences—'

'Asgard, this is not the time to argue the rights or wrongs. The sequence of the Tripodean Dream has begun. Only the Heirs of Eden can interpret because they represent the Soul, the Heart and the Ego of Earth—'

'Even though they have no training—'

'The time has come for change,' Genesis said, her vibrations overriding his. 'That is the lore of the universe. It is natures will.'

Asgard scoffed, his vibrations slowing. 'They are not equipped—'

'Enough!' Genesis said. 'They are the ones who are protected by Adam—'

'But Adam does not know it. He does not even know his name—'

'He will remember, Asgard,' Genesis said, the vibrations from her fingers singing through the air. 'He must.'

The old dreamspinner slowly dipped her hands into the blue electrical hole that filled her midriff.

'Juno,' she said, addressing a younger dreamspinner. 'Have the last dream powders from the Garden of Eden been dispersed?'

'Yes, Mother. The Atrium is clear.

'Good. Then the final part of the Tripodean Dream will be given to the Heirs of Eden this Earth night, as they sleep. Afterwards, I will give them the Gifts of the Garden of Eden. On the giving of the Gift of Strength they will have seven days to solve the riddles and unlock the key.'

'But they will die,' Asgard said. 'It is a waste. The suffering will be immense—'

'I will hear no more of your objections, Asgard,' Genesis snapped, as she lifted up her wiry, opaque outline.

'The journey for the Heirs of Eden to find the tablets and fulfil the prophecy is about to commence. Regardless of what you may think, these children of mankind are the Heirs of Eden. Nothing can stop what is coming, nothing. When the gifts are given, life on Earth will be in the Heirs of Eden's hands and theirs alone.'

SIXTEEN

A BROKEN PROMISE

'Now then, now then!' Kemp said, flicking on the light. 'What's going on here?' he said, in a mock, policeman-like voice. He looked around to see an empty room and then, slowly, Sue got up, her hair covering her face like a veil.

Then Isabella rose, too, rubbing her head.

Kemp's eyes were on fire. 'Brilliant. Blooming gold.' He pulled his phone out. 'Smile at the budgie.' The camera clicked and flashed. Kemp inspected the image. 'Lovely. You two look gorgeous. I'm gonna post this everywhere.'

Archie stood up, brushing splinters from his lab-coat.

'Archie!' Kemp exclaimed, his expression changing. 'Shit! Where did you come from?'

'I've been here all the time, you idiot.'

Kemp's manner changed immediately. 'Are you all right?' He pointed at Archie's sleeve. 'Is that…?'

Archie looked down at his hand. Blood was oozing from a gash at the base of his thumb and running over his hand.

'Satisfied?' Isabella said, as she tiptoed through the glass fragments towards him. 'Happy now?' she held Archie's arm and inspected it. 'Kemp, get the first aid box; we need to stop the bleeding. And Kemp, be useful and find a dustpan and brush.'

Isabella led Archie to the tap.

'This might hurt, Archie.'

He winced as water ran into the cut.

'There's a fragment in here. Sue, I need a towel, tweezers, and then we'll need to compress the wound.'

Archie gritted his teeth as she plucked out the tiny slivers before applying pressure on the wound.

When they'd finished, Archie turned to Kemp who stood frozen to the spot. Archie looked him hard in the eye.

'You swore, on your life, that you wouldn't do this kind of thing,' Archie said. '*You swore—on—your—life,*' he yelled. 'I held my side of the deal, but at the first opportunity you couldn't resist it, could you? It's now entirely clear to me that you value your life as pretty much worthless. What would your parents think? Do you reckon they'd be proud?'

Kemp's face fell, and the colour drained from his cheeks.

'Sorry, Archie,' he said. 'I... I didn't realise...'

With Archie's words ringing in his ears, Kemp fled.

The girls began to clear up the mess. But Sue noticed something a little strange as she swept the glass into the dustpan. After a long silence, Sue turned to Archie.

'Right, Archie. Where is it?'

'Uh?' Archie cried, feigning shock.

'Where is... what?' Isabella said.

Sue tutted. 'Oh, come along, come along, Sherlock Isabella. The storm glass, silly.'

'In fragments in the bin?'

Sue bit her lip. 'That isn't test-tube glass. That's beaker glass fragments, isn't it, Archie?'

'Beaker?' Archie replied, the corners of his mouth turning up.

'You've got it, haven't you?'

Archie couldn't contain himself any longer and laughed. 'Indeed, I have!' He slowly moved his gaze towards his trousers and pointed at his crotch. He began to unzip his fly. 'It's right here.'

'No way!' Sue exclaimed. 'Oh… my… God!'

Archie reached in and teased it out. 'DA-NAH,' he said, his eyes sparkling.

He held the test tube up in the air. 'Sorry, couldn't think of anywhere else quick enough,' he said. 'Then, when I crouched down, I lost my balance, and knocked over the beaker.'

Sue clapped her hands at Archie's story but Isabella looked horrified.

'Well, well, Archie. A storm in your pants. First time for everything, eh?'

All three burst out laughing as Archie slipped the tube neatly into the rack.

Isabella wagged a finger at him.

'Just a minute, Archie. The very least you can do is give it a wash before either of us has to handle it.'

SEVENTEEN

A POINTLESS EXPERIMENT

By the time the de Lowes returned to the stone courtyard of Eden Cottage, the charcoal colours of dusk lay sandwiched upon the buildings while, in the distance, twinkling house-lights flickered in the the expansive panoramic landscape of the Vale of York beyond.

Archie and Daisy immediately set about kicking a football. The scuffing, sandpapery noises of their feet, and the ball doffing back off the grey stone walls roused Mrs Pye who waved enthusiastically from one of the two windows in her flat opposite the farmhouse.

Isabella's mind tracked back to the conversations with Solomon and Kemp, who had both been so rude about their house.

It wasn't that bad.

She studied the exterior. Sure, it was a bit of a mishmash of an ancient moors farmstead, but it wasn't too unusual, was it?

Constructed from irregular, Yorkshire-grey stone and old, thick timbers, its slate roof was covered in moss and lichen that hung over too far, as though badly in need of a trim. Looking at the blackened, slightly crooked chimneys, the higgledy-piggledy stone arrangements, and the odd sections of glass and brick intermittently nestled into the walls, Isabella was reminded of a bag of loose, gummy sweets squished together and charred until they were all the same colour.

Architecturally, she could tell the farmhouse was deformed, but perhaps these quirky anomalies helped it blend in to the rocks and the forest beyond. Somehow, she concluded, it worked beautifully.

As Isabella entered the kitchen, she realised that this was definitely the heart of the house, a place that oozed warmth, love, happiness, and appreciation of fine foods. Bunches of rosemary, lavender, thyme, and dried, cured hams and fruits dangled from a row of black hooks, the smell intoxicating.

Even the stone slabs, laid out in great squares, bore a warm, glossy sheen from years of wear. As she looked up, grey, oak timbers fanned out in clean lines above their heads, protecting those within.

Down the middle of the kitchen ran a long, chunky, dark brown oak table fit for a banquet. Next to the table stood a pleasing, red-brick, inglenook fireplace in which the old wood-fired cooker sat, and which Old Man Wood lovingly filled up every day from the wood store next to the larder.

Two waggon wheels suspended by three heavy chains had spotlights beaming down from within the rim and, on the far wall, was Mrs Pye's pride and joy; a fifty-inch flat-screen telly.

Kemp was wrong. Even if the kitchen was a bit of a curiosity, they weren't entirely archaic.

'Well, come on then,' Daisy said, slinging a bag on her bed. 'Show me this amazing thing that's been holidaying in Archie's pants.'

Isabella unwrapped the test tube from her scarf and leant

the glass between two books on the table. Three pairs of eyes stared down at it.

'Bit foggy, isn't it?' Daisy said. 'So, does that mean it'll be foggy?'

Archie raised his eyebrows. 'Don't be silly, Daisy. This is serious science.'

Daisy giggled and elbowed Archie as they continued to stare.

'Ooh,' Daisy cooed. 'Look at those little stars. What does that mean?'

Isabella pulled out her crib sheet. 'Tiny stars means that it will be stormy,' she said, and then read from her crib sheet. '*A cloudy glass with small stars indicates thunderstorms.*'

'Wow,' Archie said, sarcastically. 'Impressive.'

Daisy spluttered. 'And... is that it?'

'What do you mean, *is that it*?'

'Well, it's very pretty, but you know, as an award-winning scientist, I thought it might be a bit... cooler,' Daisy glanced at Archie for support. 'I mean, if you wanted to know thunderstorms were coming all you had to do was watch the forecast on TV.'

Isabella shot up. 'That's what that moron Kemp said.'

'Well, maybe he's right? Have you gone to all this trouble to find out something we already know?'

'Listen, Daisy, there's going to be a terrible deluge,' Isabella fumed. 'Sue and I both dreamt about it. All I'm trying to do is prove it scientifically.'

'Don't get me wrong,' Daisy said, picking it up and turning it round in her hands, 'but how will this crappy thing help?'

Isabella sat down slowly, took the storm glass off her sister, and twisted it through her fingers.

'To be honest, I had hoped for something a little more dramatic, like the crystals speeding up or something.'

'But how would that change anything?'

'I don't know,' Isabella shrugged. 'It might give us a warning, or...' she shrugged. 'Actually, Sis, I give in. I haven't a clue. But I had to try something.'

Daisy handed it over to Archie.

'This must be the worst scientific experiment ever,' he said. 'If Kemp realised how poor it really was, then he really would rip you to bits.'

'Then don't tell him.'

'I'll never say anything again after what he did today—'

'Children!' Mrs Pye's strange voice screamed up the stairs. 'Hurry now! Tea's on the table.'

On the kitchen table sat four bowls, brimming with noodles in a thick, soupy broth. A Mrs Pye "Ramen" experiment. The children slipped into their chairs and began sniffing like curious cats.

'Have you heard?' Isabella said, taking a small taste. 'Mum and Dad aren't coming back for half term.'

'What!' she cried. 'No. Well, I'm blown apart—oh deary!'

'Can't you say something to them when they get back?' Archie asked. 'They're never here.'

'Don't eat with your mouth full, little Archie,' Mrs Pye said, before sighing. 'It isn't proper for me to tell your folks what they can or cannot do. If they chooses to be away, then it is for good reason. I know you won't think it's true but I promise they miss you twice as much as you miss them.'

Mrs Pye said this with as much conviction as she could, but she read the disappointment in their eyes and wondered what on earth it was that so completely occupied their parents' time.

In any event, she wouldn't have a bad word said about them. She only had to raise her left arm above her head or try and touch her toes to remember.

By all accounts it was a miracle Old Man Wood had found her in the woods, miles up in the depths of the forest, on the verge of death, so they said. Her face and shoulder smashed, her clothes ripped to bits and hardly breathing. He'd carried her all the way home, singing and keeping her going. He still sang that funny song, especially when he was tired.

And over the years she'd picked it up:

O great Tripodean, a dream to awaken
The forces of nature, the birth of creation.
Three Heirs of Eden with all of their powers,
Must combat the rain, the lightning and showers.
In open land, on plain or on sea,
Survive 'till sunset—when their lives will be free.
But the Prophecy has started—it's just the beginning.
And it never seems to end, and it never seems to end.

For several months, Old Man Wood and the children's parents nursed her, built up her strength, and tried to help her recover… and remember. But her memory never returned. She had no name, no address, no family, no lovers, no pets; nothing and no-one she ever recalled laughing with, or crying to.

Instead, she had had to learn everything again; although some things came to her quite naturally, like, strangely, making puddings and pies.

The first time she recalled laughing was when the babies crawled to her and gurgled in her ear, especially little Archie. Isabella, on the other hand, would scowl and point at her scars, and continued to do so until she saw past the damage on Mrs Pye's face and into her heart.

These were her first memories, and cherished ones too.

After a while she didn't want to go anywhere else. Why should she? She loved the children. She loved the quiet remoteness of Eden Cottage, with its ballooning views over the Vale of York towards the peaks in the far distance. She felt safe being close to Old Man Wood, who, although he came and went, seemed not to have a harmful bone in his body. It felt right that she should care for the children while their parents were away, for a nurturing instinct ran deep within her.

As far as her name went, Archie called her, affectionately "The famous Mrs Pie" and it caught on, though John changed the spelling. She'd been Mrs Pye ever since, living in the apartment on the top half of the converted barn across the courtyard.

EIGHTEEN

HEADMASTER VISITS

'Evening, All,' Old Man Wood said, popping his head around the door. 'Smells marvel-wondrous.'

Daisy got up and wrapped her arms around him.

Old Man Wood hugged her back, closing his eyes. 'Now then, littluns. I must say, I can't remember such strange weather. Feels like a storm is brewing right bang on top of us. An appley-big one at that. I can feel it in my old bones—'

Isabella slammed her fists on the table. 'That's what I've been trying to tell everyone. No one believes me; Solomon, Kemp, you two—'

'Whoa! Chill, Bells,' Archie chipped in. 'You've got to admit your experimentation is a bit... bonkers.'

Mrs Pye piped up, 'That nice man the weather forecaster on my television said there might be a bit of a storm. Localised—'

'Arrggh!' Isabella cried. 'NO! NO! NO! Not you as well!'

Mrs Pye turned puce and looked as though she might burst into tears.

'That's enough of that, Isabella,' Old Man Wood said, firmly. For a moment there was quiet. He furrowed his brow, as though deep in thought. 'What's funny,' he began, 'is that I've been having real clear dreams about lots of rain, flooding and storms. Thing is, I'm so old it could mean anything.'

Isabella gasped. 'You... you've had dreams too?'

The children stopped eating and stared up at him.

'Oh, yes. More than ever. Shocking stuff too. I should check those apples—'

'There's nothing wrong with them, I'm telling you,' Mrs Pye fired back from the end of the table.

'Well then,' Old Man Wood said, 'I do believe there's going to be a storm and three-quarters.' He reached across, grabbed an apple, rubbed it on his patched-up jumper, and chomped. 'Now, you're old enough to know,' he continued between mouthfuls, 'that once upon a time there was a story about a great storm and a flood that covered the world.'

Isabella groaned. 'You're not referencing the original flood story?' she said, her tone loaded with sarcasm.

Old Man Wood seemed surprised. 'Ooh. Yup. I think that's the one. You know about it, do you? With a man they called ... now, what was his name?'

'Noah?' Isabella said.

'Ha!' Old Man Wood clapped his big hands. 'There. That goes ding-dong. Been muddling that one for a while. So, you do know about it. How marvel-tastic.'

The conversation was interrupted by a banging at the door. The family stared at each other. They very, very rarely had visitors.

'Who on earth could that be?' Old Man Wood said.

Before anyone else could move, Daisy tore off to see who it was. Very shortly they could hear the sound of her footsteps returning.

'You'll never believe it,' Daisy said as she rushed in, 'it's Solomon.'

For a minute they looked at each other, not sure what to do.

'Well, don't you think you should let him in?' Old Man Wood said.

'Mr Solomon, Sir.'

'Hello, Archie, Daisy, Isabella. Please accept my apologies for the late hour, but I thought I may as well potter up and see how you're getting on. May I come in?'

They led him to the sitting room, where Old Man Wood was adding logs to the orange embers.

'Mr Wood, how nice to see you,' the headmaster said, as he eyed up the old man. Old Man Wood was just as tall and wrinkly as he remembered, and had the strangest little tufts of hair protruding from an otherwise bald and patchy scalp. In fact, the old man looked the same as he had when he met him twenty-five years ago.

He remembered thinking then what peculiar clothes old Wood wore. His trousers and shirt were made of fragments of cloth that made him look like a moving patchwork quilt. It reminded him of Archie and his curiously modified school uniform.

Their clothes must have been stitched together by the lady who was loitering in the doorway. He strode over and shook her hand. 'Isn't that road terribly narrow and steep?' he said as a way of breaking the ice. 'It must be devilishly tricky to navigate when the weather turns. Do those parcel couriers ever manage to find you?'

Mrs Pye froze, and turned as pink as a doll.

Old Man Wood rescued her by moving in and extending his hand. 'Now then, is everything in order? Perhaps I could offer you a glass of something: apple juice, cauliflower tea, my own marrow rum?'

'How very kind,' Mr Solomon said, 'apple juice will suffice. I shan't stay long.' The headmaster rubbed his hands; for a man his age, Old Man Wood's handshake crushed like iron. 'May we have a word in private?'

Isabella, Daisy, and Archie streamed out of the room while Old Man Wood poured the drinks.

'Mr Wood, I'll get straight to the point. Can you give the children the kind of assistance they need if—and I do hate to say this—if anything goes wrong?'

'Depends what kind of... wrong, Headmaster?'

'Well, say if Archie was to break his arm again. How would you get him to the hospital? And what if there's a house fire?'

Old Man Wood burst out laughing, his vibrant, joyful tones bouncing back off the walls. 'They are quite capable of looking after themselves, with or without me.'

His comments had the effect of making Solomon feel rather idiotic.

'With respect, Mr Wood,' he shot back. 'Even though Isabella has conducted herself outstandingly well in her academic studies, can we be sure she won't disgrace the school by violently interfering with the officials during our remaining football matches? And, while Daisy shows exceptional sporting ability, she is on course to fail her exams.'

Old Man Wood didn't know what to say, so he simply smiled back.

'And then there's Archie,' Solomon continued. 'Lovely fellow that he may be, he has no redeeming features, aside from a wildlife obsession and gifted siblings, to retain his place at school.'

Solomon wondered if the old man had taken in a single word.

'Mr Wood, I will be frank with you. I have no argument with your family in any way, in fact I am very fond of the children, and Isabella shows exceptional academic promise.' He removed his glasses and rubbed them on a cloth before setting them back on his nose. 'But the school exists on the legacy provided hundreds of years ago by the de Lowe family. Each successive headmaster has granted a generous bursary in favour of the family as set out in the original deeds. But I must tell you this: I am to retire at the end of the term, and I doubt my successor and his governors will be so generous.' Solomon paused and took a sip of his apple juice.

'I've heard through the grapevine that my successor—a modern, disciplinarian sort—is looking to shake up the school and I very much fear that the children's unique circumstances will almost certainly come to an end.'

Old Man Wood scratched an imaginary beard. 'I'll make sure the children's parents understand the situation entirely.'

'Good, thank you,' Mr Solomon replied. He cleared his throat. 'Are you fit and well enough to continue in the role as the children's caretaker? I worked out you must be nearing the heady heights of ninety years—'

'Oh, Headmaster,' Old Man Wood said, 'my body and mind are ticking along quite nicely, thank you.'

'I ask for the children's sake—'

'Mr Solomon,' Old Man Wood chuckled. 'When you are as old as I am, you will find that love and well-being are the things that matter. While it is hard to hold on to the memories from one's youth, we are lucky to be in possession of decent health, and blessed that Mrs Pye feeds and nurses us.' He flicked her a smile. 'But, you're right to be checking up. We don't have so many visitors up here in the hills. Have you made plans for your retirement?'

Solomon leaned back in the armchair, suddenly feeling more relaxed. Perhaps it was the apple juice.

'Yes,' he sighed, pleased to switch subject. 'As a matter of fact, I'm hoping to go to the Middle East to see some of the ancient tombs and archaeology for myself. It's a small passion of mine, if you will.' He exhaled loudly at the thought of the unknown life to come after he left his beloved school.

When the men stood up, scuffling noises scratched towards the kitchen. Old Man Wood and Solomon exchanged a smile.

'Children!' Solomon boomed. 'I have something to say to you, so you may as well come back here.'

The children emerged, sheepishly.

'I've decided the time has come to hang up my leather binder, red book and marker-pen.'

'You're leaving?' Isabella said.

'Yes, my dear, I am. It is time for some fresh blood at Upsall School. Please promise to keep this information to yourselves until I have made the announcement official after half term.'

He looked each of the children in the eye. 'I would be hugely disappointed if any of you were to exit the school before me, so I suggest you work together to improve those areas that need addressing. For example, Archie and Daisy, a mastery of the periodic table and basic algebra.' He gave them a knowing look over his half-moon glasses.

'I have a suspicion that these may feature heavily in your exams. The other thing is that I would like you to win the football trophy tomorrow. I don't mean to put any additional pressure on you both, but it would be wonderful to finish my tenure here knowing that we had reached the pinnacle of both sporting and academic endeavours. So, Archie, please try and hold your concentration for the entire game.'

'We'll do our best,' Daisy said. 'I promise.'

He smiled and headed out of the oak door.

Isabella seized her chance. 'But what about the storm, sir?'

He turned. 'Isabella, this is Yorkshire, for goodness' sake.'

'But I've studied the charts and...'

'No buts, Isabella. After so many years of service, I cannot possibly see how a small, localised storm will make the slightest bit of difference. The river has flooded only once in the twenty-five years I've been with the school. They may just have to play in the rain and get a little wet. It's as simple as that.'

He smiled at them and headed out of the oak door, his footsteps tip-tapping across the flagstones.

Old Man Wood pushed the thick bolt into the wall. 'What a fine man,' he said. 'I wouldn't worry too much about what he said. You're doing well at school, you're fit and well, and you've got friends—what more could you want, eh? Now, off to bed, right now.'

A rumble of thunder boomed high up in the night sky. Old Man Wood sniffed the air for rather too long.

'Something tells me tomorrow is going to be a big, big day.'

NINETEEN

THE DREAMSPINNERS

The grandfather clock in the hallway chimed twice, its ring echoing around the old farmhouse. Two in the morning of the next day and the children's sleep was long and deep: the night-hour of dreaming.

Four dreamspinners arrived in a flash.

Using their long, wiry legs, each dreamspinner flew across the air until they were above the children.

'You are here to witness the final part of the Tripodean Dream, for there must be no doubting it,' Genesis said, through her vibrations. 'Their sleep pattern is flowing nicely. It is time. Come.'

Genesis walked deftly through the air towards Isabella. Bending impossibly forward, as if made from soft rubber, she pushed her head and one arm into her own churning, electrically-active maghole.

If the children had woken, opened their eyes and looked up, they would have seen the old oak beams holding up the roof above and the dangling lamp with its musty-coloured lampshade and the curtains and drapes that hung across their sections: the dreamspinners would not exist. To human eyes—these creatures are completely invisible.

And neither can they be heard. The children would have caught only the gentle noises of the night outside; the rustle of leaves, or the scurrying of a mouse but never, ever, a dream-spinner.

Moments later Genesis held out microscopic-sized granules of powder at the end of a long pincer.

Fragments that hold so much power, she thought, realising that power was the wrong word. *They were far more than that, these were the opportunity of life itself.*

Genesis positioned herself so that her two long legs anchored above Isabella's sleeping head, steadying her for the dream Genesis was about to deliver. She angled her legs and soon her pincers were ready to go to work above Isabella's nose and lips.

With her ovoid, jet-black eyes, Genesis studied the girl.

Instinctively, she tuned in to the rhythm of Isabella's breathing.

IN ... OUT.

IN ... OUT.

'*Heirs of Eden*,' she thought, '*interpret this dream as best you can.*'

Beneath her, Isabella inhaled. As she did so, Genesis's legs spun at an incredible speed, the pincers releasing a microscopic dust which was drawn deep into Isabella's lungs.

Genesis plucked more blue, red and yellow powders from within her maghole and then, at exactly the right moment and in precisely the correct amounts, the dreamspinner lowered her silky legs towards the child's mouth and once again filtered the dream powders to the sleeping girl.

After every breath, Genesis stopped and gauged the girl's reaction, making tiny adjustments to the rate of powder in proportion to the volume of air drawn in.

So far, so good, Genesis thought. *Already she tosses and turns. Soon she will begin a lucid and vivid journey. Nothing will wake her.*

Genesis glided through the air, across the dark room, and

settled above Daisy where she repeated the procedure, scrutin-
ising every movement, looking for signals, and making sure her
dream was perfect.

Now, only the boy to go.

She noted the strong, intense reactions of the male sibling.
His previous haunting, wailing cries were reminiscent of
someone else. Someone with whom she hardly dared to
compare: Cain.

Genesis studied the reaction of the children, noting that the
noises they made were not just the anguished cries of their
dreams. These were sounds that exuded certainty and confidence; Daisy laughing, Archie smiling, Isabella's face beaming
with happiness.

Maybe the final part of the Tripodean Dream was a reassur-
ance that it would be worth the trouble ahead.

She dipped a hand into her maghole. *After all, there is always
balance,* she thought. *Where there is fear, there is love. And where
there is life, there is death.*

Genesis, tired and aching, addressed the others.

'Last of all, are the gifts of the Garden of Eden. And then
their journey will commence.'

Genesis's silvery-grey, ghost-like body now sat directly
above Isabella's sleeping face, her maghole emitting blue shards
of light over the girl's peaceful, pale face.

Quietly, Genesis began.

'*For the eldest, yellow dust—for hands and feet.*

'*Hands that guide, heal, and lead.*

'*Swift feet for running.*'

She transformed the end of one of her pincers into a needle
so long that it was like a sliver of pure ice that melted into
nothing and injected a tiny yellow speck into the soft flesh
between thumb and finger on each of Isabella's hands. Then,
moving down Isabella's body, she repeated the action on her
ankles, the needle entering the tender skin by her Achilles
tendons.

As she withdrew the needle for the final time, Genesis noted a fizz of electric blue energy flowing through and over the girl's sleeping body.

The gifts are undamaged by time.

Without hesitating, Genesis walked across the night air to Daisy, moving directly over her face. As she extended her legs Genesis signed again, the vibrations clear to the onlookers.

'Blue dust, for eyes to see when blackness falls,

'And ears to hear the smallest of sounds.

'With eyes so sharp and ears so keen,

'She will understand what others do not hear or see.'

A minuscule blue crystal fragment sat at the tip of the needle. With astonishing precision Genesis injected the tiny particles through the delicate tissues of Daisy's closed eyelids and into her retinas. Carefully, she slid a needle down each of Daisy's ear canals and injected the crystals directly into her eardrums. As she withdrew the needle, Genesis saw the same electrical effervescence momentarily splaying over Daisy's outer body.

So skilful was her technique that, apart from the gentle rise and fall of their chests, Isabella and Daisy did not flicker, nor spill one single drop of blood.

Now it was the boy's turn. Genesis sensed the other dream-spinners vibrating nervously nearby. She stretched out a leg and drew it slowly back in, twisting her slender pincer from side to side.

'Dreamspinners,' she announced. 'His first gift is to the heart. When the needle leaves his body it will trigger a reaction that will herald the start of their quest to open the Garden of Eden to save the Earth from damnation.'

'From this moment forth,' she continued, her vibrations like a whisper, 'clouds will build. There is no turning back.'

Genesis perched above Archie's chest, legs astride his face.

A roll of thunder drummed high above them as she steadied herself.

'Yellow gifts for hands and feet,'

'Blue to hear and see,

'But red is the one for heart and mind—for power—

'And understanding what may be.'

With aching limbs, Genesis galvanised herself.

'Red Dust, a gift of power, when strength is needed.'

And on the word "power" Genesis thrust her arm high into the air.

She paused and steadied herself, marking the exact spot on Archie's chest where she would thrust the needle. Moments later, the needle swept down and pierced the boy's heart.

His body fizzed as his chest cavity rose. Genesis held the needle as long as she dared, making sure every last speck was instilled into the boy.

As she withdrew, a terrific thunderbolt spat out, rattling every window of the farmhouse.

Even Genesis trembled. Nature had truly awakened.

A sign from one of the other dreamspinners confirmed her suspicions that Archie's sleep waves were changing. But a strange feeling filled her. A sense of exposure, something she had experienced only once before while over Daisy.

My invisibility!

She concentrated hard on the boy.

Finish this.

She dipped a leg into her maghole and withdrew her final gift. *'Red Dust,'* she vibrated quickly. *'One for strength—another for courage.'*

A minuscule red fragment flashed into the tender flesh beneath Archie's chin. But before she could fulfil the task, she heard a gasp and felt a movement.

She withdrew the needle as a pain seared into her, her face burning.

Genesis looked up.

In front of her, with a face contorted by fear, Archie's eyes were open and staring right back at her.

Candlelight filtered in to the corridor, and a soft light spread under the door into the attic room. Mrs Pye rushed in, out of breath, her red hair hanging down to her waist and her sharp eyes accentuated by the glow of the candle.

'Goodness me! Oh, my dear boy,' she said, rushing over to him. 'I never heard such a terrible scream in all me life. I thought you'd died.'

Nursing him, she dabbed the sweat from his brow.

'I... I had the strangest dream, Mrs P. I swear, I was about to be stabbed by... by a—'

'Is that right?' Mrs Pye cooed. 'Stabbed? Goodness graciousness me.'

'It had an electric hole in its middle—'

'Well, well, I never, and I'm sure it did. Now, I think you're old enough not to be getting all a-tizz with that kind of bunkum,' she continued, helping him back to bed.

'Come, now. Lie back and get yourself off to sleep.'

'Please, don't go.'

'I'm staying right here till you're back in the land of nod,' Mrs Pye said sweetly. 'Now, don't you worry about nothing.'

Mrs Pye sat on the edge of his bed for some time. When he yawned, she stroked his hair and laid him down under the duvet, his head nestling into the comfort of his pillow.

A gentle, faraway tune came to her. A song that had been sung to her by Old Man Wood, who had once sat by her bedside himself. She hummed it quietly, the music soft and soothing.

Before long, Archie's breathing slowed, and he slipped into a deep slumber.

Mrs Pye kissed the young boy on the forehead. What was it, she thought, about this funny young boy; so scruffy, so underrated, so sensitive, and yet with a curious strength she couldn't quite put a finger on.

Watching from the ceiling, her invisible status functioning once more, Genesis was relieved that the final dream had run smoothly, even if the boy might have missed out on the final part of his Gift of Eden.

If the children failed, would the blame be levelled at her?

Only time would tell.

Genesis drew her legs together and took comfort in the warm glow of electrical current that sprayed over her abdomen and nursed her burns where the boy's eyes had seared into her.

She wondered about the Tripodean Dream. Maybe Asgard was right; maybe the whole thing was foolish. *Had nature, the universe, got this completely wrong?*

Although she dared not admit it openly, she knew perfectly well this undertaking had never been designed for the children of man.

Perhaps *she* was the fool. At least she was wise enough to know that nature's wishes cannot be resisted.

And what of the old man—there to guide and help? He had forgotten everything, and this was clear to everyone. Time had taken its toll, but was he now—in a curious twist of fate—*a liability*?

Genesis stretched out her final leg, dipped it in her maghole and watched as the blue light swirled in and around it like candy floss threads spinning on a stick.

She would make sure he was given a dream every night that would somehow, *somehow*—however hard, however shocking, however desperate—stir him into action.

Something had to click, it just had to.

TWENTY

SUE MAKES A DECISION

Sleep, on this quiet, sultry night, hadn't come easily to Sue. She'd tossed and turned, but something was niggling her, preventing her from nodding off fully.

Now, as she lay in bed, she flicked through the family photo albums.

She was particularly drawn to the pictures of herself as a baby, the ones in which she lay in her cot alongside Isabella. Friends from the very beginning. Friends now, and friends until the day they would pass away.

There were only four pictures of her before she graduated to a toddler. One of the pictures was cut in half, the others were of Sue staring upwards on her tummy, always lying next to Isabella. A comforting warmth spread through her.

She wondered why she'd been visited by the dreams. Why had she been lumbered with nightmares concerning the de Lowes?

Someone had once quipped that she and Isabella might be twins, but it couldn't be possible, could it? People would have noticed. In any case, why would either the de Lowe parents or her own mother give away a child? Besides, if that outside possibility was true, then surely one of their parents would have told them by now?

She examined one picture which seemed a little more grainy than the others. She noticed, in the corner, a large, old hand. She squinted as she tried to make out the background.

She pulled out her phone and applied the magnifying glass.

The picture rushed out of focus before regaining its sharpness. The camera phone blinked and, moments later, a 'bing' on her laptop told her the image had saved itself on her computer.

A couple of clicks later, and Sue was staring at an enlarged digital version of the grainy picture.

Opening her image-editing programme, she added the picture and started playing around with the options.

Zooming in on the background, she noticed a strange brown vertical wiggle in the corner, as if it might be a wooden beam of some kind. She sharpened the image and played with the contrast.

Quizzically, she slanted her head first one way, then the other.

An upright post, on a bed perhaps?

She thought about it and realised it could be a four-poster bed.

As far as she'd ever known, they'd never had one of these; their house was modern and full of contemporary furniture. Sue knew this because these were the only items her father had left when they separated.

She looked again. That old and leathery hand in the corner, the nails thick and hard. An uncle or her grandfather, perhaps? But her grandpa lived in Australia. She first met him when she was four years old and it was one of her first real memories. And her uncle had brown, slender hands. Fit for an accountant.

Could it be …

She frowned.

Zooming out, she examined the overall image again.

She and Isabella were staring up at the lens, looking remarkably similar, although her mother insisted she was the baby on the right.

But now, zooming in on the picture, she queried this information.

She scrutinised the image. Wasn't that the same flop, the same little tuft of hair that fell forward on Isabella's brow, on the child on the right?

And then she realised whose hands they were: Old Man Wood's. And the bed had to be the old four-poster with carvings that she had seen in his room.

She noticed her pulse racing.

Twins? It was impossible.

A plan quickly formed in her head. During half-term, she'd ask for her birth certificate. If that wasn't forthcoming, she'd head to the Town Hall and ask to see the registrar for Births and Deaths. That would, at least, confirm where she was from. Then, she'd start asking questions, targeting those who might have seen them all those years ago; medical practitioners perhaps, or the local postman.

With this knowledge, she'd knock her doubts on the head once and for all. She'd need a diversion, so Isabella and her mother wouldn't ask questions, and she'd also need a companion.

Instantly, she thought of Gus. He'd been so kind to her earlier and was quite sure he'd understand the situation and, moreover, she trusted him. In return for finding him a partner for his 'doo', she'd ask him to join her investigations. He loved doing strange things like this, even if he was a bit of a dork.

And, if she couldn't find a girl to go with him to his party, she'd go herself — at least with Gus it was bound to be a laugh.

She climbed out of bed and made her way to the window. Opening the curtains, she pushed the windows open and looked out over the rooftops of Upsall.

Glancing up, the cloud loomed larger than ever and its blackness filled her soul with dread.

Back in bed, she opened her notebook. She read over exactly what she'd written down moments after she'd woken up, stains of her sweat still marking the pages.

All she had to do was tell Isabella. At least, that would unburden her from the feeling that a heavy chain hung around her neck.

She lay back and closed the book. Yes. She'd tell Isabella everything before the game. All the weird stuff, every little detail she could remember.

And then, after that, in secrecy, she'd get to the root of the twin thing once and for all.

She returned her diary to the desk and made her way over to the window, peering out over the eerie night sky dotted with pinpricks from lights in the distance.

As she looked, she heard a piercing cry from somewhere outside, the haunting notes of a scream caught on the wind. It chilled her to her core.

Quickly, she shut the window and raced back to bed, as a series of huge lightning bolts flashed out of the sky.

She rushed back to bed and lay panting. If that wasn't a cry of intense pain, then it was the cry of someone wrestling with agony.

Noting the direction, Sue wondered if the sound hadn't come all the way from Eden Cottage.

TWENTY-ONE

CAIN'S LUCK

Asgard shifted. 'Time is moving, Cain,' he said. 'On Earth, the storm spills its anger when the Earth's sun moves to the highest point in the sky. It is time to go to the boy. It is known that one of his Gifts of the Garden of Eden failed.' Asgard hesitated. 'His "courage" may not be with him.'

'Excellent, excellent!'

'Soon, the boy sleeps. He has seen the Prophecy in his dreams but much of it he does not understand. Death confuses him for he is young. His confusion relates to your mother, the female Founder of the Garden of Eden. To him, she is known as the Ancient Woman. He dreams of her murder but it frightens him.'

'Her death and her end,' Cain muttered. 'The power of life. I will use his fear of her murder to manipulate him.'

'Indeed. Now come with me. Hurry.'

'There is hardly a stone unturned in your scheme,' Cain said. 'But hear me out one more time. How will the boy trust a spirit?'

'It may not be enough to remain invisible,' Asgard said. 'Can you bear garments?'

The ghost scratched a non-existent chin. 'There is a long,

light overcoat with which I use to visit my primitive subjects. I have the strength to wear it for a short time.'

'Then gather it,' Asgard said. 'And bring anything else that you think you may require.'

Cain drifted away, his invisible presence marked only by the swaying movement of dust and papers wafting off the floor.

Shortly, he returned wearing a rimmed hat, a scarf, and a long overcoat.

Asgard stretched out a spindly opaque leg. 'You will soon feel the strong sensation of my energy. It is my maghole pulling you in.'

'Yes. The force is powerful.'

'Now crouch down, and dive like a bird as you have done before. Do this quickly.'

A tingling, gassy fizz vibrated through his ghostly frame as he neared Asgards maghole.

'When you are ready, Cain, go!'

Cain thrust forward, a mild burning sensation shuttling through him, and a millisecond later he found himself lying on a worn carpet in a dark, creaking house.

He scanned the room, vibrations from objects and walls filling his mind with a picture, a sense of the world around him.

'You have little time,' Asgard said, 'and you must do the rest alone. Return to the fireplace at the bottom of the house when you are done, and hide in the chimney. I will be back before the sun rises, before the old man stirs.'

Cain floated towards the stairs.

'Remember,' Asgard called after him, 'make an ally of the child.'

'I know he fears the murder of the Ancient Woman,' Cain replied, 'so I will play on it.'

'Perfect. Arrange a place and time to meet him before the storm breaks, when he understands the power and the fury that is to come and when he realises they have no chance. Go now, in haste, Cain, and do your bidding.'

TWENTY-TWO

ARCHIE MEETS CAIN

Archie woke, his brief sleep disturbed.

He exhaled loudly, opened his eyes, and looked out into the blackness of the room.

Was there someone at the foot of his bed?

'Daisy? What d'you want?'

A windy chuckle came back at him. It wasn't either of his sisters.

Archie shuffled into a sitting position, stretched his arms out, and searched the room. Before long, he was able to make out a figure. A human figure, wearing a long coat and a wide-brimmed, cowboy-like hat.

Archie slipped back under his duvet, terrified. 'Who is it?' he called out in a weak voice.

'Aha! Hello!' the voice said, huskily.

Shivers raced up Archie's back. 'What can I... er... help you with, Mister?' Archie eventually stammered.

'You are the boy, aren't you?'

This wasn't the kind of question a burglar would ask.

Archie couldn't think what to say, so he remained silent as his eyes adjusted to the light.

'Ah! Forgive me for another little intrusion,' a deep, crisp voice said, 'but I have something I really must share with you.'

The cloaked man approached. As he neared, he raised his head.

Archie's eyes bulged. Beneath the hat, he saw straight through to the curtain.

'Now, boy, I need to speak with you again about a rather urgent matter. The thing is, this time I need a favour.'

'No!' Archie reeled. 'Not you, *again*?' he blurted.

'I tell you what,' the ghost said, moving closer, 'perhaps you need a reminder?' In a flash, Cain whipped out his knife.

Archie froze as the knife whizzed through the air towards him, and moments later, he felt a nick just under the left side of his jaw. A drop of blood ran down his chin. Archie sidled down his bed.

The ghost moved closer, inspecting the damage. 'Goodness, now it matches the other side,' he said coldly. 'Now, you do believe I exist, don't you?'

Archie's bones rattled.

'Good,' the ghost said. 'Let's be quite clear about that straight away.'

Moving a little further from the bed, he said, 'you might be aware that you are on the threshold of something rather extraordinary. There are mortal challenges you must face. I am sure you know of them...'

'The dreams?' Archie stuttered.

'Precisely,' the ghost said, chuckling. '*The dreams.*'

Archie shivered. 'I don't understand.'

The ghost sucked in a mouthful of air. 'You've heard about the Garden of Eden?'

Archie's brain fizzed. Why was this ghost so interested in a place that only figured as whispers in his mind?

Archie kept as still and as quiet as he could, hoping like mad that the ghost would say his piece, not mutilate him any further, and go away.

The ghost stared at Archie for a few moments. 'Well, the Garden of Eden is where life began, where all things were created. But more recently it's been, how should I say, put on... standby. The thing is, there's a slim chance it may operate again, which would mean terrible things must happen to my mother.' The ghost paused as though taking stock. 'Everything clear so far?'

Archie had no idea what the ghost was talking about, but agreed anyway.

'Excellent,' the ghost said. 'Now this event is known as the Prophecy of the Garden of Eden, and it involves you, my boy,' he leaned in. 'I would like to help you in your quest, and, in return, you can lend me a hand. How do you say it, a tit-for-tat arrangement?'

Archie tried to remember to breathe and his eyes strained in their sockets. He sensed the ghost was smiling thinly at him.

'In due course,' Cain continued, 'I need you to take good care of the Ancient Woman, see that no harm comes to her.' His voice trailed off as he searched Archie's face. 'You do know about the Ancient Woman?'

Archie stayed silent.

'She's my mother,' the ghost continued, 'and a sad old woman who's been hanging on to a mere thread of life for an awfully long time. But she'll never see any of it again because, like me, she's blind. Eyes gauged out, a rather gruesome affair.' The ghost paused solemnly.

'One day, maybe, I'll tell you more about her, but, to cut a long story short, boy, she took the noble but worthless step of sacrificing herself to keep a spark alive.'

'A spark?' Archie said, barely able to squeeze the words out. 'Of what?'

'A spark of life, I suppose.'

Archie thought he'd better play along. 'If you save your mother, will it mean you stop being a ghost?'

Cain was thankful Archie couldn't see his face. 'Of course

not,' he sobbed, trying to bury the amusement in his hurt voice. 'My body is gone, but my spirit is forever.'

'But will I stop having dreams about... about killing her.'

'If you help me,' the ghost said, his voice suddenly changing. 'Then I solemnly promise that from this moment forth, this is exactly what will happen. No more violent, murderous dreams, young man.'

Archie exhaled. 'What... what do I have to do?'

'In due course, you must protect her, that is all,' the ghost whispered. 'There are some people that would want the old woman dead. These people may think they are right, but rest assured they are mistaken. Dreams often show what you fear; they indicate the opposite action to what you must do in reality. In this case, you must protect her from harm—do you understand? I'm really asking so little.'

Archie smiled. Looking after the Ancient Woman seemed entirely reasonable especially as he'd not only tried to kill in his dream, but also because she didn't really exist.

'Yep,' he answered, his voice unreasonably high.

'Splendid,' said the ghost, whose invisible gaze seemed to rest on Archie for rather too long.

Archie breathed a sigh of relief.

In the event that this entire conversation hadn't taken place in an unknown part of his brain and in lieu of his appalling dreams, looking after this Ancient Woman absolutely had to be the right thing to do. I mean, who in their right mind would kill an old woman in cold blood?

Maybe the ghost was on their side—even if it was a bit knife-happy—but perhaps ghosts were whatever you made them out to be.

TWENTY-THREE

SOLOMON'S DANCING

Dancing! The blasted Scottish reels, that's what he'd forgotten!

I never, he thought. *All that twirling, stamping and clapping. The sets and the doe-see-doe-ing, and as the host, he'd be expected to lead from the front! What had made him agree to that?*

Solomon shook his head and rubbed his eyes. *Drat.* He hadn't done any reeling for years and it wouldn't do to make a tit of himself in front of his esteemed guests.

He climbed out of bed and studied his watch. Early, even by his standards.

Drawing the curtains, he levered the windows open and frowned at the enormous cloud hoping it might have blown away overnight. Fresh air brushed through the room and he breathed deeply, the oxygen waking him.

He hummed a tune while moving downstairs to his office. He flicked through his old vinyl records until he came to the 'Scottish Reeling Classics'. Blowing the dust off, he pulled out the black disk and placed it over the gramophone deck.

He'd start with the "Dashing White Sergeant".

The sound crackled as the reeds of the bagpipes filled with air.

Solomon, clad only in boxer shorts and string vest, moved a

couple of chairs and exercise books off the floor. Placing a hand behind his back, while imagining a circle of his guests, he 'set' to an imaginary lady, clapped and turned. Then he began to hop up and down on the spot.

Yes, that was it. Set, clap to your partner, turn, figure of eight, and bow.

The music of the Highland Band filled the room. Solomon skipped through the song, growing in confidence as the memories flooded back.

Hop, clap—and turn—bow, and twist.

After the third tune, he collapsed into his armchair, and sipped a glass of water.

He wondered about his guest list. *Pity,* he thought, *that the de Lowe parents couldn't make it.* He shook his head. *One minute they were here, the next they'd gone.* No wonder the faces of the children had dropped when he'd passed on the news.

But such was the archaeologists' life, he supposed.

In the public eye of archaeology, they were very much seen as stars in their field, even if they didn't show it. They would have fitted in perfectly with the guest list of prominent men and women of the area.

His train of thought moved on to the children. He had to admit the set-up up there on the moors was more than decent. The old man looked well, Mrs Pye obviously cared for the children splendidly, and the house was in good order. Solomon wondered if he shouldn't have talked to Isabella further. Oh, well, the deed was done, and it was another thing he could tick off his list.

A passing thought struck him. He wondered whether he should ask the de Lowe children to come along to the party. Perhaps they could help the catering staff with their chores. He nodded at the thought. Isabella was his most gifted pupil, a prize-winning scholar, and Daisy their greatest athlete. He could make a bit of a fuss of them and introduce them to his guests.

And Archie could look after the coats, although he'd probably lose them.

He walked over to the gramophone and turned over the vinyl record. Inviting them to his party was a sterling idea. He'd ask the children after the football match, as a surprise. A consolation prize, or a reward for Daisy? And the gesture would also show Isabella that he took her seriously. After dinner, there was a disco so what better way to get everyone going than by having a few of the youth around to energise the dancing? Rumour had it that Daisy was a very bouncy dancer, particularly, he'd heard, at a type of movement called "rave".

Solomon smiled as he bowed to the music, clapped his hands, and, with one arm in the air, spun and hopped his portly frame around the room until the music ran its course.

He pondered this thought as he selected another disc from his collection, 'Disco Hits of the Seventies'. A cracker, if he recalled.

The music came on. Solomon nodded his bald head in time with the beat.

Feeling his body come alive, Solomon thrust a hand high into the air, and gyrated his hips.

'Daisy de Lowe,' he said, as he jived with the music, 'will be second fiddle to these kinds of shapes!'

TWENTY-FOUR

CAIN OFFERS A PLAN

This boy—this Heirs of Eden—has absolutely no idea what is going to happen, Cain thought, as he hovered into the middle of the room. *He has found no meaning in his dreams. Do people now ignore visions? If so, these Heirs of Eden will never survive the storm, let alone find the cave of riddles.*

Cain understood that the cave was the place which held the secrets to finding the tablets that would lead them to the Garden of Eden.

It is time to execute the plan.

He floated back to Archie's bedside. 'There is another way,' he crowed.

Archie didn't move a muscle, the leadenness of sleep preventing him.

'I want you to consider joining me, physically, as my flesh and blood.'

'Join you,' Archie said, trying hard to stifle a yawn. 'Really?'

'Not right now of course,' Cain continued. 'I'd like you to think about it. But bonding with me will save your life.'

Archie stretched his arms out wide. 'Save my life,' he repeated, involuntarily closing his eyes. 'Sure it will.'

'Good-good. I'm thrilled... delighted,' the ghost said,

suddenly feeling the weight of the coat. 'About the knife,' he continued. 'I don't have time to explain things in depth, so occasionally it pays to use other means.'

'But, Mister... sir,' Archie said, summoning his energy and his courage. 'If I did this bonding thing, what's in it for me?'

'For you? Ah yes!' the ghost crowed. 'What's in it for you, aside from maintaining your human existence on this planet?'

The spirit drew himself up as best he could.

'I hold the secrets of ages past, boy. I will give you strength and courage, so that you are feared and respected. You will have the strength of a horse and the courage of a lion. I give you my word. All you have to do is meet me tomorrow morning. Somewhere quiet and safe. Then, I will show you what is about to happen and when you know the facts, you will choose to join me freely.'

His voice turned darker.

'A terrible time is coming, boy. You have seen the prophecy and, deep down, you know it is a hopeless situation. I offer you salvation.'

'The prophecy?' Archie stammered.

'Yes, indeed,' the ghost crowed. 'Meet with me in no more than nine of your hours, and no less than eight, before the sun rises to its highest point. Tell me a place where no one will see us.'

Archie tried to think. 'Er... there's a back alleyway above the bank above the football field by the school,' he said, trying to swallow a yawn. 'You'll know you've found it when you see two houses leaning in, sort of head-butting each other. It's usually pretty quiet.'

'Excellent,' the ghost gushed. 'Wear a long overcoat, like mine, and a scarf. Do you have a scarf?'

Archie didn't, but he lied and said he did.

'And do you like sweet treats, boy?'

'A bit, I suppose,' Archie replied, thinking what a strange question it was. 'Old Man Wood's the sucker for sweet things in our house. He's always dipping his fingers in the sugar bowl, and getting told off by Mrs Pye.'

The ghost chuckled. 'Is that so?'

A groan from the bed nearby signalled that Daisy was stirring.

'I must leave. We meet before noon in the alleyway,' the ghost whispered, as he drifted to the door. 'Tonight's chat, young man, is our own little secret. Any tongue-wagging and our deal is off.'

Cain stopped, as if an idea had popped into his head. 'Tell me your name, boy?'

'Archie de Lowe.'

'I will save you, Archie de Lowe.'

Archie caught a glimpse of the knife.

As the ghost reached the door, he turned. 'Be in no doubt that your life will change forever in a few hours from now. The strength of a horse and the courage of a lion! You will never regret it.'

Archie nodded. 'What... what's your name?' he asked.

'Ah, yes. The finer details.' His eye sockets bored into Archie, who felt as though his heart was briefly being sucked out. 'I am the ghost of Cain, Frozen Lord of Havilah, Son of the Ancient Woman. Do you have a cup of water, boy?'

Archie pointed to the table just behind him.

Cain hovered to it and dropped something in the cup. 'You will need this. Drink, and it may give you strength.'

And with those words, Cain slipped quietly out of the door.

Archie fell back on his pillows and rubbed his eyes. *What the heck was that about?*

He didn't know what was real and what wasn't anymore. He knew, though, that there was no way he was going to turn up at this meeting with the ghost, whatever powers had been offered to him in return.

Lions and horses! Twaddle.

He studied the clock. Three-thirty-five.

He did a quick calculation. Eight hours from now and it would be… bang in the middle of the football match. Nine hours and the game would just be finishing.

Another classic Archie timetable cock-up.

He breathed a sigh of relief. Problem sorted; he wasn't missing the game, certainly not for a knife-wielding ghost, whatever the cost.

Hugely relieved, Archie closed his eyes and drifted back to sleep.

Gaia raced across the air to the boy, anchored her legs either side of Archie's head, and spun a hazy-styled dream.

Cain, forever banned from leaving Havilah, had discovered a way to the Heirs of Eden only hours after the last part of the Tripodean Dream had been given! This was beyond comprehension.

With any luck, as the sun rose and humans readied themselves for a new day, his meeting with Cain might feel as if it had never happened.

TWENTY-FIVE

HAVILARIAN TOADSTOOL POWDER

While talking to Archie, an idea so simple, and yet brilliant, popped neatly into Cain's head.

Cain pulled a small jar out of his pocket and examined it, smiling.

Havilarian toadstool powder; a lethal poison, with the power to kill those who came from the Garden of Eden. In one stroke, he could reduce the old man to a spirit. Just like him.

Adam's value would be nullified, not that he had much worth anyway. *But why not take the chance, while he had it?*

Cain reached the hallway. *No signs of Asgard. Good*, he thought, *better the dreamspinner doesn't know.*

The ghost cursed. Wearing a coat for such a long time had drained his strength. He let the garment cascade to the floor as he headed down a corridor and arrived at an open door. Slipping through, he instantly sized up the energy in the room and before long, the outlines of a table and chairs, and the vibrations of plants and foodstuffs came to him.

Turning to his left, he discovered the strong vibrations of a smouldering fire—a cooker. He thought about sweet foods, like honey or, how did the boy say it, *sugary-things*?

Yes! There, near the cooker, in a small container. Sweet granules, exactly as he'd hoped.

It's easy to see, he thought, *and to understand how energy spins, fires and vibrates around every single thing when one has had aeons of time to practice.*

Cain cursed. With his strength sapped by the coat, pouring the Havilarian toadstool powder into the bowl was more of an effort than he'd bargained for. By concentrating hard, he completed his task and before long he picked out tiny shrill squeals emanating from the container.

Perfect. The fungi are alive.

Cain drifted out of the room, along the corridor, into the living room, and back to the fireplace.

He felt for the aura of the dreamspinner.

Nothing.

Above him, he could hear yawns. The old man stirring. Feet padding on the ceiling above.

Come on, Asgard, where are you?

A moment later, the stairs groaned with a heavy footstep.

Cain didn't want to hang about. Even though he knew he couldn't be seen, he certainly didn't want to be found in the house of his father, the home of his greatest enemy.

As the footsteps neared, a small vibration squeaked out. 'Cain, it is Asgard. Dive straight ahead. Do nothing else.'

'About time,' Cain snapped.

Without waiting to be prompted, Cain knelt down and sprang towards the dreamspinner, hoping like mad it was the right place. As he left, he heard a small cough as Old Man Wood entered the room.

TWENTY-SIX

SIMILAR DREAMS

Archie stretched his arms and thrust out his chin. As he did so, he felt the sting of a fresh cut. He froze. Cloudy images of the previous night rushed in. He dashed into the bathroom and stared back at his reflection.

A small incision, just as he expected, mirroring the cut from the night before.

Archie couldn't believe it.

And why were the words "horse" and "lion" swimming in his head?

'The weight of a horse and the looks of a lion? Nah,' he said aloud to his reflection, shaking his head. *The head of a horse and the body of a lion?*

Archie sprayed water on his face. *The bite of a lion and the kick of a horse? No, no.* Deep in thought, he headed towards the kitchen, letting the water spill onto the floor as he went.

Mrs Pye looked up as Archie came sloping in. 'You taking an elephant for a walk?' she said.

'Elephant?' he repeated, before realising what she meant. He tried not to break into a smile.

'What is the matter with you lot?' Mrs Pye complained. 'Slumping and skulking and screaming in the night.'

Archie coughed. 'Oh. Isabella and Daisy had a bad night again. I think they're talking about some, er... girlie things. You know...' Archie mumbled.

'Periods?' Mrs Pye squealed. 'Daisy's becoming a woman now, is she? About time, I suppose.'

Girlie things? Archie went bright red. Oh dear. This was absolutely the last thing on his mind.

He changed the subject, fast. 'My throat's sore, Mrs P, and my head hurts. It's like someone's tightened a clip around my neck.'

'Come here and I'll take a look.'

Archie sidled over to the sink, and Mrs Pye took his head gently in her hands. 'What are these cuts on your chin? Have you been playing with your knives again?'

'Of course, I haven't,' Archie said, weakly. 'Caught my face on something in the woods.'

Mrs Pye looked at Archie suspiciously. 'I won't tell anyone about your knife throwing, you know that. I know you like to sneak off to that old potting shed and practice, though heaven only knows why.'

She took his hand, before feeling his forehead and the back of his neck. 'It's your eldest sister who doesn't approve.'

Mrs Pye finished her medical. 'Well, you is a bit sweaty, young man. Could be a fever coming on.'

She rubbed her chin, thinking about what might be the best cure. 'I reckon you need a couple of...'

'Apples?' Archie suggested.

Mrs Pye raised her eyebrows. 'How did you know?'

Archie smiled. Mrs Pye's medical knowledge was virtually non-existent and Old Man Wood's extraordinary variety of apples in the orchard just happened to be her number one cure for everything.

❄

After an unexpectedly large breakfast they returned to their room. Archie felt it was time to question his sister. 'Daisy,' he began quietly, 'last night you called out "Tripodean Dream" several times. Why?'

A shadow fell over her face. 'Another nightmare,' she began. 'I've had three, each one utterly disturbing, but this dream was the best... and the worst... and the weirdest.'

She turned to her sister for support. 'They've been so real. I could smell things, and understand everything. Birds, trees, and plants talked to me. *Talked, Archie*! It's so... so complicated and bonkers and confusing. I don't know where to begin.'

Daisy scrunched her face up and ran a hand through her hair, trapping a finger on a thick hair knot.

'One minute, there's this knackered old woman telling me about a wonderful, beautiful place. The next minute I'm in a terrifying storm, like an endless hurricane, and the storm is chasing me. Lightning, mudslides, and tonnes of water coming after me, beating me to death...' She tailed off, scratching the back of her neck.

'What is it, Daisy?' Isabella asked.

'I dreamt I reached a sanctuary. It was only then that I was safe from the storm. Kind of like heaven, but with pictures on the walls.'

She shook her head. 'I still don't know what it's supposed to mean.'

Isabella set her books down on the table and pulled up a chair.

'Daisy, in your nightmare, what happened to this Ancient Woman?'

'Well, I'm pretty confident this haggard old woman kept trying to tell us something,' she said. 'But each time she did, she died.'

'Are you sure?'

'Yeah,' Daisy said, her eyes wide. 'A violent, horrible death, different every time. And it was like being there, standing next to her. I could feel myself screaming.'

She took the stunned silence from the others as a green light to continue. 'Look, I know it sounds nuts, but this Ancient Woman knew about us... she knew *everything*, even though I think we were on an entirely different planet.'

Her eyes searched her elder sister's face, urging her to believe and her bottom lip began to tremble, as tears moistened in her eyes.

'I've tried to blot it out, but I think I'm going crazy.' She noticed Isabella's face creasing. 'Bells, you OK...'

Without warning, a teardrop spilled from Isabella's eye.

'Oh, God. Not you as well!' Archie said.

'Yes, me too!' Isabella cried, lines of water now streaming down her cheeks. 'Same, exactly.'

Archie's eyes nearly popped out of his head. 'But this is madness—'

'I know. It literally doesn't make any sense.'

Archie was confused. 'You're sure it was just like Daisy's dream? You're not making it up?'

'Yes, Archie! It's the truth,' Isabella insisted. 'I swear it. Three intense, clear dreams just as Daisy described but making no sense whatsoever. I've never been so amazed or happy or terrified, and what's more, just as Daisy said, it always ends in death.'

She burst into tears. Daisy handed her a tissue and she dabbed at her eyes before continuing.

'It's like flying into a cloud and every now and then, as you get used to it, you find yourself back in the cloud, trying to figure out what's going on.' She grabbed another tissue.

'I've never been so amazed or happy or terrified, and, as Daisy said, the dreams ended the same. In some form of death.'

'Can you remember anything significant, or different?' Daisy asked.

Isabella clenched her hand. 'I kept seeing lightning and rain. Torrential, terrible rain. You know how I've been going on about this deluge, well it terrifies me. It's as if this stupid storm wants to target us, alone, until we make it to a weird cave, just as you said.'

'And, Bells, you say you saw this Ancient Woman,' Daisy asked. 'What did you think of her?'

Isabella thought for a moment. 'She'd been stuck, abandoned someplace, I think. She's pathetic, desperate, waiting. Waiting for...'

'For what?'

Isabella shrugged. 'I don't know. Us, perhaps?'

'But her eyes had been gouged out, so she didn't know where she was.'

'Exactly, Daisy!'

'And even though she had no eyes, she had an aura of gentleness, kindness, and love,' Daisy continued. 'She was disgusting to look at, though. All shrivelled up, like one of Old Man Wood's prunes.'

'Probably even more withered,' Isabella added with a thin smile. 'I don't know how she's still alive. It was as if she held the key to something we had to find.'

Archie had become noticeably quiet over the past few minutes and as if by instinct, the girls noticed.

'What about you, Archie?' they said in unison.

Archie swivelled and faced the girls, his face ashen.

'Yeah,' he said, shakily. 'I've dreamt of this storm and this Ancient Woman on three occasions—just like you.'

The girls gasped.

Archie stared at them, his eyes brimming with tears.

He dropped his head.

'The thing is, in each of my dreams, it's me who kills her.'

TWENTY-SEVEN

OVERCOAT

Eventually, Isabella spoke.

'Look. I know it's odd, but these are only dreams, you know. And dreams are just part of our minds worrying about everyday stuff. Dreams aren't real, however much they appear to be.'

'If you don't think there's any truth in them,' Archie said, 'then why did you go to such lengths to make a barometer and a storm glass? You must have thought there was something to it.'

Isabella thought for a moment. 'Sue had had a similar dream and I suppose I wanted to try something—anything—to prove or disprove the dreams, scientifically.'

'So, four of us have had the same dream,' Archie said. 'Perhaps there's a sleep demon out there giving dreams, and we happened to catch the same one?'

'Don't be silly, Archie,' Isabella sneered. 'Sleep demons don't exist.'

'They might,' Daisy said, 'but Sue had the dreams and she lives miles away,'

Archie guffawed. 'She sleeps here most of the time—'

'The Fitzroy storm glass thing!' Daisy exclaimed. 'Where is it?'

Isabella stood up, plucked the glass out of the fire grate, and placed it on top of the mantelpiece.

The children stared at it, as though it held the answers to all their problems.

'It's still cloudy with little stars,' Archie said, mischievously.

Daisy focused more intently. 'Wow,' she whispered, entranced, 'those little stars are belting around.'

Isabella sighed, 'Listen, Daisy, I don't know what it means or what it's supposed to show. To be honest, it's not my finest work.'

Daisy wasn't convinced. 'Just out of interest,' she said, 'for simple-minded people like me, who never saw it before, what was the glass like when you began this mad project?'

'Cloudy,' Archie said, drolly, 'just as it is now.'

'Thanks, Archie, very helpful,' Daisy said. 'Well, I can see an epic game of pinball going on in there,' she said. 'There's way more going on than simply cloudy—can't you tell?'

Isabella strode over and squinted. 'There's nothing here but a foggy substrate,' she announced. 'You're wasting your time, Daisy. Come on you two, get your things. You've got this big match to play today, or had you forgotten?'

Daisy frowned. 'You think we should just ignore it, Bells. The dreams, the cave, the Ancient Woman, everything?'

'Yes, I do,' she replied.

'Really?'

'Absolutely one-hundred percent. It's purely a coincidence, that's all. These dreams are more than likely parasites of fear for some reason or another.'

The twins grabbed their sports bags, Daisy stealing a last glance at the storm glass before Isabella popped it into her bag.

'We need to get a move on,' Isabella said, hoisting her bag onto her shoulder. 'My guess is that, somehow, this big cloud sitting above us has made our brain patterns react oddly in advance of a storm breaking. With my scientific hat on, I'd say we ignore the whole thing. Yorkshire storms are never that bad.'

The twins shrugged. Isabella was the school boffin and, much as they hated to admit it, she was generally correct.

'I realise I'm pretty rubbish at Chemistry,' Daisy said, earnestly, 'or whatever science category your storm glass belongs in, but I'd keep a really close eye on that Fitzroy storm thing-a-me-thing if I were you.'

They filed down the stairs and found Mrs Pye waiting for them. 'Now then,' she said, giving each of them a hug. 'Goals galore for you, Daisy, goal saves for you, Archie, and as for you, Isabella, just make sure you don't go running onto the pitch beating up the umpire—you heard what that nice headmaster said.'

Mrs Pye gave her a friendly nudge.

'Now, away with you—and I expect to hear heroic tales when you get back.'

The children had barely stepped out of the door when Old Man Wood's deep voice stopped them short.

'Best of luck today, little ones,' he called out. 'There's one heck of a big dark cloud over our heads. If lightning starts, remember to run for cover. You understand?' He was quite sure they weren't paying him the slightest bit of attention. 'Do you recall that ditty we used to sing about different types of cloud? Now, how did it go? Ah yes':

High and light, no need for flight.
Low and grey—stay away.
Grey and round—rain around.
But black with a crack—is a devil's smack.

'So, I'll see you early afternoon. Best of luck, Daisy. Your school is relying on you, you heard what Solomon said.'

The children waved.

'His stupid poems,' Daisy said quietly.

'*Wait*!' he yelled from the doorway. 'Did any of you leave this coat? I found it in the corridor.' A large overcoat dangled over his arm. 'Nice one too, with an unusual pattern on the lining. I'm sure I've seen it somewhere before.'

Archie missed a step and stumbled, righting himself before his nose split the floor.

Old Man Wood noticed. 'Yours, is it, Archie? Looks a touch big for you, mind.'

Archie doubled back, his body trembling. Without looking at Old Man Wood, he inspected the coat and shoved a hand inside one of the pockets. The hairs on his back shot up.

'Back in a second,' he yelled, as he flew up the stairs.

Archie sprinted into the attic room where he spied the cup of water, tinged slightly blue, exactly as he'd left it. In one movement, he drained the glass.

'Everything all right, Archie?' Old Man Wood asked.

'Fine,' Archie answered.

'Right-oh,' Old Man Wood said. 'Your coat then?'

'Oh, yeah, it's a friend's. Must have grabbed it by mistake, in a rush.'

'Big fella, is he?'

'Yeah, I suppose,' Archie said, as casually as he could.

Old Man Wood handed him the garment, but as he did so a knife slipped out of the pocket and tinkled onto the hard paving stones.

'A knife, Archie? You know you shouldn't carry one of those at school.'

Archie's heart skipped a beat. 'It's only plastic. A stage knife, you know... drama stuff.' He smiled, bending down to pick up the knife, just beating Old Man Wood to it. 'The bloke who owns the coat is the lead part in the play.'

'He certainly has an interesting taste in knives,' Old Man Wood commented, raising an eyebrow. 'Well, on you go, young Archie, and remember to get in the way of those footballs.'

Archie ran to catch up with the girls. As he went, his heart thumped like a huge bass drum and his head buzzed with a mixture of dread and excitement.

Old Man Wood immediately knew it was a beauty; a knife worthy of a powerful man. From the clinking noise it made when it fell on the paving, he would have bet a coin or two that it was made from a mixture of alloys, possibly titanium and steel. From the way the light reflected through the stones on the handle, he'd have taken another wager that its jewels were unique; most likely rubies and pink diamonds.

It certainly wasn't a plastic knife. Oh no, not in a million years.

He couldn't remember how he could tell a cheap knife from a proper knife, but he had shown Archie how to master a knife-throw all those years ago: how to test the balance, and weight, that would determine the revolutions and thrust of the weapon.

Old Man Wood mulled this over, wondering what light his brain might shed on the subject. No, nothing there, just a deep penetrating pain in his mind, like toothache.

And why did that funny old coat stir his curiosity? The lining had taken his breath away, was it the pattern that made him feel nervous and thrilled at the same time?

He'd seen thousands of patterns of snakes and trees, or snakes slithering around poles, all the way through his long life but now, as he replayed the moment he'd noticed the lining for the first time, he experienced the curious feeling again, as if the snake had actually moved, or rather, slithered into the tree right there on the fabric itself.

Old Man Wood paced around the room.

He'd noted the buttons too. A matching crest of a snake winding through branches.

Nothing I can do about it now, he told himself, *whatever it might mean.*

Suddenly, a thought smashed into his head, electrifying his entire body.

He sat down in his large, worn armchair, cupping his face in his big leathery old hands.

What if the material of that jacket wasn't from Earth?

He'd never seen a fabric that had the ability to change shape here on Earth before, but, if he remembered correctly, the marks of the snake and the tree were from... the Garden of Eden?

A surge of energy rushed through his body, making him feel strong for a second or two. He pulled himself together, noting how his heart thumped in his chest.

Maybe it's time to research those old wooden carvings, he thought.

He'd start on the stairs and then try his bedroom. He didn't know what he might find but he had a sense about him that they might shed a clue on that strange coat's true home.

TWENTY-EIGHT

THE JOURNEY TO SCHOOL

Assured by Isabella's dream diagnosis, the girls had a spring in their step as they headed down the track. From the top of the hill, the banks on either side of the road gradually increased in height, as if a giant digger had gouged the lane out of the hillside. The lane acted as a drain taking the water off the hill, and even in the driest summer a constant trickle dribbled from the moors to the river below.

Branches of oak, ash, maple, wild cherry, crab-apple, blackthorn, and hawthorn made a thick canopy high above the road and today, it was coloured in a mat of rust, red and gold autumnal colours.

On a clear day it looked as if glitter had been sprinkled on the track as sunlight flickered through the trees. Today it was almost pitch black, and the tree roots supporting the bank twisted through the rock and soil, reaching out like the arms and legs of decaying corpses. Sue still called it 'the big graveyard ditch', but the children were used to it as it was their daily walk to school. The idea of it being scary had long gone.

Nonchalantly, Archie told the girls that the coat was Kemp's dad's, and they must have got muddled up in the cloakroom. But although he slumped along quietly, his heart was thudding in his chest, and his brain worked overtime as he tried desperately to remember what had happened during the night.

The girls didn't bother to question him further.

For someone as disorganised as Archie, mistaking a coat was as common as being late for a lesson.

Half way down, they stopped by a large oak with a huge bough that leaned over the road. Daisy climbed nimbly up the steep, tall bank, using the roots as handgrips. At the top, she uncoiled a rope wrapped around the branch and tossed down the slack end.

Archie went first. He took off, climbing the rope until his feet settled on a large knot at the bottom. Swinging backwards and forwards, the warm wind rushed through his hair.

As the line slowed, he jumped down, running to a stop.

'Pathetic, Arch,' Daisy said. 'What's up with you?'

'Nerves,' he replied. 'I'm not really in the mood.'

Isabella went next. She sat on the knot and swung backwards and forwards at a leisurely speed, while Daisy waited impatiently until her time was done, as she always did. Finally, Daisy mounted the rope and asked Archie to pull her up the hill as far as he could.

'Watch this,' she said, her eyes glimmering. 'Proper swinging."

Archie let go, and Daisy soared forwards, hair flying, until she was horizontal with the bank, touching the canopy. She swung back, screaming in delight, and bashed into the bank on the other side.

'Daisy! Enough. We've got to go to school,' Isabella said, trying to catch the rope. 'Kill yourself on the way back, but we're running late as it is.'

'Typical,' Daisy said, coming to a stop and tucking the rope around a protruding root system. 'It's always the same thought; we'll be too tired, or it'll be too dark, or some other rubbish excuse.'

'Daisy,' Isabella replied, 'after today, you have all of half term to swing yourself, and your brother, into hospital. Right now, we need to get a move on.'

At last the steep track levelled out and the height of the bank lowered, like at the end of a playground slide. At the old wooden bridge, the children peered over the handrail at the water running beneath and looked for fish gliding in the pools next to the chunky oak uprights.

Isabella noted how, in the strange light, the school tower to their left looked enormous compared to the tiny boathouse by the river. She wondered if the old rowing boat they'd once played around in was still fit for purpose.

Soon, they arrived at the lush, velvety green football pitch. White posts balanced safety ropes to keep the spectators at bay, and, set back from each corner, the moveable floodlight towers dominated the pitch like metallic giants standing guard.

Daisy ran across the bold, alternating stripes with its tattoo-like, fresh white markings. She practised kicks, flicks, and tricks and commentated loudly on the goals she was going to score later.

Much to Archie's amusement, she included the crowd noises, which were like the "huuuuhhh" you make when breathing on a window pane.

Before long, they were across the playing field, and heading up the steps to their form rooms.

TWENTY-NINE

KEMP TRIES TO MAKE UP

Archie noticed Kemp sitting quietly at his desk, reading a book.

Let sleeping dogs lie, he thought, *especially unpredictable dogs.*

Without any fuss, Archie made his way to the other side of the room, draped the coat over the back of his chair, sat down, and put his head in his hands. He desperately tried to remember what the ghost had said; a meeting, something about a lion and a horse? After writing down a couple of variations, Archie realised it might be something to do with strength and courage.

He remembered that he would be saved, *but from what exactly?*

Hadn't he agreed on something as well, such as joining the ghost in some form of partnership? It didn't make any sense but, and it was a huge BUT, the ghost's coat and dagger were right here in this room. So it couldn't be a false memory, regardless of Isabella's certainty that their recent experiences were mere figments of their imaginations.

Archie teased the nicks on each side of his chin. *Another reminder.*

He pulled out a piece of paper, and nibbled the end of a pencil.

"*Possible meeting places*" he wrote.

He searched his brain.

Was it down by the boatyard, or up by one of the big willow trees? He wrote both down, but shook his head. No. Neither option carried weight. He wondered if it was the alley above the football pitch, and he wrote that down as well.

He underlined it twice and leaned back in his chair. That one rang a bell, but a muted bell, filled with cloth.

His thoughts were interrupted by a friendly but slightly painful wallop on his shoulders. It was Gus Williams who had bounced into the room.

'Morning Archie. You're not by any chance writing a "to-do" list are you?' he said, sarcastically.

Archie smiled. If Kemp looked like an otter with big lips, Gus was a laughing donkey.

'No, don't be ridiculous,' he said.

Gus read the list. 'Lost something?'

'Nah. Just trying to remember a dream.'

'Oh, well that's okay,' Williams said, cheerily. 'So long as it wasn't a big and complicated one?'

'Well, as a matter of fact, it was.' Archie smiled. 'Now, go away and leave me to think.'

'News alert!' Williams announced to the room, his grin almost completely covering his face. 'Archie de Lowe is thinking! Give him plenty of room, oxygen at the ready.' Gus leant down again. 'Next, you'll be telling me Daisy's caught the same bug,' he whispered. 'Bon chance!'

He smiled and sprang off like a big, energetic puppy to his desk at the back of the room.

Kemp had listened in to Archie's conversation with Gus. He'd bet money Archie had forgotten something again and by the looks of it this time the object was more important than usual.

Kemp stood up quietly. 'Morning, Archie, everything cool?'

Archie groaned. *First Gus, now Kemp.*

'Not really, Kemp,' he replied.

'Lost something?'

'No,' he started. 'Well, kind of.' Archie groaned. 'Actually, I had another dreadful nightmare. I'm trying to remember it.'

'Oh, yeah?' Kemp replied.

'Yeah,' Archie said. 'A couple of really strange experiences, but, poof... and now it's gone for ever.'

Kemp laughed. 'Want to talk about it?'

Archie stared at Kemp. 'I told you, I'm not talking to you after what you did yesterday.'

'Really?' Kemp sighed. 'Look, I had a think and last night I decided that I'm going to change. No more jokes, no more pranks. I promise—'

'You said that before, and let me down. In fact, you lied to me. Christ! Kemp, I had to own up for your stupidity, and you made me feel like an idiot. It's lucky Isabella didn't believe me.'

Kemp sucked in his cheeks. 'I've told Jackson and Pulse I don't want to be part of the gang. When I'm with them, I act like a... well, like a total knob. I don't know what comes over me. The bottom line is I'm actually sick of it, too.'

Kemp noted Archie's look of disgust. 'Arch, if you don't believe me, go and ask them,' he continued. 'They're over there in the corner playing on their phones like happy little freaks. Seriously, I don't want to hurt anyone anymore. I really don't.' He dropped his voice and briefly stole a look over his shoulder. 'I want to be your friend.'

'Blimey, Kemp, this isn't the time. Right now, I've literally got a nightmare on my hands. I'm not going to trust you until I know you mean what you say.'

'What do you want me to do? I've promised I won't be nasty to either of your sisters. I'm going to put all that anger behind me. I won't even speak to your sisters if you don't want me to.'

'But I bet you've already arranged with your Sutton mates to give Daisy's a kicking, haven't you?'

Kemp winced. 'There's not much I can do about that now, is there?'

'The only reason you're being "Mr Nice" is because if they kick her out of the game we'll lose and she won't play in the team after half term. That would leave room for someone else, wouldn't it. And that person will probably be you.'

Kemp's expression had changed. 'You know what, Archie,' he spat. 'I meant what I just said. Throw it back in my face, why don't you.'

On hearing raised voices, Jackson and Pulse instantly towered over Archie. With one huge hand, Pulse picked him up by the collar.

'Back off boys, let him be,' Kemp ordered. The muscle released Archie and sloped reluctantly back to their desks.

The classroom had fallen silent but Archie wasn't finished.

'See what I mean, and boy it's rich, coming from you,' Archie said, holding his ground. He looked Kemp in the eye.

'I swore on my life that I wouldn't tell anyone about the glass and I kept my word. You, Kemp... well, you're a lying, deceitful disgrace to your dead parents, your aunt, your school and, more importantly, to yourself. Frankly, you disgust me.'

THIRTY

AN ABUSE OF POWER

The dreamspinner was astonished to learn a couple of things. First, that it was Cain who knew about the children's dreams and their gifts. Second, that Archie had no idea about his own gifts; but Cain knew enough about them to exploit him.

Gaia thought it through, reaching the same conclusion. One of *them* must have gone to Cain. But dreamspinners were neutral in all things. They did not meddle, they never had.

Only four dreamspinner elders had seen the gift ceremony: Genesis, Asgard, Juno and herself.

Was Genesis bitter about appearing in front of the boy? No, it didn't add up.

What about Asgard? He was the one who had objected to the Gifts of the Garden of Eden being given to children, but he was also the most passionate dreamspinner when it came to giving dreams.

Or Juno, the quiet one?

Yes, Gaia thought, maybe it was her. But why? What was her motive?

Another thought whistled into Gaia's mind. Cain was a spirit, so what if he had travelled through one of their magholes, or perhaps the maghole of another dreamspinner, to escape Havilah?

It was the only possible explanation she could think of.

She searched her vibrations.

Nothing close by.

This dreamspinner would have to be caught in the act. But dreamspinners moved so fast through the universes, it was as if they were a multi-dimensional fluid.

Catching one would not be easy.

THIRTY-ONE

ARCHIE TELLS KEMP

The silence hovering over the room was broken by the metallic ring of the bell. moments later, the upright figure of Mr Steele came striding in, twiddling the ends of his moustache.

'As you know,' he boomed, 'there is no class-work today.' He stared around the room. 'Gosh,' he continued in a softer voice. 'Silence! Oh, hallelujah!'

The classroom remained noiseless.

'Have I missed something?' Steele continued, as his eyes flashed from pupil to pupil trying to make out what had caused this unusual lack of bedlam. 'No? Very well.' He peered at his notes.

'Our school day looks like this; footie for those playing footie and that is, de Lowe, de Lowe, Nugent, Allen and Alexander. Can I have hands up for those who are likely to be watching?'

The remainder of the class except for Kemp, Jackson and Pulse thrust their hands into the air.

'Excellent. I take it you have other things to be getting on with, Pulse?'

Pulse shrugged.

'You know, you three aren't the best advert for this school

and today is what we like to call an "open day".' Steele said this very slowly. 'It means we should all be on our best behaviour for the parents and prospective parents who are visiting because they are thinking of sending their wonderful children here.'

Kemp stole a glance at Archie, who was still looking troubled. Just beyond Archie, Williams was smiling his big toothy smile straight back at him and raising his eyebrows.

Was Williams trying to provoke him with his eyebrows?

He put his hand up.

'Yes, Kemp.'

'Actually, I'm watching the football as well,' he said.

'A change of heart, huh, Kemp.'

'Sure, you could say that.'

'Well, I'm glad to hear it.'

Kemp caught Williams' bulging eyes again. He knew exactly what he was implying.

'So Jackson and Pulse, just you two. Correct?' They nodded dumbly. 'In that case, you will report to Mr Pike in the Maintenance Department. There are leaves to sweep up and fences to paint.' On cue, the class burst out laughing. Mr Steele waited until the noise was bearable.

'Come on. Simmer down. Mr Pike is expecting you to be ready for work at kick off time, which will be eleven o'clock precisely.'

'By my watch,' Mr Steele said, hitching up his sleeve and twisting his arm as though showing off a priceless treasure, 'the time is approaching half past nine. After I have dismissed you, you have an extended free period. Please use this for last minute drama rehearsals; like learning your lines, Mr Ford; or practising your clarinet, Miss Buxton; or for recital practice before the programme this afternoon, Mr Anderson.'

Steele stuck his nose in the air and twitched his moustache. It was a signal that he was going to say something profound. 'Now, about the weather. There is a rather large cloud b*rrr*ewing right above us.' He rolled the 'r' rather dramatically.

'To put your small minds at rest, our headmaster has been in touch with the Met Bureau to find out if this might be a cause for concern. I am happy to report that, as far as they know, there are none. Later this morning and this afternoon, there is a high chance that we may get a little wet; indeed there may even be a possibility of a heavy downpour. But all school activities are scheduled to go on as usual.

'Daisy de Lowe, please remove that lipstick from your desk. Now, remember, class, just in case lightning strikes, what would be the best course of action to take? Anyone? Ah, yes, Alexander?'

'Put up your umbrella, sir.'

'No, you do not, Alexander. And stop laughing Allen, and please desist flicking paper balls at Daisy.' He glared at the boys, 'Umbrellas, as you know perfectly well, are for repelling water. I'm talking about lightning strikes.'

Steele raised his eyebrows in anticipation. 'Kemp, what would you do?'

'I'd get the hell out of there before I was shrivelled to a crisp.'

The class laughed.

'Well, it's better than holding up an umbrella, but where would you go?'

Little Jimmy Nugent put up his hand.

'Yes, Nugent.'

'I've been told that, if you get in a car, the rubber tyres would earth the strike, wouldn't they, Sir?'

Mr Steele clasped his hands together. 'Very good, Nugent, and you're absolutely correct. Either rush indoors fast, or hop in a car—'

'My granddad,' Nugent continued, 'got killed by a bolt of lightning in 1983, while walking his old bull terrier called Plank across the park—'

'Did he, Nugent?' Mr Steele sensed one of Nugent's stories coming on. 'How fascinating. Perhaps you might be kind enough to fill me in another time.'

Steele turned back to the pupils. 'Now, class, do your best today and make us all exceedingly proud of what we have here at Upsall school. After the spectacular events, enjoy a safe and relaxing break. You are now dismissed.'

The pupils instantly divided into several small groups. Archie remained in his chair, twiddling his pencil.

Kemp quietly made his way over. 'Come on, Archie, it can't be that bad. You look terrible. I can help if you want... if we're still friends?'

Archie shrugged. 'Sure. Sorry about the outburst, been a bad morning, that's all.'

'Sounds terrible—'

'You have no idea,' Archie replied. 'Really, if I told you, you would never, ever believe me.'

'Try me.'

Archie sighed. 'Nah. You'll only laugh.'

'Go on. I promise I won't tell a soul.'

'Look, Kemp, we've been there—'

'If you don't talk to someone, it just gets bottled up. My shrink told me that.'

Archie fingered his pen. What did he have to lose?

'You won't believe me,' he heard himself say.

'I promise you I won't judge. I'll listen. That's what friends are for, right?'

Archie exhaled. 'Okay,' he began. 'If you really want to know, last night I was visited by something that, as far as I could tell, was a ghost.'

'A ghost?' Kemp coughed. 'Really?'

'Yes. Really.' Archie fired back. 'I told you2 you wouldn't believe me.'

Kemp eyed him suspiciously and raised his hands. 'Cool. A ghost... carry on.'

Archie rubbed his forehead. 'Well, this ghost promised me stuff if I met up with him.'

'Yeah? What did you say?'

'I think I kind of agreed. I was half asleep. What would you do?'

'I'd probably agree too,' Kemp said. 'Was it a nice ghost or a nasty ghost?'

'Bit of both, I think. It was wielding a knife, but at the same time I'm pretty sure it wanted to help.'

'Well, for starters that's all right,' Kemp said, sounding like an authority on the subject. 'The ghost had a knife and it didn't kill you. That's decent.'

Archie hadn't thought of this. *But it had cut him.*

'Any idea where you're hooking up?'

'That's the problem,' Archie replied. 'I can't remember. I thought it was a dream, so I agreed to everything and said the first thing that came into my head.'

'What makes you think it wasn't a dream?'

Archie pointed at the coat. 'This,' he said pointing to his chin, 'and this.'

'An overcoat! Bleeding heck, Archie.' He wondered if Archie hadn't entirely lost his marbles.

'I know,' Archie said, realising he probably sounded idiotic, 'but I swear it's the same coat the ghost was wearing. I remember those buttons with the snake winding up a tree.'

Kemp thrust out his jaw and furrowed his brow. 'How do you know it isn't Old Whatsisface's?'

'Old Man Wood,' Archie said. 'His name is "Old Man Wood".'

'Yeah right, chill your boots,' Kemp said, holding the coat up. 'I mean it's pretty big—about his size—are you sure he wasn't... giving it to you? You know, offloading it before he took it to the vintage clothes shack.'

Archie shook his head. 'No, definitely not. Old Man Wood

only has patched up clothes, certainly not an overcoat like this one. Anyway, there's more.'

'More?' Kemp raised his eyebrows. 'Blimey. I mean, great.'

Archie turned his head up. 'See these. They're cuts from the knife I was telling you about—'

'From the ghost?'

Kemp inspected Archie's face. 'Nah, I don't believe you. You could have got those from a bramble or from that hare you rescued when you ran to school yesterday.'

Archie shook his head. 'No, honest to God, look how neat they are.'

Kemp looked closer. 'You're one-hundred percent sure?'

'Yes.'

Kemp guffawed. 'Look, Archie, everyone knows ghosts don't carry things like knives or hit people—'

'This one did.'

Kemp struggled to contain his laughter. 'Don't get me wrong, Archie, but it doesn't stack up. Why would a ghost want to harm you?'

Archie thought for a second. 'To prove it was real.'

Archie felt in the coat pocket and slowly withdrew the knife, shielding it from prying eyes.

'Here. Look.'

Kemp's eyes fell to the gap under the desk where Archie held the knife and he swore under his breath.

'Blimey, Archie, that's a beauty,' he said. He could hardly tear his eyes away. 'So, what did this ghost say?'

'This is where it gets blurry,' Archie began. 'He said he was on a mission to save his mother, and said she was going to die. I think I agreed to protect her at any cost.'

'Epic. He sounds all right to me,' Kemp said. 'I'd do anything to protect *my* mother.'

Archie realised he'd hit a nerve. 'Sorry, Kemp. I didn't mean—'

'Chill, Archie, I know you didn't mean anything by it.' Kemp was fully intrigued. 'Was there anything in it for you?'

'Well, as I said, I think he mentioned a partnership of some sort. That's the part I can't remember. I would find out at this meeting, I suppose, not that I can go.' Archie laughed and turned a little red. 'I think I agreed to meet it bang in the middle of the football match.'

Kemp chuckled. 'Blimey. Even with the dead, your planning skills are garbage.'

Archie screwed up his face. 'Somewhere along the line, he went on about power and strength, or something,' he scratched the desk thoughtfully. 'Maybe it's in my head from a general lack of sleep?'

Kemp was intrigued, but also concerned about his friend. If Archie's story was completely made up, this was nigh on madness, or genius. You had to hand it to them; these de Lowe kids were damn interesting.

Archie studied Kemp's face. 'You think it's bollocks, don't you?' He put his head in his hands. 'I've been sucked in, haven't I?'

Kemp shrugged. 'Probably your old Old Man Woody friend playing a joke or something—'

'Or I've been hallucinating from one of his bitter apples?' Archie added.

'Yeah,' Kemp said, as though this could have been perfectly normal. He'd heard about the old man's curious apple collection. 'Probably one of those. I can't believe you didn't see it all along.' He slapped Archie on the back. 'You ought to be getting along, don't want to miss your warm-up.'

Archie cocked his head and looked at his watch. 'Rats! Is that the time?' He gathered his things together. 'Hey, Kemp, thanks for the chat. Please don't think I've turned into a nutter.' He slung the bag strap over his shoulder. 'Promise me you won't tell anyone about this.'

'You are all nutters, that is definitely true,' Kemp said. 'But you, Archie, are the only one worth your salt.'

Archie noted that the look in Kemp's eyes had turned harder. Maybe his thoughts had moved on to his sisters.

Archie ran to the door. 'See you later.'

'Sure.'

Kemp shook his head.

If it wasn't strange scientific experiments, or an infatuation with ghosts, or girls being brilliant at games designed for men, then it was some other random thing in the de Lowe family. Extraordinary disorganisation, say, or manic recklessness, or unbelievably old helpers and absent parents.

Mr Steele reappeared. 'Time to lock up,' he said. 'Please grab your things as the school won't re-open until after half term. Take everything you need.'

Chairs scraped against the floor as the remaining students stood up. Kemp slipped into his overcoat and gathered the contents of his desk, dropping them haphazardly into his bag. He tucked in his chair and headed towards the door.

'Kemp,' Mr Steele called out, 'haven't you forgotten something?'

Kemp looked puzzled.

'Your coat?'

'What coat? Oh, that? It's Archie's,' he said quickly. 'But, er, don't worry, I'm seeing him later. I'll take it for him.'

At that moment, he saw the slip of paper covered with Archie's scrawny handwriting.

Kemp scanned it for a second, and noticed the underlined location. Was this where he was meeting his so-called ghost.

He folded the paper and crammed it in his pocket.

'Jolly good,' Mr Steele said running his hand over his chin. 'Have a nice break, Kemp. It's good to see you've decided to watch the game after all. That's the kind of spirit we like to see in you.'

THIRTY-TWO

STORM GLASS SHATTERS

Archie tore down the corridor, almost colliding with a bevy of girls.

Daisy stood in the middle of the pack, holding centre stage.

He reddened. 'Daisy, shouldn't we be getting ready?'

'We've got plenty of time,' she studied her watch. 'It's only just gone ten. At least half an hour before we need to change.'

Archie blushed even more and shook his wrist. 'Yes. Sure. Right.' It wasn't going well.

Individually the girls were fine, but as a group they scared him to death.

'I'm going to see if I can find Isabella,' Archie said. 'Want to join me?'

Daisy crossed her arms. 'No. Not really.'

Archie's face went purple. 'Please,' he squeaked.

Daisy caught his eye, and *that* look.

'Okay, Ladies,' she said, stealing an eye back at Archie. 'I'm off to do battle with those big, bad, beastly boys, and kick the damn house down.' They shrieked their approval. 'Wish me goddamm biiiig luck.'

Each of the girls made a big play of kissing her on her cheek, before breaking into a chant.

'GO, GO Daisy de Lowe! GO, GO Daisy de Lowe! GO, GO Daisy de Lowe!'

'Go Daisy! Go Daisy! GO Daisy…'

Daisy put one hand in the air as she waltzed away, wiggling her hips and fluffing up her wavy blonde hair.

As the twins turned the corner the chanting changed to the old *Queen* anthem:

D-D-L

D-D-L

D-D-L—

SHE WILL, SHE WILL, ROCK YOU!'

'You're awfully glum-faced,' Daisy said, as they headed down the stone corridor. 'What have you done now?'

Archie groaned. 'Something insanely foolish. I told Kemp about my nightmare.'

'You…dwerk!'

'Look, I don't know why I did it. He'll probably tell everyone, like he usually does.' Archie caressed his temples with his fingers. 'It's social suicide.'

'Yup, it most certainly is,' Daisy replied as she pinched him playfully on the cheek. 'When will you ever learn? Kemp's a moron. It's really that simple.'

They found Isabella in the physics lab with Sue. They were running over an experiment, their heads buried in calculations while an assortment of rubbery tubes and glass devices lay strewn over the counter.

Daisy was bouncing with energy.

'Ready to go, girls?' she said.

Her jollity didn't really have the same effect on the science students.

'Daisy,' Isabella said, in her most serious tone. 'I want you to wear these, in your boots.'

Daisy looked at her in amazement. '…my boobs?'

Isabella rolled her eyes. 'Don't be stupid. *Boots*, not boobs.'

Daisy fingered the rubbery, gooey material handed to her.

'What is it?'

Isabella peeled off her lab glasses. 'In short, it's a de-energising unit that we've created.'

'A what-erising-unit?' Daisy said. 'Jeez. Why?'

'Just in case, that's why.'

'I don't understand. Can I put it in my hair?'

'No! Just do it, will you,' Isabella demanded. 'One for each boot.' She handed her a second. 'You too, Archie.'

Archie studied it. 'What's it for?'

Isabella squealed. 'Listen. It's just in case either of you gets struck by lightning. It might help you not fry, that's all.'

Archie stuck the strips to the insoles in his boots. 'Look, aren't you're taking this a bit far, Bells—'

A huge roll of thunder shook the building rattling the windows. They looked at each other.

Isabella raised her eyebrows. 'These could save your life.'

'Where's your Fitz-storm glass-thing?' Daisy cut in, her tone serious for once.

'Next to Isabella's desk,' Sue said, wafting a hand.

Daisy picked the storm glass up and quickly put it down again.

'I don't mean to be rude, science-y nerd folk, but have you analysed this lately?'

Isabella marched over as though it was a complete waste of time.

'What?' she snapped.

'This storm test tube thing of yours,' Daisy began. 'Have any of you noticed:

a) how hot it is, and,

b) that it's literally crammed full of crystals moving incredibly fast?'

Isabella stared at the cloudy glass tube for a moment or two.

'I have no idea what you're talking about, Daisy. Yes, it might be a little warm, but so what? As I told you earlier, I'm not sure how it works.' She dismissed it with a wave. 'We've already moved on.'

Daisy shrugged. 'Well, I'd keep an eye on it, if I were you.' She stretched out the gooey strip.

'Please, Daisy,' Isabella said. 'Fix it to the bottom of your shoe using the sticky Velcro patch or in the insole.' Isabella sounded irritated by the intrusion. 'Now, run and get changed or you'll be late.'

Daisy skipped off, singing to herself and punching the air.

As her footsteps receded down the corridor, Archie picked up the storm glass. Immediately, he put it down again.

'Whoa! It's boiling, seriously. Try it.'

'I've just done that,' Isabella said.

Sue put her finger to the glass.

'OW! Scorching!' she sucked her fingers. 'Isabella, it's steaming!'

'A mild expulsion of water vapour, that's all,' Isabella said, nervously.

'You think so?' Sue said, as they started to back away.

'No, not necessarily,' Isabella admitted.

The test tube was beginning to glow, steam seeping out of the top.

'Has anyone added anything to it?' Isabella asked.

Archie and Sue shook their heads far too much.

The activity in the test tube increased. They could hear crystals popping against the glass.

'Get out!' Isabella yelled. 'It's going to blow!'

They ran for the door, shutting it firmly behind themselves before diving to the floor. Seconds later, the storm glass blew into smithereens.

Sue shivered. 'What does it mean?' she asked.

'I think it means that we were right all along.' Isabella's voice quaked. 'Here, above us, lies the storm from hell.'

THIRTY-THREE

SUE AND ISABELLA

'It's time for direct action,' Isabella said. 'Solomon clearly doesn't want to know about the storm, so we're going to have to either sabotage the match, or figure out a brilliant exit strategy—'

Sue couldn't face direct action. 'An exit strategy gets my vote—'

'Good,' Isabella said. 'Now, if I can somehow get Arch and Daisy over the bridge, then I think we'll be fine. When we get to the lane, the canopy of the tunnel should protect us from any heavy rain, it's that old and strong. Trust me on this.'

She looked at Sue and grabbed her hand. 'It's you that I'm worried about.'

'*Me?*'

'Yes.' Isabella confirmed. 'Have you thought how you'll get out of here? You'll either need to get home, come with us, or scramble to high ground. Have you ever driven a car?'

'Of course I haven't. Stop being ridiculous—'

'I'm not, Sue. I'm deadly serious... you could steal one.'

Sue glared at Isabella. 'I'll think of something, but you're getting weird.'

'That's not good enough,' Isabella snapped back. 'You need a plan, and pronto. Why don't you come with us?'

'I can't. I think Mum wants me back, but I haven't heard from her.'

'In that case, immediately start engaging that brain of yours for viable getaway solutions.'

As the two girls trudged slowly back from the science laboratories in silence, they could feel the buzz of the crowd making its way down towards the football pitch.

'I feel so edgy about this match,' Isabella said, as a couple of boys ran past nearly knocking her over. 'What if Daisy gets kicked and then can't run? They lose, the storm breaks and she can't get home?'

'Isabella, that's not going to happen—'

'And what about Archie? He's all over the place, have you seen him? He looks ill, the poor boy. I'm worried he won't save anything. He's even more scatter-brained than ever.'

'Well, it is the final—'

'I know that,' Isabella said. 'It's just... I've got this hollow feeling deep inside me.' She closed her eyes and shook her head. 'I think I hate football—'

'What tosh! You love it,' Sue replied. 'Thing is, you're jealous of Daisy, just like everyone else—'

'Doesn't mean I like it.'

Sue laughed. 'Listen, you're her sister and as sporty as a mole, so it's only natural for you to want her to do well.' Sue looked up at the sky. Her heart seemed to skip a beat. She whistled.

'Blimey,' Isabella said, her tone betraying her nerves. 'Solomon's floodlights are on and it's not even eleven.'

Sue frowned as she inspected her watch. 'Every time I look up, my body starts shaking like jelly. We've got five minutes till kick off... I think.' She slowed and grasped Isabella's arm as if setting herself up to say something important.

'Listen, Isabella,' she began, 'I've been meaning to tell you something super-important—'

'Important?' Isabella noticed that her friend had gone a little pale. 'You put the wrong mix in the storm glass—?'

'No. It's not about that... it's about—'

'You definitely added something to it though, didn't you—?'

'Isabella, I haven't touched it. I'm quite sure it did what it did perfectly naturally.' Sue added. '*It's about you*. This is personal.'

'Me?' Isabella's mind whirled. 'What? You've got a boyfriend and you haven't told me—'

'For goodness' sake,' Sue squealed. 'Bells, you know full well I haven't—'

'Okay, someone out there fancies *me*—'

'NO. Of course not. Listen, Isabella—this has absolutely nothing to do with boys—'

'Sure?'

'YES.'

'Good,' Isabella said, 'they're such a waste of—'

'It's *about* you,' Sue said.

'Me?' Isabella said. 'You... and... me?'

Sue shrieked. 'For crying out loud, Isabella. NO! *Will you please let me speak*?' She took a deep breath. 'It concerns YOU, in fact it concerns all of you de Lowes. You, Archie, and Daisy. All those things I told you about? Well, there's more.'

'More?'

'Yes! I wrote a whole lot of stuff down the moment I woke up. I'm pretty sure it's about you, and in some way you're linked with—'

'Linked? With what?'

'SHUT UP! Listen to me for just a minute.' Sue said, trying to compose herself. 'What I'm trying to say is that—'

The long shrill of a whistle and the roar of the crowd swept over them. Sue followed Isabella's eyes towards the floodlit football pitch.

'We're late!' Isabella cried. 'Your watch is slow again.'

Sue tapped the face of the dial and compared it to the clock on her mobile. When she looked up, her friend had already gone.

What was I thinking? I bet someone's scored.

'Come on, keep up!' Isabella yelled over her shoulder, as she took off down the shingle path. 'You'll have to tell me later! I mean, it's not like it's life or death, is it?' she yelled.

As Sue watched Isabella zoom away with extraordinary speed she slowed and caught her breath.

'Bells, there are things you absolutely... must... know,' she said, her voice trailing off into the dark morning light.

Sue felt empty, the moment lost. Everything that had happened in the last hour had started to confirm that what she'd seen, heard—and felt—was about to come true. If there was even the tiniest chance of this happening, she needed to tell Isabella everything.

Because, increasingly, it really was about life or death.

THIRTY-FOUR

KEMP FINDS SOMEONE

Kemp reached into his pocket, pulling out Archie's scrap of paper.

He leaned against the stone wall outside the school hall and held it up. If that Old Man Wood had played a prank on Archie and given him the coat to wear, then what were the others capable of? Perhaps this was an elaborate set-up, dreamed up by Isabella in order to get him into a fight with Gus Williams.

Kemp could smell Isabella's cheap perfume all over this.

He glanced up. The sky was ridiculously dark and ridiculously huge.

Then again, what if Isabella's experimental madness had solid foundations?

Kemp's eyes returned to the paper. He read the middle, double-underlined, option.

'Alleyway behind kissing houses.'

Kemp thought about it. If he was going to meet a knife-wielding ghost in a quiet spot, this was a pretty good choice. It had the advantage that you could get out at both ends, and it was close enough to the playing fields for a quick getaway.

Clever Archie. Not just a scruffy lad.

The alleyway was also the perfect place for a fight. He

clenched his fist. He remembered the look on Williams' face, the glimmer of madness in his eyes. Kemp twisted the fabric on Archie's coat. It was nice and strong, and light, too. A layer of protection if Williams came at him.

Kemp sucked in his breath. It was a set-up for sure. It had to be. After yesterday's performance, Archie had been duped by his sisters.

Oh, well.

Kemp tapped his pocket, feeling the metal object within.

If he was right, and Williams was coming after him, then Gus Williams was in for a mighty sharp surprise.

From the road above the football field, Kemp scanned the crowd lining the perimeter of the pitch. They stood four deep behind the barrier rope at times, with smaller kids kneeling at the front. Kemp ached to be part of it, to have them cheer *him* on.

He'd never play alongside Daisy de Lowe, though. Never. Just the thought of her running beside him made his stomach heave.

He kicked a loose stone on the ground, which skipped across the raised pebbles and smacked a small boy in the knee with a dull crack.

The boy collapsed on the path as Kemp clenched his fist. *Nice one*, he thought, wishing it had been Daisy de Lowe's knee.

Kemp climbed further up the slope, towards the houses above the playing fields. He kept going until he was on his own, high above the pitch. As he walked, he thought about how he could occupy himself over the break with his dreary aunt. Last time, he'd nearly died of boredom, being dragged around endless museums, antiques shops, and flea markets. Sure, his aunt was pleasant and she tried hard, but her never-ending jollity and the way she talked to everyone about the same things over and over again drove him mad.

She was too nice, too wet, and too dull.

His mind turned to his parents. They would have done

awesome, cool, outdoor stuff, and they'd all get stuck in together, like sailing, or mountaineering, or holidaying abroad.

He imagined a trip by the side of the river next to a large campfire staring at the stars, his mother by his side playing guitar and singing, and his father smiling and sharpening a hunting knife.

It was a fantasy, of course; the idyllic family life he'd never have. Every time he thought of it, an overwhelming sadness entered his soul. He couldn't remember if his mother used to sing to him and he had no idea what his parents even looked like; but to him, the fantasy felt right.

A long rumble boomed in the sky above. Kemp spied another round pebble, and took a mighty swipe with his heavy, black boot. The stone connected sweetly, skipped a couple of times and then, on the last bounce, lifted quickly and seemed to whistle past the head of someone lurking by a lamppost near to the alleyway.

What was an old bloke doing standing over there in the first place? He didn't even flinch! Bloody weirdo. The stone must have missed him or else he'd have been knocked out cold.

Kemp put his head down and sauntered on as if nothing had happened. A few paces on, Kemp noticed a man just inside the entrance to the alleyway. He was sure no one had been there a moment earlier.

His heartbeat quickened.

Kemp pretended to read Archie's bit of paper while he studied the man who was hunched over, and shrouded in a long, dark cloak, with a thick scarf wrapped round his chin and nose. He had a kind of wide-brimmed hat pulled down over his head in such a way that Kemp couldn't identify his face. And he leaned on a stick like a blind man.

Maybe, Kemp thought, *this* is Archie's ghost.

THIRTY-FIVE

SOLOMON'S PARTY PLANS

Solomon leant on the oak door, and listened to Isabella's footsteps receding down the corridor. He let out a sigh. Had she believed him? It was hard to read her expression.

Isabella's persistence was admirable, if misplaced. No, no. Nothing was going to stop today's celebrations going ahead; not a big storm, nor a few drops of rain.

Goodness me, he thought, *this is Yorkshire, the finest county in all of England, God's Own Country! Thunder and lightning go hand in hand with the rough landscapes of the moors and the dales.*

Kids these days were too soft.

He chuckled to himself. Telling her he'd just put the phone down from speaking with the Met Bureau? *What brilliant nonsense to throw something scientific back at her.* And it had stopped her in her tracks.

But why mention a weatherman called Mr Fish? It was an implausibly good name for a weatherman.

Returning to the soft leather armchair, he picked up his schedule; a busy morning lay ahead. The Press were due shortly, and there were place names to sort through for his banquet in the school chamber.

Solomon hoped that sister of Isabella's, Daisy, would play

her heart out again. What a player! He'd never seen the like. She was Maradona, Pele, Messi, and Ronaldo, all blended into one slender slip of a girl. Brave as a mercenary, tough as leather, quick as a pike, and slippery as ice. This was a day he'd anticipated for years and how much sweeter it would be if they won the cup.

He sighed before returning to the matter of wondering who he should sit next to tonight; Geraldine Forbes, perhaps? The star of Summerdale, the endless TV soap.

Yes, a perfect match.

Famed for her gritty Yorkshire one-liners, in reality she was a delightfully attractive lady, with beautiful green eyes and lips as full as cushions.

He pictured the scene in his mind; the hall decorated to the nines in the school's scarlet and light green colours, candles accentuating the Gothic arched windows, and trophies and cups sparkling in the atmospheric light. *Magnificent!*

It would be a banquet that the governors, his friends, and their exclusive guests, would never forget.

Afterwards, he'd make his retirement speech and he'd receive warm, generous, and heartfelt thanks from those whose lives he had touched. Yes, he mused. It would be a glorious swan song and nobody, certainly not Isabella de Lowe, was going to stop it. Best, he reasoned, to keep them on side with a couple of harmless white lies.

His mood turned from happy to jovial. Mr Fish. Ah yes! The forecaster who in 1987 told the entire nation there was little need to worry, shortly before a devastating hurricane ripped across England causing insane damage and destruction.

Solomon laughed out loud and dabbed his brow. What if Isabella rang up the Met Bureau and asked to speak to Mr Fish?

Whatever will they think?

THIRTY-SIX

KEMP'S FIGHT

A roar rang out from below. Kemp spun back to the game, picked out the chant of *"Daisy de Lowe, GO, GO, GO"* and smacked his fist into his hand.

Dammit. She must have scored.

He reached into his pocket and his hand touched a waxy piece of paper, like a sweet wrapper. With a frown on his face, he tried to work out how it had got there. Of course, it was from a pack of Haribos he'd stolen from one of Daisy's girlie friends at break. He'd stuffed the sweet in his mouth and nonchalantly tossed one of the wrappers into the headmaster's rose garden where it stuck comically on a thorn and flapped in the breeze.

So, how come this wrapper was folded, and in his pocket?

He opened it up but strangely, the sweet paper not only looked larger than he remembered, but scribbled all over it were random lines like spaghetti plonked on a plate.

Just as he was about to trash it, a few of the lines started to look familiar. *Faces?* he thought. Kemp scanned it, turning it sideways and then round again. Three figures came out at him, like a "magic eye" puzzle revealing itself on the wrapper.

There were three clear images staring back at him.

Then it struck him. It was the de Lowes! Absolutely, definitely, them, all smug and cheerful, and ghastly.

As he studied it, their faces seemed to melt away into the paper, like slush dripping through a gutter.

The next time he blinked, he was staring at nothing. Not a damn thing.

He turned the sweet paper over.

Blank.

Kemp felt a surge of excitement run through him. Was this some kind of joke?

He slapped his cheeks and rubbed his eyes.

When he looked at the wrapper again its colour was changing gradually from white through grey to almost black, like the vast cloud above them. Then, the words "HELP ME" started to form in tiny molten streaks of lightning on the paper, as if they were being lasered into it.

His heart raced and unsure what else to do, he crumpled the paper up, and tossed it in the gutter.

For a moment, a dizziness bordering on nausea overwhelmed him. Instinctively, he started walking faster and faster, as if walking might make what he'd seen go away.

Kemp bounded up a series of wide stone steps back to street level and tentatively made his way towards the street's dark, oak-beamed dwellings. He peered down the dark alleyway but it was empty, save for the black wheelie bins guarding it like mini soldiers.

As he took his first step under the buildings, he noted how the houses on either side weren't leaning over the street as if they were kissing, more leaning towards each other like fighters braced for combat.

He heard a groan from the crowd below, and moved to the roadside to figure out what was happening.

Bodies lay strewn over the pitch like a battle field. Had Newton won a penalty?

And was that Archie staring up at him?

He waved back, before turning, and walking into the alleyway.

Halfway down, he slowed, sensing something behind him. Who? A teacher? Nah, unlikely. They'd be watching the game, or making last minute plans for the performances later on. In any case, by now they'd have said something.

Then he realised it had to be Gus Williams. He almost spat his name out. Williams was coming after all, and it was exactly his style to creep up on people like this.

Kemp curled his fist into a ball.

'Williams,' he said, 'I'm warning you. Stop, and walk away, NOW.'

Still no reply.

He could feel the presence edging closer.

Kemp bent down pretending to tie his boots. His pulse raced. He readied himself. He sensed the person behind him was now only a couple of paces away.

'I've been waiting for this,' Kemp said, and in one movement swung around and threw his biggest punch. His momentum carried him forward, his fist unstoppable.

But it wasn't Williams. It was the old man he'd seen earlier.

Instead of connecting, his arm careered through the man, propelling Kemp onto the grey stone. His head cracking the paving.

'You don't have to do that, Archie,' a gravelly voice from behind the scarf said. 'We're on the same team now.'

Kemp was struggling to get to grips with what had happened.

'Believe me, it is excellent news. Even better that you have arrived on time.'

The old man moved almost directly above Kemp, his face covered by the scarf and hat. 'And I sense that you have brought my coat. Very well done; did the old man find it?'

Kemp was horrified, and his brain was contorting like spaghetti. 'Yes, he gave it to me,' he lied.

'Are you ready to join with me, Archie de Lowe?'

Kemp's skin crawled. Everything Archie had told him was completely true. He needed more time.

'Join you?' He said, scuffling backwards, trying hard to keep his face hidden. 'Er, can you remind me again? I was very tired last night.'

The ghost hesitated. 'Well, let me put it this way. I've got what you want.'

'What I want?' Kemp repeated. No wonder Archie was freaked out. 'What do you mean?'

The old man moved to one side and appeared to look up towards the sky.

'Why me, of course.'

'You?'

'Yes, me,' said the ghost. 'You see I'm the only one here who can help you escape from this place. And you have only about fifteen minutes in your time to decide.'

Kemp's brain went a little fuzzy. Fifteen minutes? In *your* time? Decide what? Kemp stole a look down the alley.

He needed to get away, fast.

The old man sensed his unease. 'You see, in a very short time the skies will open and it will rain for forty days and nights in a way you cannot even begin to imagine—'

Kemp looked confused. 'What... forty days and nights?'

'Yes. That's what I said, forty days and nights—'

'Forty days and nights—?'

'Yes!'

'What … like Noah's Ark—?'

'STOP repeating what I say and listen!' the old man spat.

The words seemed to smack Kemp around the face. He lost his footing and slipped.

'If you think what I'm saying is any way over the top,' Cain said, bearing down on him, 'I can assure you that in a short while, all of this—everything here, everything—will be destroyed.' The ghost gestured, almost triumphantly.

'Archie,' he continued, his voice mellow once more, 'there is a shift happening, a shift in time, a shift in the way of the universe and it is happening right here, right now. You are part of this, Archie. The wheels are turning and they cannot be reversed.'

Kemp reeled, and wondered if he should try playing dead. A chill swept through him.

'Are you ready to join me, Archie de Lowe?'

Kemp's skin crawled. He summoned his energy.

'Ey, look here,' he said gruffly, 'I don't mean to be rude, but I think you need help.' He felt a slither of confidence returning.

The ghost laughed. 'Look, Archie. You see that thing there—' he indicated the vast cloud.

'Yeah, right,' Kemp said. 'So? It's a large, dark cloud. Big deal. Excuse me, freak, but I'm outta here—'

'No—you—are—not,' the old man said, spitting each word out so severely that Kemp slipped to the ground once again.

'Out of all the people on this puny planet, I've selected you. So be grateful, boy, because I'm giving you the chance to save your life. There is no other way for you.'

Kemp squealed, and looked down the passage. What was holding him back? Why didn't he go for it? Why didn't he say that he wasn't Archie? He felt oddly dizzy, as if a force was holding him against his will.

'I see you need convincing,' the old man said, his voice as smooth as honey once more. 'I'm going to show you something to... reassure you. All I'm asking for is a little co-operation.'

The old man took a step back.

Kemp stood up, his knees barely able to hold him.

'You see, I'm going to tell you the story of what has happened so far, and then I'm going to tell you what happens next. Do you understand?'

Kemp nodded.

'Good. Let me tell you about that piece of paper in your pocket, and how I will generate your image in the lightning,' the ghost said, this time softer. 'Then, Archie de Lowe, I'm going to show you who you really are and how we are going to help one another.'

THIRTY-SEVEN

THE GAME

Isabella dashed down the touchline.

'Sue, thank God I've found you,' she said. 'What's up with you? We're on drinks duty!'

'Heck,' she said. 'You're right. My stupid watch...'

They rushed over to the old Volkswagen Combi ice cream van, known as the "catering-cart" which acted as refreshment centre and mobile sweet shop.

Isabella and Sue pulled out a few tables, and lined out paper cups ready for jugs of orange squash. A steady stream began queuing for drinks, chocolate bars, and crisps.

Sue took the money while Isabella handed out cups, but Sue could barely keep up.

Isabella was working at an astonishing speed, darting here and there, handing out confectionery and drinks. She talked to everyone about the current score, or Daisy's brilliant goals, or the curious weather.

'How did you manage to serve all that in ten minutes?' Sue said, as she squeezed a few more cups into the overflowing bin bag. 'We've made a killing.'

Isabella breathed a sigh of relief. With no rain thus far, perhaps Solomon was right after all. Maybe the cloud would break later that afternoon. From inside the van, she looked out over the scene. The crowd was still three or four deep the entire way around the pitch, and she could just make out the steep rise of the bank on the far side that led up to the village.

The floodlights shone down, giving the players a strange, quadruple shadow. If it hadn't been nearly midday, there would have been no reason to suspect that they weren't playing a night match.

'Isabella,' she called out. 'Get a place just left of the halfway line. I'll join you in a minute after I've cashed up.'

The feeling of dread that Sue had experienced before was building again. The vast black cloud seemed to be growing denser, sinking lower in the sky.

Instead of watching the game, Sue knew she should get out of there and run to higher ground, but she was instantly swallowed up by the drama, and swept away by the skills of Daisy de Lowe.

A heavy challenge sent Daisy flying. The crowd swayed, and spilled onto the pitch.

The noise levels increased.

'That was late. Too damn late,' Isabella shouted, peeling off her scarf.

'Careful, Isabella. Watch it,' Sue said, firmly. 'You mustn't go nuts because you'll get expelled. I promised Sol—'

'It was deliberate and dirty—'

'NO, Isabella!' Sue snapped. 'Hold your tongue.'

'But they're targeting Daisy exactly as Kemp said they would. They're going to kick her out of the game!'

Sue closed her eyes. Great, just what she needed! Ten minutes to go, and Isabella sizzling like a firework.

'What was that noise?' Isabella said.

'That gargantuan thing up there?'

'Th... thunder?' Isabella said, momentarily removing her eyes from the action.

Sue nodded nervously, half wishing to make a run for it.

Several members of the crowd started to leave, while others gestured upwards.

This is it, Sue thought. *This is where it starts, exactly as I saw in my nightmare. It even feels the same too. I've got to tell Isabella. I've got to tell her NOW.*

A ghastly feeling of panic swept over her.

They should stop the game. Get everyone away.

Sue's thoughts were interrupted as Daisy stole the ball and sprinted down the field.

Daisy skipped inside one tackle, then dummied inside looking for support.

The crowd roared, but, from nowhere, a couple of Newton boys smashed into her from opposite angles. All three lay on the ground as the ball was kicked away by another Newton player.

Play continued, but it was a poor decision.

'Yellow card,' yelled a senior boy. 'C'mon ref!'

The atmosphere flipped. Suddenly, late tackles flew in and players were being kicked indiscriminately out of eyeshot of the referee.

One of the Newton strikers stole into the penalty area, as a massive crash of thunder reverberated around them. At that exact moment, little Jimmy Nugent, running back, tapped the forward's foot and the player fell face-first onto the turf.

The whistle shrilled and the ball was placed on the penalty spot.

'I don't believe it!' Sue said, quietly, 'the end of Daisy's dream.' She turned. 'Isabella, what on earth are you doing?'

Isabella was scribbling furiously in her notebook. 'Just watch for me a minute. You know, commentate, like they do on telly.'

She didn't need to. The groan told her everything.

'What happened?'

'The ball trickled past Archie. All he had to do was put his foot out. Two-all.'

'He is absolutely useless sometimes,' Isabella said.

'Well, he's only in the team because no-one else would do it.'

'And to keep Daisy company, though, to be fair, he has improved, ' Isabella said, as she thrust the paper into Sue's overcoat pocket. 'Ye of little faith, Sue Lowden,' she said. 'You'll see, I bet Daisy scores again.'

Another roll of thunder boomed and cracked. More spectators started running away.

Sue's stomach lurched. It was now or never.

'Isabella, we've got to get out of here, now. I mean it. But listen to me first. There's something important I've got to share—'

'Please, Sue. Just shut up!' Isabella snapped, her eyes on the action. 'Get the ball to Daisy de Lowe,' she roared. 'Give it to Daisy!' Isabella turned to Sue. 'Listen, hun, tell me whatever is so damn important at the end, okay. There's less than five minutes to go and it's two-all in the most important match of my brother and sister's life. Can you please just give it a break for five minutes? Five minutes. That's all I'm asking.'

With that, Isabella sidled out onto the pitch, ran down the touchline, and dived in among the spectators further down.

Archie stomped around the penalty area, his face burning with shame at the unsaved goal.

For some reason, just before the Newton player stepped up to hit the penalty, it had come to him. The person he'd seen way up on the steps heading into the alley was definitely Kemp. For a start, his hair was a complete giveaway, and he was wearing the ghost's long coat, which made him look like a monk.

And then, just as the guy hit the ball, all he could think of was running over to find out what the hell Kemp was up to.

In the next instance, the ball had trickled past him into the goal.

If Cain *was* there, and Kemp had gone to find him, would Cain know the difference between them? Would he care?

Archie kicked the base of the post. The more he thought about Kemp and the ghost, the more it confirmed that his feelings on the matter were right.

All I ever do is look on hopelessly, he thought. *When will I stop being so pathetic?*

A slow-burning fury moved through his body, an anger borne of frustration and annoyance. It began to build up in him like a glowing light, as if he were being charged up like a battery.

Archie was about to kick short from the goal kick, but, from out of the corner of his eye, he saw Daisy in yards of space on the halfway line, catching her breath after the last attack. It was worth a try. He pushed the ball ahead, ran up, and thumped it hard. The ball rose high into the air.

Daisy saw it, her eyes never leaving the ball. She took it down in her stride and, with a burst of speed, tore past one player, then another. She then stopped so suddenly that another player over-ran, and she side-stepped one more player who fell over. The crowd roared.

'… *She will, she will — ROCK YOU!*'

Daisy side-stepped again and, with an injection of pace, flew towards the penalty area with real menace. Four Newton players lay sprawled on the floor, leaving only one more to beat.

'Go on Daisy, you can do it,' Archie screamed.

Archie watched as the remaining defender was sold a beautiful dummy, which Daisy seemed to do with such ease that it was laughable. As she pushed the ball past him and effortlessly made her way around, he slid out a leg and tripped her up quite deliberately. Daisy stumbled and fell but she wasn't giving up. She crawled towards the ball and then, even as she lay on the ground with the ball wedged between her knees, she managed to keep moving.

But a warning cry went up as three Newton players and the

goalkeeper converged on Daisy. It looked as if Daisy had fallen into a trap as the Newton boys cocked their legs and kicked out, striking more of Daisy than the ball, kicking her again and again in a kind of frenzy.

And still she refused to give the ball up.

The crowd swayed and screamed before falling silent.

They could quite clearly see Daisy's face contorting in pain as the assault rained down on her, and then all hell broke loose.

THIRTY-EIGHT

SUE TELLS OF HER DREAM

For the first time in her life, Sue could feel a sensation of utter panic building up in her veins like one of her bubbling chemistry experiments. A series of flashes filled the sky, mirroring the extraordinary scenes of fighting on the pitch. Lightning fizzed then crackled.

For a brief moment, the light formed a picture of a boy in the sky.

Sue gasped. *A boy?*

A thunderclap smashed overhead so loudly that the crowd cried out. Shrieks and screams filled the football field.

Sue fell to her knees, barely able to think, her body shaking. *No! It can't be! It's not possible. It's... it's... Kemp's face!* The lightning was Kemp's face super-imposed in the cloud. How was this possible?

She looked around. *Where was Isabella?* She couldn't have gone already. Sue followed the eyes of the crowd.

Isabella was striding towards the pitch.

Oh hell.

'No! Isabella,' she yelled. 'Stop!'

There was no reaction.

Without thinking, Sue took off after her.

'Isabella, LISTEN!' she yelled as she ran. 'It's you!'

She ran faster.

'The dream is about your family, the de Lowes.' She sensed Isabella slowing down.

'You must ALL survive until sunset and find a cave. Do you understand?' She took a deep breath.

'Survive till sunset,' she screamed. 'YOU MUST ALL STAY ALIVE!'

Her voice was petering out and she realised her yelling was making herself hoarse. She sucked a deep breath in again.

'Find clues in Eden Cottage,' she hollered. 'You must find the clues.'

Sue coughed and then repeated the last part, adding,

'Get home. All three of you!'

She noted some of the crowd staring at her as if she was a madwoman. But she didn't care, not one little bit.

Archie couldn't believe it.

First Sue screaming nonsense at Isabella, and now this!

And where the hell was the referee?

He thumped the goalpost, shook his head, and looked up. The giant, angry bruise of a cloud stretched above him like a monstrous airship. It sagged so low in the sky that he felt he could jump up and burst it as easily as pricking a balloon.

The heady smell of damp filled his nostrils as another crack of thunder escaped. Archie felt his blood boiling inside him. Five Newton players surrounded Daisy who had dragged herself up, and was rubbing her shins.

Then one of them pushed her over.

Anger flooded through him. *No one*, Archie seethed, *does that to my sister.*

He tore down the pitch, the crowd baying and shouting as the referee desperately tried to separate the fighting players.

'NO! Don't retaliate, Archie—' he could hear someone yelling. It was too late, though. Hell had broken loose.

One of the Newton boys was holding Daisy's hair and leering at her, screaming in her face. Archie grabbed him by the collar and threw him away, the boy sailing through the air and landing in a heap on the ground. Archie punched another boy hard on the nose. He thought he heard crunching sounds, then found himself receiving blows although he couldn't feel them.

Blood coursed through his body. He felt strong and powerful. Invincible.

A couple of Newton boys jumped him but he picked one up with one hand and tossed him over his shoulder. The other boy he wrestled to the ground until the boy under him squirrelled away. Then he found another hitting Jimmy Nugent. He smashed the boy hard in the stomach and tossed him to the side like a piece of litter.

The whistle shrilled again and again.

Finally, a sharp, stern voice rose up out of the melee. It was Isabella. Archie could see her nearing them a sense of steel in her determined walk. *Oh no!*

Archie looked around. Three Newton boys and the referee stared at him with their eyes wide open.

Was it in fear?

This was a sensation he'd never experienced before.

Archie wiped his brow and allowed himself a smile.

Weirdly, it felt strangely good.

THIRTY-NINE

SOLOMON'S PENNY DROPS

'Sir,' a small boy said, running up to him. 'Sir. What shall we do?'

Solomon smiled, badly. 'I've been assured that there won't be any rainfall until this afternoon,' he said. 'I'm sure we'll be fine.'

'But, Sir. We don't think it's safe.'

Solomon stared up at the throbbing deep bruise that filled the sky to the horizon. His heartbeat quickened.

'If you're worried, make your way indoors. Are your parents around?'

'No, Sir. They're coming to the music concert this afternoon.'

'Then I suggest you go to the library and find a good book. How does that sound?'

The boy ran back to his friends, and together they scampered over to the old tower.

Solomon's knees were shaking. In fact, now that he noticed, his entire body shook, as if he'd been swimming in the cold sea. Nerves about the match, probably.

At the back of his mind he wondered about Isabella's warning. I mean, *really*? Bah! It wasn't going to happen, was it?

BOOM! CRACK!

Solomon felt the ground shake.

'Sir—'

'The team need your immediate support,' the headmaster said, loudly, when suddenly he noticed the players attacking one other.

Oh Lord.

Moving quickly, he headed down the touchline.

'Coach,' he shouted.

The coach swivelled on his heels and ran towards him. 'For goodness' sake, watch out for Isabella de Lowe. If anything happens to Daisy—'

They watched as the Newton boys set upon her.

'Goodness gracious me. I'm quite tempted to get stuck in myself.

'Best you don't, Headmaster,' Coach said. 'What's the ref doing? He's standing there like a bleeding' dummy!'

They both stared at the scene, their mouths open.

'Boss, shouldn't we call it off?'

'No, no. It's so nearly over—'

'Who's on earth is doing that yelling?' Coach asked.

'Well, I never,' Solomon said. 'That's Sue, isn't it? Whatever is she going on about?'

'No idea. Something about it being their fault?'

'Whose fault?' the headmaster queried.

'The de Lowe's. If you ask me, they've all gone mad… Bloomin' Nora, is that Archie? It's not poss—'

'Lord above…. he's duffing them up! Whatever has the world come to,' the headmaster said. 'Steel, Coach. Over there! Isabella's on the march. Be good fellows and grab her before this melee gets even more out of hand!'

FORTY

DIRECT ACTION

'Stop it! All of you.' Isabella screamed as she strode towards the players with a formidable sense of purpose.

The teams almost instantly ceased brawling. Isabella's direct approach had that effect on people.

'Pathetic, all of you,' she shouted, pointing at various individuals. 'It's like a wrestling match for the Under 5s. Newton, you three especially, should be deeply ashamed of yourselves.'

Isabella scooped up the ball. 'As for the refereeing; a disgraceful performance. Twelve deliberate fouls totally unaccounted for and you haven't even got the balls to book them, let alone send them off for repeated violent conduct.'

The football smacked into the referee's hands. 'You should be struck off—?'

Before she had a chance to finish, she was grabbed by Coach and Mr Steele who hauled her off her feet and away to the side line.

The referee responded by pointing belatedly at Isabella.

'You'll be dealt with later by the authorities,' he roared, blinking, trying hard to pull himself together.

Why couldn't he remember the procedure for dealing with a brawl? It felt as if his brain had emptied.

'And along with that madwoman,' he continued, 'Upsall goalkeeper and number eight, and Sutton players five, seven and four,' he said pointing at the players, 'Get off this playing field!'

He waved his red card at Archie and the other players and scribbled in his book.

Another huge slap of thunder exploded almost directly overhead. The ground shook. A terrible prickle tiptoed up his spine, sending his hairs erect.

'Direct free kick to red,' he said, pointing to a spot fractionally outside the penalty area. 'And the quicker we're out of here, the better.'

The ref studied his watch. 'Last minute,' he announced.

That girl was right, though. His had been a truly woeful performance.

Daisy dragged herself up and flicked a fleck of mud off her shorts.

What a crazy match! Her being kicked to bits, Sue screaming at Isabella, Isabella going mad again and screaming at everyone else. Archie missing a total sitter and beating up the opposition like a prize-fighter before getting sent off, while thunder crashed overhead, lightning fizzed, and everything was incredibly deafening.

Now, with the last kick of the game, she had a chance to win the match. *Boy, pressure kicks don't come much bigger than this*, she thought. *Better make this a good one.*

'Come on, Upsall. Come on, Daisy de Lowe, you can do it,' roared the small section of crowd still remaining.

Daisy rubbed her tired, bruised legs, and drew her hands through her muddy blonde hair. She fixed her boots and selected a slightly raised patch of turf on which she carefully placed the ball.

She stood back and studied her route to goal. Twenty, twenty-three yards perhaps? Perfect. Just as she'd practised time and again with Archie.

She rubbed her eyes and concentrated hard. It was now or never. Everything she'd ever played for came down to this one kick.

She sucked in a large mouthful of air, her eyes focusing on the ball so intently that she felt she could see its entire trajectory and the precise spot on the leather where she aim her boot.

The whole atmosphere of the crowd, and the rumbling sky seemed to disappear for a moment, leaving behind a strange hush.

The referee blew.

Daisy exhaled. She'd take her time. One minute left and, if she had it her way, one kick to settle it. That's all she needed.

FORTY-ONE

SUE DISCOVERS A NOTE

There was more, Sue thought, but she'd finally said what needed to be said. Thank goodness she'd had the presence of mind to scribble down her dreams the moment she'd woken up.

'*GO! Run! Run... all of you,*' she screamed at the spectators. 'The storm's going to break.'

Thunder rolled.

She sprinted up the slope towards the buildings.

As she passed the top end she spied Gus leaning on the lamppost, near to the leaning houses. She headed directly towards him. 'Gus, what are you doing?'

'Following Kemp. He's been acting weird all afternoon. Are we winning?'

'Listen, Gus,' she said as she caught her breath. 'Rain,' she panted, 'like you've never seen... get out of here... fast. You've got to believe me.' Her hand touched some paper in her pocket and she pulled it out. She remembered; it was Isabella's note.

Gus rolled his eyes.

She read it out loud.

'*Sue, there's a boat in the old shed. Key under a pot by door, oars on the side. Think there's a canopy in cupboard... just in case. Love you. Be safe, Isabella.*'

Sue kissed it in relief. *Clever, brilliant Isabella.*

Gus grabbed the note. 'What is it with you two?'

'Look at the sky, Gus. When that "thing" bursts it will rain harder than you can possibly imagine. In minutes, the water will flash flood. I've had a premonition. I'll tell you about it'

'A premonition? Blimey. Cool. You sure?'

'Absolutely. No one has a chance. Can you drive? Do you have access to a car?'

'Yes, a little, but no! You?'

'Me neither,' she fired back. 'Some of the kids have gone but I'm going later, after the music concert.'

'Same,' Gus said, trying to keep pace with her.

'Then we're stuck, Gus. Properly screwed. There's no way out.'

'Screwed? What are you talking about, Sue? Why should we be stuck?'

'Look up, Gus,' she said. 'That massive black thing up there. I promise you I'm not crazy. I'm being absolutely deadly serious. That cloud isn't holding an ordinary storm inside its belly. When it lets go the result will be catastrophic. Come on, keep up.'

Gus frowned. 'You're really serious, aren't you?' he said, the smile slipping off his face.

'Never more so.' She stopped to catch her breath. 'Please, Gus, I need your help. Will you help me? Please?'

Gus scratched his nose. He liked Sue, and he'd certainly never seen her quite so animated. 'Okay,' he found himself saying. 'I'm going to have to trust you on this one. Where do we start?'

'Oh, great! Thanks, Gus,' Sue said, moving in and bear-hugging him. If she was going to do this, better to do it with big, strong Gus Williams than by herself.

'First off, provisions. Food: high-energy snack bars; choco-lates; lemons; dried fruit; tinned food like tuna and baked beans; sweetcorn; a couple of lighters and firelighters; bottled water,' Sue rattled off, 'and blankets—'

'Blankets?'

'Anything you can get hold of.' She urged him to keep up. 'You're the Scout leader, aren't you? Grab stuff we can survive on.'

'To the shop, then,' Gus said, smiling keenly and feeling rather important.

'I've got about twenty pounds from the footie snacks and drinks. I'll pay it back later.' Sue did some calculations in her head. 'Actually, that's probably not enough. Have you got anything?'

Gus shoved his hands in his pockets and pulled out some change. 'Just short of four quid.'

Sue grimaced. 'In that case, Gus, I hope you don't mind but you're going to have to steal. Come on, there's not a second to lose. When we get in there, grab some bags and start filling them. Don't hesitate or stop, understand? When it's done, I'll throw the money on the counter and we run. Got it?'

'Blimey, Sue. What if we get stopped?'

'We won't. Oh, and if necessary, use force.'

Gus nodded, and handed over his money. His eyes were bulging with surprise. 'Where are we going afterwards?'

'The boat shed.'

'Boat shed? What boat shed?'

'By the river.' She waved her hand in its rough direction. 'We should have time to sort out some kind of cover and find survival things, then we're going to have to hope for the best. I don't know what we'll find when we get there, but, right now, it's our only chance.'

Gus smiled. He loved a girl who meant business and if there was to be some weird catastrophe, at least Sue had the whole thing planned.

FORTY-TWO

ARCHIE FINDS KEMP

Even before the referee had brandished the red card at him, Archie turned and ran.

He had to find out what Kemp was up to, and fast. If he was right, there wasn't much more time left.

His stomach churned, and darkness seeped into his bones.

Thunder crashed and boomed as spectators began to flee to their cars and the school buildings.

Archie sprinted and scampered up the steep bank, pulling himself up on the longer tufts with his hands and using his studs to give him grip. At the top of the bank he caught his breath.

Another dramatic roll of thunder rattled the ground as Archie watched Isabella kicking and screaming as she was hauled off the football pitch. People were streaming away, pointing skywards.

Wow. What a mental couple of minutes.

And where did his strength come from?

He shook his head and smiled. *Was it from the strange glass of water left by the ghost?*

He spied the alleyway and ran over, the studs of his boots clacking on the stone beneath him. He thought for a minute about taking them off but really, was there any point? *This ghost,* he thought, *couldn't really exist, could it?*

He peered down the alleyway and saw two shapes.

A sudden burst of lightning brought the pair to light and he could make out Kemp's hair, as well as another figure beside him wearing a long coat and a kind of wide brim hat. Archie's heart pounded. They were moving towards him.

OMG. Wrongo. The ghost *did* exist and Kemp had got there first.

Archie shrank down, wiping rivulets of sweat off his forehead.

Cain was blind, wasn't he? He'd gone on about the fact that he didn't have any eyes, like the Ancient Woman, so perhaps the ghost couldn't see Kemp.

So, what were the chances the ghost thought Kemp was him?

Archie stood up from behind the wheelie bin so that only his head might be seen. Kemp was about ten paces away and Archie could definitely make out that the figure next to him was a ghost by the simple fact that he didn't have any feet and his face was mostly covered by a scarf.

A crackle of lightning fizzed above them and from the light it momentarily threw out, Archie saw Kemp's terrified face, an expression he'd never seen before on his friend.

One of pure terror.

Archie gasped.

Kemp's eyes widened as their eyes met.

Now, he could discern the ghost's words, like 'power' and 'magic' and 'strength'.

Archie was stunned. *This spook, Cain, really did think Kemp was him!*

The ghost held Kemp around his left arm and Archie wondered if Kemp was bringing them towards him, or if it was the other way around?

He listened harder as they came to a stop just on the other side of the wheelie bin.

He heard Kemp's quivering voice. 'Tell me again about the Prophecy,' he said. 'I need to be absolutely certain before I make my final decision.'

'Did you not listen, Archie?' the ghost complained.

Archie reeled. *Archie? What was Kemp playing at?*

Why was he asking Cain to tell him about this Prophecy one more time? It seemed a pretty odd thing to do.

Or was it for his benefit?

'I need to be sure,' Kemp croaked.

'Very well.' Cain tipped his head to the sky as though sniffing it. 'But we are running out of time.'

Archie stole another look at Kemp from around the corner of the wheelie bin. When he caught sight of Kemp's face, tears were streaming down his cheeks.

Why was Kemp crying?

He crouched down and listened to Cain's deep, powerful voice. 'There is a great shift that occurs every now and then in the way of the universe, Archie,' the ghost began.

'When this happens, the world changes. There is a change in the world's relationship to its surroundings, the infinite and beyond. The process of these movements have been given to you in the form of dreams. These dreams are the Prophecy of the Garden of Eden and they are given to three people who are known as Heirs of Eden,' the ghost paused. 'You and your sisters are the Heirs of Eden. You are the chosen ones, charged with undertaking the tasks that have been shown to you.'

Archie's gut turned. *WOAH! Chosen ones! Blimey. The strange creature above Daisy must have been feeding her dreams, just as I thought.*

The ghost carried on. 'It is complex, and this is not the time to tell you the ways of the universe. All you need know is that the Heirs of Eden face fearsome challenges. The first of which is a terrible storm aimed entirely at you. If any of you do not survive the storm, it will rage for forty days and forty nights. It will wash away the world, bit by bit,' Cain paused. 'And when the waters recede, there will be a different world and a new beginning.

'I tell you now. You children stand little chance. There is no ark to save you, nor any place you can go where you will not find yourselves shot at by lightning or washed out by torrents of rain. The earth will slip down hillsides, the rivers will swell, and trees will crash down. There is nowhere you can hide. I do not tell you this with any joy, but the storm was designed when men were strong, lived long, and knew how to fight with nature through other means such as magic. You are about to enter a time you are not equipped to cope with. Do you understand?'

Kemp nodded and his eyes bulged. 'Why?' he croaked.

'Young man, the Prophecy is a measure; a test, if you like, to see if the people on this planet are equipped to move into a new age. It was designed to test the strength, courage, intelligence and the spirit of mankind.'

Cain stopped for a moment and chuckled.

'You and your sisters, the Heirs of Eden, are the measure of human life on Earth. Together you must survive until sundown and locate the cave of riddles.'

'Then what?' Kemp stammered.

'Then, the destructive force of the storm will cease and the Heirs of Eden must look for the clues that will open the Garden of Eden and save Earth in the form you know it today.'

Cain sniffed the air. 'There is no more time,' he barked. 'The storm breaks in a few moments.' The ghost faced him. 'Now boy, it is time for you to willingly make a choice.'

FORTY-THREE

GUS IN THE SHOP

Gus hurried after Sue, his arms nearly dropping off with the weight of the shopping bags.

In the shop, he'd rushed round shovelling everything he could find into three carrier bags, much to the proprietor, Mr Ranji's, increasing curiosity. Sue was on the other side doing the same, when she ran up to the counter and literally threw money at the shopkeeper. Notes fluttered through the air like leaves and coins sprayed the counter. Sue spun on her heel and fled out of the door with Gus right behind her, burning with shame.

'Come back here!' Ranji shouted. 'Stop! Stop them! Thieves!'

Gus bit his lips and shrugged his shoulders, as a sort of apology, then ran off as fast as his legs could carry him. He headed down the hill, hoping like mad a thunderbolt wouldn't smack him.

When he took a little breather, he spotted Kemp in the alley looking nothing less than petrified.

What the hell was he up to?

There wasn't time to dwell. He ran to the boat shed after Sue.

Sue's fingers shook so much that she couldn't lift the plant pot under which the key sat. Eventually, Gus put his bags down and calmly tried it for her. The old and rusty key stuck in the lock, turning only fractionally. Gus forced it first one way and then the other, loosening it gradually until it clicked and let them through.

If that was the condition of the lock, he thought, *then what sort of state will this boat be in?*

The door whined open, as another crash of thunder and lightning crackled in the sky overhead. Gus shivered, and brushed away a few old cobwebs.

'When was the last time this was used?'

'No idea,' Sue replied, searching for a light. She flicked a switch and a solitary light bulb sparked into life.

In the middle of the boat house, covered by a large tarpaulin, sat an old rowing boat resting on two large pieces of wood. It had three bench seats, and Gus reckoned it was probably twelve feet in length by four feet wide. He laughed.

'This is it? This piece of junk is going to save us? It should be in a museum!'

He dragged off the tarp, shook away the dust, and whistled as he inspected the vessel. Layers of peeling varnish and thick dust covered the wood.

'We need to build a canopy,' Sue said.

'Why?' Gus quizzed.

'So we don't spend the entire time bailing water out, that's why.'

Gus pulled the oars off the wall and nestled them in the rowlocks before searching the boathouse for wood. He found several lengths of two-by-four inch cut timber, as well as planks intended, he supposed, for repairs.

'How long did you say we would be stuck in this?'

Sue shrugged. 'How should I know? A day, a week'

'A week?'

'Maybe a month?'

'Jeez. A month.' Gus sprang into overdrive. He ran around the room finding things that might be useful and tossed them into the boat: rope; wood; a couple of buckets; a crabbing line, and a fishing net. He found a handy-looking wooden box and a sealed plastic container, which he told Sue to clean before putting in the matches and anything else that needed to be kept dry.

How would they anchor down the canopy? What would they sleep on? What would they drink?

He yelled over to Sue, who was still busy cramming the tarpaulin under a seat.

'A month? Really, a month! You think so?'

A huge crack of thunder smashed overhead.

They cowered.

She stretched her arms out. 'How long is a piece of string?'

Gus spied four, fifty-litre plastic containers. He ran over and smelled them. No foul odours. Good. He took two to the tap, rinsed and filled them before heaving them up onto the boat. It creaked ominously under their weight.

'Make room for these,' he instructed Sue, 'one at each end.'

Gus tied the two empty ones to either side to act as bumpers or emergency buoys.

With this task complete, Gus spotted more loose planks on the far wall. He marched over and without hesitating, levered the first plank off. As the nails bowed to the pressure and the length came away, he pulled two more weatherboards away and slipped them into the boat. 'Hammer and nails,' he yelled out. 'Have you seen any?'

Sue pointed in the direction of an old workbench.

It was a long shot, but if there were any tools it might make all the difference. He flew through the drawers and cupboards, finding paint and rags, paintbrushes and sandpaper. He dragged out a thick canopy and laid it aside. How would he attach it? To the right, another pile of workman's bits was covered by two large, crumpled dust sheets.

He handed the dust sheets to Sue, indicating that she needed to shake them out and fold them away.

Underneath all this he discovered a selection of wood-working tools hidden in an old, blue canvas bag.

Gus thumped the air. Clearly, someone had set out to repair the building and left everything behind.

Right, Gus thought. *I reckon I've got approximately twenty minutes to build a world class, life-saving canopy.*

FORTY-FOUR

KEMP AND ARCHIE

Archie trembled. Everything Cain said rang true.

Archie heard Kemp's voice, strangely muffled, saying 'So, there's little hope for me and my sisters.'

'There is always hope, young man,' the ghost replied. 'But in comparison to the thickness of a rainbow, the chances that the three of you will survive this storm are but an atom wide. You are a child. You have neither the strength, nor the skills, to combat what lies ahead. You have no magic, and you do not understand nature. What chance do you have?'

He paused for effect.

'None. That is why you must join me now, Archie. And while your world is washed away, I alone offer you the chance to escape through me. You have the opportunity to start again. All I need is the use of your body.'

'Will this help save your mother?' Kemp said.

The ghost seemed a little surprised. 'Yes. You have seen her and you know that she holds a great secret within her that others seek to destroy. By joining me, Archie, she will be saved. I guarantee it.'

Cain was laying on the charm. His persuasion was intoxicating.

'Here, on earth, the suffering will be great. Together, Archie, we can build a new future. I am nearly useless without you, and you are helpless without me.'

Kemp looked over at Archie whose astonished face had risen from the other side of the wheelie bin. 'But, I still don't understand,' Kemp whimpered.

Cain growled. 'These things are beyond your understanding. Open your mind and offer me your body for both our sakes.'

Kemp tried to make a run for it. He attempted to loosen the grip on his arm by charging at the rubbish bin.

'GO!' he screamed at Archie. 'RUN!' But the ghost held him tight and forced him to the floor. Kemp whimpered at the stabbing pain in his hand.

The ghost moved into Archie's path and began to unfurl the scarf wrapped around his face. 'I see,' he said. 'There is another.' His head moved. 'And only one of you is Archie. You have tried to deceive me,' the ghost said. 'It is your choice, Archie. If you choose to come with me, you will be saved, and my mother will be saved. Run, and you will almost certainly die.'

He released Kemp, who stumbled to the floor. 'Which is it going to be?'

Kemp's cheeks were streaked with tears. He caught Archie's eye, and stared at him, imploring him, begging him to understand.

Kemp began to speak to his friend. 'Kemp, you are my only friend,' he said, 'and, not long ago, I swore on my life that I would never hurt you or your family. I screwed up.'

Archie frowned. *What? What was Kemp talking about? Had Kemp figured that the ghost was blind?*

Kemp began again, 'Run, Kemp, save yourself. GO!'

'Uh?' Archie said, confused.

'Yes, Kemp, you moron, get out of here! Flee to safety, while you have the chance.'

Archie stared at Kemp.

And then Kemp said it again. 'Look, Kemp, you great big oaf. Go now while there's still a chance. Leave this to me, but promise me one thing.'

'What?'

'Look after that fishing rod.'

'Fishing rod?'

'Blimey Kemp, how dim are you?' he said. 'Go! Now. Run you idiot—GO!'

Archie stared deep into Kemp's tear-stained eyes and saw a spark of light.

Archie curled his fist into a ball and punched his friend lightly on the shoulder. He winked and mouthed the words, 'Thank you'.

'So long, Archie de Lowe,' Archie said. 'See you in the next place.'

Taking a deep breath, Archie turned, and fled for his life.

FORTY-FIVE

ARCHIE RUNS

'It has started,' the ghost cried, his hat angled upwards towards the sky. 'Something more powerful than you can possibly imagine has begun.' He raised an arm towards the lightning and thunder.

'If you want to see your friend for the last time, follow his path but I doubt he will last long. You too may run now, but you would be a fool, Archie de Lowe.'

Kemp moved towards the end of the alleyway.

People were scattering even though the players were still on the pitch.

Kemp watched Archie hare towards the steep bank and out of view. Then he reappeared, running flat out, waving his hands in the air, sprinting towards the football field.

Kemp shifted his gaze slightly to see Daisy, with a wall of Sutton players between her and the goal, about to strike the ball just as Archie ran onto the pitch.

BOOM! CRACK!

With a deafening roar, a massive thunderbolt flashed out of the sky right on top of Archie.

Kemp's heart missed a beat as he watched Archie collapse to

the floor like a rag-doll, his body spasming one moment, then still the next.

Smoke drifted from his body and sounds of screaming filled the air.

Kemp recoiled. Everything the ghost had said had happened; the sweet paper, the lightning in his own image, and now the thunderbolt aimed at Archie who lay dead on the ground.

Laid back Archie with his scruffy hair, who was always late for everything. His fishing pal, the only person to whom he'd ever told the whole story about his parents.

He'd sent him to his death.

Cain hovered behind him. 'I am nothing more than a sad ghost,' he said, almost forlornly. 'I was stripped of my flesh and bones, but not my spirit. It means that I cannot move or touch anything with any great purpose, so I require flesh and blood to partially restore me. This is where you come in. I cannot do it alone.'

The ghost removed his scarf and sniffed the air around Kemp, who felt a chill on his neck.

'Rest assured, boy,' the ghost said softly, 'I have no intention of taking your life, only *borrowing* it for a little while. When my work is done and my mother is safe from harm, I will put you back near this spot. That is my solemn promise. But nature's curse is now upon us. A decision needs to be made.'

Kemp remained frozen to the spot.

'You must freely decide,' the ghost continued. 'The window is closing so you must decide now. I very much doubt you will get such an offer from the storm.'

FORTY-SIX

THE STORM BEGINS

Confusion reigned as players and spectators ran hard towards the cars and houses above the football field. Screams filled the air.

Archie prised his eyes open and attempted to focus. His head! It pounded as if a gigantic road-roller was travelling back-wards and forwards in his brain.

He caught the sharp, acrid smell of burning hair.

When his eyes finally hooked up with his brain, he could make out a burning net and a smouldering goalpost.

'Archie!' Daisy cried as she rushed over. 'Please...'

Several inaudible words mumbled out of his mouth.

'Archie!' Isabella screamed as she tore across the pitch.

She placed her hand on Archie's forehead then felt for his temperature, checked his pulse and inspected his tongue.

'Thank God!' she said, cradling him. 'I thought you were toast. Say something—can you... move?'

Very slowly he lifted an arm, his fingernails black and his clothes singed.

He smiled weakly.

'At least he's showing signs of usual mental stability,'

Isabella said. 'Daisy, grab the tracksuits! I'll make sure his internal organs are functioning correctly.'

Shortly, Isabella declared that Archie was well enough to try a couple of little sips of water.

Archie shut his eyes then opened them. Then he slurred a series of inaudible words.

'My strips must have saved you!'

'Urgh?'

'The strips you stuck on the bottom of your boots.'

Daisy returned with their tracksuits, slipping into hers before helping Archie into his.

'We won!' Isabella said. 'You did it!'

'Don't be ridiculous,' Daisy scoffed as she pulled Archie's top over his stiff hair.

'I'm not,' Isabella replied. 'The ball is in the net. It was blown into the goal. You actually scored!'

Daisy didn't know whether to hit her sister or cry. 'No,' she said furiously. 'I missed and Archie got fried. Look at him, it's a miracle he survived—'

'But you're fine now, aren't you, Archie?' Isabella said. 'Anyway, you're wrong. Your free kick was heading towards the corner flag but the lightning bolt deflected the ball into the goal. I swear it. The charge of particles must have generated a force to deflect it without blowing the ball up. It is therefore, the most extraordinary goal of all time—'

'Shut up! Please,' Daisy snapped. 'Stop it.'

Coach was running over towards them. He went straight to Archie and checked him over.

'WOW-ee,' he whistled. 'That is one lucky escape, young man. I thought you were brown bread. It looks like the Gods spared you. You may feel a little groggy for a while, but, amazingly, I think you're gonna be all right. Try standing if you can.'

Archie, with the support of a person on each side, stood.

'How do you feel?'

He couldn't quite hear or see them. He tried smiling.

'That's the match ball in the net, isn't it, Coach?' Isabella asked. 'I've taken a picture of it on my phone, for safekeeping.'

Coach clapped his hands. 'You know what, Isabella, you're right! Looks like we're the ruddy champions. We're only the bleedin' winners!' He slapped Daisy on the back, almost knocking her over. 'Quite amazing...' He stopped mid-sentence and looked up, his tone serious once again. 'Listen, if you think you can make it, Arch, you'd better get off now, up that funny track to your cottage. Otherwise, I'll give you a lift back, via the school.'

'Thanks, but don't worry, Coach,' Isabella said. 'It's not so far. We'll get him back in one piece, I promise. Anyway,' she continued, addressing Archie, 'you're not *that* poorly, are you?'

Coach eyed them. 'You sure? Well then, you'd better get going then. Best scarper before another of them thunderbolts zaps us.' He patted them on their backs. 'As fast as you can! I reckon it's going to bloody piss down.'

Coach skipped off towards the car park singing loudly. Then he yelled back at them. 'Great goals, Daisy, and bloody brilliant hairdo, Arch. You're all ruddy legends!'

Archie wavered a little and Daisy caught him. 'You really think we can get back home?'

Archie was trying to say something. But it came out slightly askew.

'What is it?' Isabella said softly.

'Storm!' he said, his words slurred. 'Go.'

Angry rolls of thunder boomed around them.

'Is anyone else finding this very loud?' Daisy asked. 'I've had to put tissue in my ears. Look!' And she pulled out the paper. Suddenly Daisy's face went pale.

Isabella spotted it. 'What is it?'

'I think there's another in-coming thunderbolt.'

'*What!*' Isabella said.

'RUN! NOW!'

They hooked Archie's arms around their shoulders and set off.

'I can hear particles gathering way up there in the cloud, I think. Like snap, crackle and...' Daisy said, nervously, '...pop.' She stopped.

'DIVE!'

A moment later, a massive crack tore across the sky and unleashed a lightning bolt which smashed into the exact spot where, moments earlier, they had been huddled together. The ground smouldered.

'Bloody hell,' Isabella whispered, her knees buckling, her heart thumping. 'That was close. It's like it's after us.'

'It is,' Archie mumbled. He closed his eyes and tried to work more saliva into his mouth. 'We have to survive... until dusk.'

'That's exactly what Sue was yelling about,' Isabella said. 'Survive till sunset.'

'Where do you get that nonsense from?' Daisy said. And then she twitched.

Isabella noticed. 'What is it, Daisy?'

'Another one coming—I think I can hear it again. Crackling like fat in a pan!'

They reached the tree and slipped under the branches.

'We should be safer here,' she whispered.

Daisy held her hands over her ears as a couple of tears rolled down her cheeks. 'My God, look out. Here it comes!'

A lightning bolt crackled and smashed into the branches. The children screamed as a huge branch sheared off and crashed a couple of metres away.

They ran out hugging each other.

'**OH, NO!**' Daisy cried, her ears screaming in pain.

'What is it now?'

'It's like... like a power shower has just been switched on.'

A warm wind swirled and nearly blew them off their feet.

Then the first few large rain drops like mini water balloons began to plummet out of the cloud.

'We need to move, NOW!' Isabella cried. 'This is the storm from hell we predicted—'

'*Predicted?*' Daisy yelled.

'Yeah, Sue and I ...' Isabella's voice trailed off. 'We've got about five minutes before this playing field becomes a river.'

'Oh, well that is simply marvellous,' Daisy yelled.

Isabella and Daisy folded Archie's arms across their shoulders so he was properly supported.

'You've got to move your legs, Arch,' Isabella implored. 'HURRY!' she screamed, forcing the pace. The rain intensified as the wind blew in several directions at once. In no time, in front of them, on top of them, and behind them, a wall of water sluiced out of the heavens, pounding them, beating them hard on their heads and shoulders and backs. Isabella removed her coat and draped it over their heads. For the moment at least, it acted as a shelter.

'Where's the bridge?' Daisy shouted above the din of the rain. 'I can't see ANYTHING!'

Isabella slowed and stared at the ground. Water heads downhill, so it's got to be this way. Without knowing why, she pointed her free arm ahead of her, closed her eyes and allowed it to guide her.

Soon the feel underfoot of soft wet turf made way for hard gravel.

They followed, but every step was tricky and they couldn't be sure exactly where they were going. Isabella rubbed the ground every so often with her foot to feel the hard path underneath. By the time they reached where they thought the bridge should be, the children were cold, soaked through, and exhausted. And, worryingly, water was spilling out of the river at an alarming rate—up to their ankles and rising fast.

'Bind—tighter—scrum!' Isabella yelled, 'We've got to move together, rhythmically, in time. I'll count.' She realised they

couldn't hear her so she signed with her fingers: ONE, TWO...
THREE and then she flicked out her thumb.

'Where's the bridge?' Daisy screamed, before suddenly
losing her footing. They hauled her to her feet.

Isabella shook her head, imploring her to keep going.
'DON'T FALL.' She turned to Archie to see if he understood. He
nodded.

Isabella counted each agonising step, the force of the water
gaining by the second, pushing hard at their legs. Every breath
was a struggle and their heads bowed from the pressure of
water crashing down upon them.

Isabella had no idea where she was headed. She simply
trusted her hands and, as if by a miracle, they guided her to the
handrail. She breathed a deep sigh of relief. They shuffled onto
the bridge, still huddled together, their feet searching for the
wooden boards.

Daisy suddenly went stiff, holding the others back. She
turned to the others, her eyes bulging.

Collectively they realised what she meant.

'RUN!'

They scampered up to the brow of the bridge, Daisy leading
the way holding Archie's hand on one side, when suddenly she
dived, hauling Archie forward with all her might.

Bits of wood splintered around them, the noise deafening.
Daisy picked herself out of the water, her feet grateful for the
feeling of land, and discovered Archie next to her. He was fine;
but where was Isabella?

She scanned the area as best she could but even as she called
out Daisy knew it was hopeless; she wouldn't be heard over the
din. The only thing she could hear was the roar of the rain and
rushing water flushing everything downstream. And Isabella,
she feared, was now a part of it.

FORTY-SEVEN

OLD MAN WOOD'S WORRY

As the morning wore on, fear consumed Old Man Wood with a feeling of utter dread, as if a toxic soup stewed in his stomach and a splinter played darts with his heart.

Whatever he did, this anxiety would not go away. He marched around the house looking for something—anything—to alleviate this terrible feeling.

He studied the wooden carvings, tracing his fingers over the rich detailing on the panelling in his room. He inspected the old pictures for a clue, anything that might shed some light on the nightmares he'd had to help dilute the worry that filled him from the top of his head to the tips of his toes.

Did the carvings and paintings mean something? *If so, what*?

Was a vital clue staring him in the face?

The more he played with this notion, the greater and deeper his feeling of despair grew, like a festering skin boil.

He wondered if he shouldn't go down to the school and watch the football match, but it didn't seem right.

Instead, he headed up to the ruin to check on the sheep and cattle.

The herd appeared restless and jumpy. The same as him, he thought, as if the animals sensed something unusual was about to happen. He made sure that the shelter was sound, before counting them: eleven sheep, three cows, six bullocks, and Himsworth the bull.

Old Man Wood sat down on a grey boulder at the head of the ruin and looked out across the vale. In front of him a sheer drop of solid rock disappeared into thick forest seventy metres or so below, before levelling up near the valley floor. He could just make out the river curving around the rock face and, from there, it slipped around the corner.

Old Man Wood shuffled his boot in the dirt. He was too old for this, too old for riddles and memories.

But why the dreams every night, and what were they trying to tell him? Why did he have that aching feeling in his bones which he hadn't had for ages?

He stood up as a deep roll of thunder boomed and crackled through the valley and kicked a stone which flew off the ledge and sailed through the air before crashing into the canopy of the trees below.

Looking out at the school buildings in the distance, lost in his thoughts, Old Man Wood saw a lightning bolt shoot out of the sky right into the heart of the village. This was followed by another, and then another. Each one came with a blast of light so bright and a crack so loud that Old Man Wood shielded his eyes and his ears.

A searing pain walloped into his chest. He bent over and cried out. The sky fizzed as another huge bolt crashed out of the sky directly onto the playing field.

This time the pain was unbearable and Old Man Wood crouched low, clutching his chest, struggling for breath.

Was his pain linked to the storm? He needed to lie down.

Old Man Wood straightened up as best he could and stumbled back down the pathway, stopping occasionally to view the tempest playing out over the school.

Wasn't it funny, he pondered, *how the storm seems to focus only on the school?*

As he concentrated on this thought, his feeling that the children were in terrible danger accentuated. He hurried back, lay on his bed, and massaged his heart, as another thought crossed his mind.

If the storm broke, how, in all the apples in the world, would the children return home? The river would swell and the track to Eden Cottage would act like a storm drain. What if they were trying to get home and were swept away?

He dabbed his handkerchief on his forehead. He had to *do* something.

But as he was preparing to get up, an instant tiredness washed over him, and a powerful urge to close his eyes enveloped him like a strong drug.

His head fell back onto his large pillows and a moment later the old man was snoring like the throbbing of an old tractor engine.

FORTY-EIGHT

KEMP JOINS

Kemp stumbled, dizzy and sick with fear. He faced Cain head-on for the first time.

All Kemp could see was a transparent gap between the hat and the overcoat. His teeth were chattering. 'If I don't—?'

'You'll almost certainly die, or be drowned in the rains. Or in the landslides, or the tsunamis which will sweep the land…'

'Will you kill me?'

'Me? Kill you?' the ghost chuckled. 'No. As I said, I'm just going to *borrow* you for a while. Why would I kill you when my purpose is to save so many? You must *trust* me.'

Kemp looked up at the sky which fizzed with electricity like an angry nest. A terrible boom rattled every bone in his body as a thunderbolt walloped into a nearby chimney pot spraying terracotta tiles into the alley.

His head vibrated like a jack-hammer smashing up a road.

Kemp stared down the path, preparing to run. As his eyes focused on the dark shadows between the buildings, he found himself looking at a familiar face: Gus Williams laden with shopping bags. They locked eyes for several seconds before Williams simply ran off, as though someone had called him away in a hurry.

'Dreamspinner!' the ghost barked, impatiently. 'Open up. It is time to go! This boy is not the Heirs of Eden.'

'Wait,' Kemp croaked. 'Please! What do I have to do?'

'You must want to survive and you must absolutely desire with all your soul to go with me.'

Kemp looked about. His mind was made up.

'I agree,' he said.

Cain roared with delight. 'Reach into me and put on my coat and hat, child. Do it quickly.'

In a flash, Kemp threw off both of his overcoats and moved in close to Cain. As he did, he felt a strange coolness wash over him.

'Ignore that I am here,' the ghost said soothingly, as Kemp fumbled with the cloth. 'Put the coat on, as you would any other.'

Kemp grabbed the collar and pushed his arm into the sleeve, amazed by the sudden freeze that enveloped it. Then his other arm slid in. Kemp had a wonderful feeling of a deep strength building up in him, as though a syringe was powering him with a thick energy fluid.

The sensation started in his fingers, moved up to his wrists, through his elbows and in to his shoulders. All too soon, it spread down through his loins and into his legs and feet.

A syrupy liquid, like freezing treacle, coursed through every vein and into every muscle and sinew of his body.

Kemp drew the coat across his chest as the curious feeling crept towards his heart and lungs.

He cried out and stretched his arms wide, as the ice-like goo rushed into his vital organs and washed through his body. He let out a cry of pure ecstasy, his shouts bouncing back off the old houses.

Kemp only had one more thing to do. He lifted up the hat and pulled it down over his head. Suddenly, he could feel the cold charge oozing up his neck and through his mouth.

He shut his eyes, enjoying the extraordinary tingling sensations of the liquid ice entering his brain and slowly dispersing through the back of his skull, tickling parts he never knew existed.

The surge of power moved around the skull and headed towards his eyes.

As it flowed into his eyes, everything changed. With a rapidity that took him completely by surprise, Kemp felt a searing, burning pain crashing into his head, expanding like a balloon filling with air.

'What's happening?' he screamed. 'MY GOD, *my eyes*!'

He desperately tried to rip off the hat and wrestle out of the coat.

'My head! MY EYES! What have you done to me? Help me! *HELP! I'm burning!*'

As Kemp carried on screaming, the ghost chuckled.

'Welcome to me,' Cain said, his voice laced with triumph. 'Welcome to the burnt-out body of Cain, the Frozen Lord of Havilah.'

FORTY-NINE

SOLOMON ROUNDS UP

Solomon felt a sharp pain in his chest. He looked at the school-children and the adults streaming away from the pitch.

In an instant, he knew what to do.

He ran to the Newton coach. 'Go, directly,' he ordered. 'Please don't argue, get in your bus and drive as fast as you can away from this place. I believe this fearsome cloud is about to break.'

He didn't wait around. He ran on, sweat breaking out.

'Children,' he boomed. 'All those staying till later, do not go back to your classrooms. Run directly to the library in the tower. Hurry, there is not a moment to lose. Grab anyone you see on the way.'

Solomon rushed towards the buildings and ran, panting, into the classrooms.

'Run to the tower, now!' he roared, rushing in. 'Leave your things, just go there this second!'

A terrible realisation filled him. Children were scattered around the school. The noise overhead, like heavy artillery fire, made his eyes water.

He bumbled into the gymnasium, where a last rehearsal was underway.

'Stop what you're doing!' he ordered, climbing on to the stage while trying to catch his breath. 'Go to the library, immediately.' He hoped his firm tone would not go unnoticed.

Children poured out of the entrance. 'Good. Hurry,' he called out after them. 'You too, Mrs. Rose.'

He rushed back into the yard and shot into the canteen.

He gasped for breath. 'Chef!' he said, as an idea popped into his head. 'Take as many provisions as you can to the library, this instant. Bread, milk, anything.'

'Are you all right, boss?'

'Pile the contents of your fridge, the store cupboards, the larder into containers this very instant and head directly to the tower.'

The chef stared at him in disbelief and stole a glance towards his assistants.

'Do it NOW!'

'Everything?'

'Yes, chef, as much as you possibly can. Just trust me. There's not a moment to lose. And remember milk and orange juice. Do it now—all of you,' he roared.

They hesitated.

'DO IT NOW! GO! There's no time!'

Solomon sped out of the kitchen as fast as he could, ran outside across the yard and into the art department. He struggled to breathe. 'Skinner, Moloney, run to the tower this instant,' he gasped, falling into a chair.

He wiped his specs. Who else?

The building splintered from a lightning bolt, the sound rattling the windows.

Good Lord. The changing rooms!

Then he heard the whooshes of wind, no doubt whipped up by oncoming rain.

No time!

Out he shuttled, his body screaming at him to stop.

Three boys sat on the benches, staring out of the window.

'Don't just sit there,' he cried. 'Come with me.'

'Where to?'

'Safety,' he gasped, collapsing onto the wood.

'Sir, are you all right?'

Solomon clenched his eyes. 'Yes, yes. Now run! Go to the library. I'll follow you.'

'But, Sir?'

'GO NOW!'

The headmaster took several deep breaths. He'd rounded up as many as he could.

Where were the de Lowes? Then it struck him. They would be heading home across the playing fields. A twenty-minute walk at the very least.

He summoned his energy and threw himself through the door, rushing out into the corridor and then down the stairs.

As he ran outside, he saw far off in the distance three figures huddling together, heading slowly towards the bridge.

Oh my God, he thought, a feeling of utter despair gripping him. *They haven't got a chance.*

But as he sucked in a lungful of air to call out to them, the first drops of rain thudded into him.

Moments later amidst deafening noise and visibility of precisely zero, the headmaster knew he had to seek safety himself.

But how?

FIFTY

GUS AND THE CANOPY

Water edged through the cracks of the boat house and stole down the sides, drumming like a giant carnival on the barn's tin roof.

Gus stared in disbelief at the rain. *Holy moly,* he thought, *she's bloody right.*

Quickly, Gus stretched the canopy, which in truth was a thick, heavy-duty plastic sheet covering the length of the vessel from bow to stern. It would fit perfectly. Then, he formed a tent frame over the boat, hammering in nails as fast as he could go.

He stepped back. *Uneven,* Gus thought, *but it would do, so long as the nails held.*

Gus listened. It needed to be super-strong. He'd take more wood and prop up the mid-section if he had time later, once they were underway.

Next, he nailed two rough planks on both the port and starboard sides, leaving a gap in the middle for the oars. As fast as he could, he nailed batons over the canopy on the outside, repeating his action on the other side. In no time, the boat was covered in a tight tent. Better still, if it worked, water would run off the canopy into the river and not inside.

Sue looked on in awe. She tried where she could to help,

amazed at his dexterity and speed. Gus didn't come across as the brightest spark in school, but my goodness he was practical.

She ran around the boat pulling bits of the canopy tight while Gus hammered, sawed and stretched the plastic sheeting. So immersed in their project were they, that they hardly noticed water seeping in, up and over the floor.

'Almost time to batten down the hatches,' Gus yelled, smiling.

Sue ran up and hugged him. 'I couldn't have done this without you,' she said, and she genuinely meant it. Sue climbed in and sat under the canopy as a deep sense of foreboding filled her. She desperately hoped they were doing the right thing, and she hoped like anything that Isabella and the twins had fled to safely.

Gus slipped in a few remaining planks and a couple more of the two by four inch sections. He grabbed the remaining nails, the hammer, a saw, a small axe, a hand-drill and a chisel, and threw them all in the box. Just before the water covered the whole floor, he scanned the shed looking for anything else. Sue's umbrella, for starters, and a couple of old empty paint pots with lids. More rope, string, a whole reel of strimmer cord, and another large dust sheet, this one already neatly folded. He rummaged through the cupboards like a man possessed, and found an untouched bag of barbecue briquettes. He threw them in; maybe they'd need fire.

Sue packed them away. Then with a few last-minute alterations, as the water reached the upper limits of his boots, Gus clambered in to the boat, hoping like mad that with the weight of the fresh water, the timber, and the both of them, they wouldn't exit through the bottom.

The vessel creaked as it rose. No holes nor rotten timbers so far.

Sue shook, holding her hands against her ears as thunder and lightning blazed outside. It felt as if they were waiting in the depths of the Colosseum before being fed to the lions in front of an angry, baying crowd. The boat continued to rise, finding its buoyancy. Then it started to drift.

'Here we go,' Gus yelled. 'Hold on tight.'

A moment later, the boat clunked into something.

Gus squeezed past Sue to the bow. He looked out and muttered something under his breath.

'What is it?' Sue cried. 'Is there a problem?'

'Technical difficulty,' he said, scratching his chin. 'Pass me that hand axe.'

Sue scrabbled around in the box and handed it over.

Gus disappeared, and set about trying to smash the weatherboards. A short while later, his banging stopped. 'It appears,' Gus said, popping his head back under the canopy, 'that the water has risen higher than the gap the boat was meant to go through.'

'What does that mean?'

'It means we're stuck!' he said, smiling his huge grin again.

'For crying out loud,' Sue howled. 'Can't you get the boards off?'

'What do you think I've been doing? Knitting?'

'So how are we going to get out? I was hoping we might be able to save Archie and the others.'

Gus raised his eyebrows. 'There's a window directly above, so panic ye not. I've got an idea,' he said. 'Pass me the saw, and move to the other end, please.'

Gus took the saw and stood on the seat right at the prow of the boat. He began sawing as fast as he could through the timbers surrounding the window. The boat sloshing from side to side.

After several minutes of sawing and hacking, Gus put his drenched head back under the canopy. 'Don't think that's going to work, either.' He smiled again. 'Rain's quite warm, though.'

Sue looked appalled. 'What are we going to do?'

Gus stretched out his legs, closed his eyes and took a deep breath. 'We wait.'

'Wait!' Sue roared. 'You must be joking. We'll drown if we stay in here. Can't you see that?'

Gus ignored her and smiled toothily again. It seemed to act as an anger-deflecting shield. 'You know what we haven't done?' he said, his large eyes sparkling.

'What?' Sue snapped.

'Named our vessel.'

Sue eyed him warily. 'Seriously, Gus, before we start thinking up names, do you actually think we'll get out of here?'

He raised his eyebrows and shrugged positively.

'How do we get out?' Sue said, raising her eyebrows back at him. Getting a straight answer out of Gus was proving to be a bit of a nightmare.

Gus jabbed a finger upwards.

'God?' she yelled, sarcastically.

Gus's whole body galloped up and down with laughter.

He moved close to her so they could hear each other without yelling. 'No, you banana-cake, through the roof. So long as the water continues to rise,' he peered out of the end of the boat, '— and it is rising, just as you said it would, then up we go.'

Sue grimaced. 'Really? You sure it'll work?'

'Oh yeah. Far easier this way. There's corrugated iron sheeting up there, they'll lift off and then, whoosh, into the river we go.'

Sue couldn't help but admire his confidence, although she wasn't convinced. Wasn't corrugated sheeting heavy, especially with water beating onto it? 'So, what do we do now?'

'Well, let's see. We could start by naming our boat. It's definitely good luck before a maiden voyage. You got any ideas?'

'Not really. You?'

'Yeah,' and he smiled his big smile again.

'Well, what is it?'

Gus opened his eyes wide. 'I think we should call it the "The Joan of".'

'That's it?' Sue said. She looked mystified. 'The Joan of"...

what? What does that mean? It doesn't make any sense. That's not a name for a boat.'

Gus feigned a look of shock. 'Now, come along, brain-box. This little teaser shouldn't be difficult for super-smart Sue Lowden.'

FIFTY-ONE

OLD MAN WOOD'S DREAM

Old Man Wood hadn't reacted to any of the dreams given to him. The dreamspinner worried that if Old Man Wood could not understand his dreams, then what chance would the children have with theirs?

Were the dreams proving to be too complex, too terrifying? Were the dreams suited to a different time? Perhaps their dreams needed a different blending of powders to aid interpretation?

Gaia dipped a hand in her maghole, removed the dream powder and rubbed a couple of fingers together. This wasn't the time for reflection, that would come later. While the children were still alive, for the time being at least, she needed haste.

She would give Old Man Wood a dream that would stimulate action and, at the end of the sequence, she would add a powder that would simulate a shock. Yes, that was it. He needed something to get his brain working, to unlock his memory, so that he might help the Heirs of Eden as he'd been entrusted to do.

Gaia worked fast, her slender claws moving like a blur in her maghole. In a flash, she was plucking tiny specks of dream powder out of her maghole and feeding them to the old man as he inhaled. Gaia took her time, and, digging deep into her memory of powders, knitted a dream ending with a reminder of a potion that Old Man Wood had stored away a long, long time ago.

Gaia stared down at the old man. *Maybe this time we will see a positive result,* she thought, before inverting into her maghole and vanishing.

Old Man Wood tossed and turned as the dream filled his head. He looked down and found himself wearing a pair of shorts. He was running and he felt young again; roughly the same age as the twins. His skin was smooth and his mind was alert. He had hair! He dragged his hands through it. What a lovely feeling. As he ran, air filled his lungs.

On his feet, he wore a pair of football boots. Red ones, just like Archie's. He looked up. A football was flying towards him, and his immediate reaction was to duck out of the way. But out of the corner of his eye he spotted Daisy yelling at him. What was she saying? Pass it? He went towards the ball but it was too fast and it bounced off him straight to an opponent.

This wasn't as easy as it looked.

Daisy swore and chivvied him to chase the player.

He took off and was moving at speed. To his delight, Old Man Wood found himself gaining on the player. He lunged for the ball but missed and tripped the boy.

The whistle blew. 'Do that once more and you'll be booked,' the referee said.

Old Man Wood caught his breath and brushed mud off his knees.

Daisy was there in an instant. 'What do you think you're playing at?' she said. 'There's hardly any time to go. Don't make stupid fouls like that. We've got to win or we're never playing again.'

The other team lined up a shot and the ball was cruising towards the goal. But Archie danced into the path of the ball and caught it smartly. In a flash, he punted the ball wide.

One of his players passed the ball to him. This time he managed to control it and he slipped a neat pass through to Daisy. Daisy, now on the halfway line, jinked past one player, and then sped past another, her blonde hair bobbing up and down as she went. Boy, she was quick. He found himself sprinting just to keep up.

A defender forced her wide and she played the ball inside to him. Looking up, he passed it to Isabella on the other flank. He couldn't remember Isabella ever liking football, but she neatly passed it back to him just as she was clattered by an opposition player.

He couldn't help laughing at the horrified expression on her face.

Now Daisy was screaming for the ball.

Old Man Wood found himself running with the ball and it felt brilliant. He did a dummy, just like Daisy had, slipping past the player in front of him. He knocked the ball forwards, finding Daisy, who held off a challenge and stood with the ball under her foot.

In a flash, she turned on a sixpence, the ball rolling under her other foot. Totally foxing the defender, she headed towards the goal. Old Man Wood felt himself sprinting into the area as Daisy smashed a shot at the goal.

He held his breath as the ball sped toward the goal. It whacked against the post and rebounded directly into his running path. From the corner of his eye, a defender was flying towards the ball. He knew he had to get there first, so he sprinted harder, cocked his leg back, and kicked the ball as hard as he could a fraction before the defender got there.

The ball screamed into the roof of the net, tearing a hole, and was still rising just as the defender crunched into his foot.

A heartbeat later, and a lightning bolt smashed out of the

sky directly into him. A surge of energy fizzed through his entire body, through every sinew and fibre and particle of his being.

It took his breath away.

When at last the sensation wore off, he peered down to find a bottle of gold liquid sitting on his lap.

Then he woke up, with a start.

FIFTY-TWO

KEMP'S PAIN

The last thing he remembered was diving head-first towards the electric body of a weird spidery creature and then being sucked into a void. He must have passed out.

After the euphoric sensation of the icy power sluicing through his every sinew, Kemp experienced a pain like he had never felt before. His whole body raged with fire, the burning excruciating but, as he dissolved into Cain, Kemp kept repeating his name and his birthday, and his mother's and father's names and his school and his favourite colours and everything happy that he could ever remember.

When he opened his eyes it was as though he was seeing through a grey filter. He could see grey shapes and objects, but nothing clearly; no precision, no detail.

He sensed he was lying on a bed. He shut his eyes, and tried to see if he could lose the pain—a constant, driving, nagging ache. He could sense that he was in a body that was gently rising and falling—his body—but it was surrounded by something else. Ash? Soot?

Kemp felt woozy and weak, and utterly helpless. Nothing he did seemed to make any difference. He had no control, but maybe he could use this time to think.

Cain stirred.

Kemp felt this like painful pins and needles in every orifice of his being.

Suddenly Kemp felt his entire body taken over and his brain and eyes and body seemed to fade away, like a gas lamp being extinguished.

And he suddenly wondered if death might have been an easier option.

FIFTY-THREE

ISABELLA DISAPPEARS

Isabella's world went blank. When she came to, her entire body tingled and every nerve and sinew sizzled as if she were enveloped within a giant pin-cushion.

She coughed, spluttered, and violently ejected water trapped in her lungs. She gasped as her hands and feet instantly kicked into action, her arms and legs moving faster than she could ever have imagined just to keep her head above water.

She breathed, luxuriating in the intake of air.

Her hand grappled with a shrub branch. She tried to hoist herself up, but it fell away plunging her back underwater. When she surfaced, visibility zero, she knew she needed to touch down on the cottage side of the river.

Treading water, she did a quick calculation. If the river ran from the moors down into the valley, she had to land on the left bank as it went with the flow. Isabella kicked until she could feel the water pushing against her before twisting with all her strength and swimming at an angle into the current.

Moments later, she touched on something spindly and woody. She pushed her legs down and was relieved to find the water was up to her waist. With her feet on firm ground, she clambered across the bush and kept going until her knees hit on solid ground the other side.

Isabella coughed, spluttered, and retched, as though her insides were coming out. Without hesitating, she continued uphill, searching for the cover of a tree. She found one, leaned in and put her head in her hands.

Tears built up and for a moment they rolled freely down her cheeks. *Daisy! Archie! They'll think I'm dead.*

She imagined them waiting for her.

Please, please keep going! Every minute spent waiting is a minute wasted.

She wondered what had happened to Sue. Did she find the boat? In any case, that little boat would fill with water and sink in minutes. The whole thing was hopeless.

Isabella felt herself welling up, but a ripple of water washed against her shins. She had to move. Finding the others was futile now. She'd head uphill from tree to tree and find cover wherever she could.

She had to survive.

FIFTY-FOUR

CAIN'S ADMIRATION

'Look at us, boy,' Cain whispered. 'Well, look at me. Aren't I *magnificent!*'

Cain studied his body in a tall mirror ringed with dull gemstones. Morning light seeped through a vast window. 'You're here, boy,' he said, as his voice echoed off the walls. 'Right here inside me. That's right; half ash, half man... or boy. Only a fraction ghost.'

Cain examined his reflection.

His borrowed eyes weren't anything like the proper article, his vision was filtered by a grainy film. But, what a sensation to see anything at all when, for thousands of years, he had tuned into the vibrations and presence of things using his highly developed sixth sense.

He studied his hands and turned them over. He clapped, the noise a muted thud. Ash puffed up and floated quietly through the air.

Oh, the joys of having a body, he thought, *whatever form it took.*

Cain removed his overcoat, took off his hat, and returned, naked, to stand in front of the mirror. His figure was the same size as the boy and his torso was covered in layers of flaky ash in every conceivable hue of grey. *How utterly remarkable*, he thought, as he rotated his hips from side to side.

His chest was a boyish replica of the one he remembered. His pectorals and abdomen were not so hard and toned as perhaps they once were, but the sinews and muscles on his thighs, calves and buttocks were pleasingly accentuated by the light.

His feet, he noted, were unusually large. He sprang up on his toes, only to find that a couple of digits simply dropped off. Cain stared, fascinated, as they instantly regrew.

In the reflection of the mirror, Cain moved close. His face appeared sallow and partially skeletal, with a flaky grey chin that jutted out more than he cared to see.

He nudged his thick plump lips, prodded his flat nose, and admired his eyebrows. He touched his hair, a mass of ash swept back off his forehead, and admired his eyes that sparkled like polished coals.

Then he noticed a strange cluster at the top of his legs. Wasn't this awfully important? Instinctively, he reached for it, but to his horror—and just as he remembered its purpose—the appendage severed, slipped through his fingers and careered to the ground.

Cain squealed.

His concerns were short-lived. Moments later it reappeared and he and his organ were reacquainted.

Cain's mood brightened.

'Thousands of years without one,' he roared, 'and instantly it falls to pieces!'

Cain realised his new body was a by-product of his incineration all those years ago.

His eyes narrowed.

How could he forget the burning and the eye gouging when his powers were taken away from him?

The verdict from The Council of One Hundred in the Garden of

Eden, he remembered. *Oh yes, the very bad deal. Part of his original punishment.*

Cain flexed up and down on his knees. He had movement; real, gravity-based movement, and physical presence. None of this 'floating around' nonsense, none of this walking through walls and doors and people, although this skill did, from time to time, have its advantages.

Cain, Frozen Lord of Havilah, is back! He could almost taste the fear of the strange creatures that now populated Havilah; trolls had moved into the forests close to the silvery sea, a tribe of Neanderthals had swept over the pink mountains that surrounded Havilaria and some marsh-men had dammed the planet's great river at its mouth. The dragons, snakes, lizards, and reptiles, once controlled by his undefeatable reptilian beast called Gorialla Yingarna, had risen in numbers, with many now living on the outskirts of the city of Havilaria.

The rumours once said that Cain would return from the ashes to free his frozen people from the domed puddles and, remembering this, Cain knew that he needed to make the most of his new form, and fast, which was exactly what he intended to do even if it meant he had to forcibly drag the boy along with him.

First, he would check up on the Heirs of Eden's progress towards their demise, now that their journey through the storm was underway. Perhaps he still had a chance of blending with an Heirs of Eden, instead of this rather cumbersome specimen.

Asgard's dream-spinners were watching the Heirs of Eden. When they were close to deaths door, they would let him know.

Cain smiled. Everything was slotting into place.

And when that time came, in an instant, he would be there.

FIFTY-FIVE

DAISY GETS ARCHIE BACK

Daisy shivered, grateful that the rain was not particularly cold. Daisy knew that even warm rain quickly chills, and there was just so much of it. She ventured from one side of the path to the other, as far as she dared and screamed once more for Isabella, but she knew it was hopeless; she couldn't see and she could hardly hear her own voice.

With every movement, her bones ached and her joints screamed out, as if her energy reserves had gone past empty. If only she hadn't just played a game of football.

She stamped her feet and jogged up and down, and concentrated hard on the water further down. For a moment, she was sure that she could see, much further down on the river bank, a body climbing out of the water. She shook her head. She must be imagining things, like a mirage in a desert.

She put a hand around Archie and hugged him close. His body warmth was like a hot water bottle. He seemed better, his eyes clearer, and he smiled when she touched his odd hair.

But the shock had rendered him dumb, as though his tongue had been cut out.

What had Archie said earlier? That the storm would follow them until sunset. *How did he know?*

She didn't need him like this, she needed him on full alert, thinking and helping.

Perhaps, she thought, *he needs another shock.*

She slapped him on the cheek as hard as she could.

'Blimey, Daisy!' he yelled, rubbing his cheek. 'What did you do that for?'

'Got you back,' she mouthed, kissing his forehead. 'Sorry —necessary.'

'There was no need to hit me,' he yelled.

Daisy hugged him tight, and spoke into his ear. 'Aw, but it did the trick. Come on, Arch, we've got to go.'

'What about Isabella?' he cried, waving his arm downstream.

'She's a strong swimmer,' she said. 'She'll be fine. Come on!'

Daisy saw him check his watch.

'What are you doing that for?'

Archie's face dropped. 'It's only two-forty-five. Sunset at what, five-fifteen, five-thirty?'

She could tell he wished he knew.

'Every second of every minute gonna count then,' Daisy said, bluntly. 'Come on, Arch. No time to be hanging around.'

FIFTY-SIX

MRS PYE WORRIES

Mrs Pye sat in the kitchen, fretting and fiddling with a bunch of herbs, her hands shaking.

She heard noises in the courtyard. The sounds weren't the sounds of a soccer ball scuffing over the paving slabs, which she associated with Daisy and Archie. Nor was it Old Man Wood returning from the cattle. He'd been back a while.

This was more like something being torn in two, and then crashing sounds audible even over the beating rain.

Must be my imagination playing tricks, she thought, as she returned to her task of flavouring a large beef casserole.

She concentrated on lighting the fire, before her ears instinctively pricked up. Those sounds, again.

Opening the front door, she reeled as a wall of water poured like a waterfall over the low, extended roof. Seeing a branch jumping about in the water nearby, she realised that the sounds she'd heard must have been trees crashing down around the house.

A pain, like a stubborn splinter, pierced her. For the first time in years, the long, thick scar beneath the mop of bright orange hair on her forehead throbbed, giving her a pressing headache.

She'd never seen or heard anything like it. Instantly, she recognised the gravity of the children's situation.

The longer it went on, the more she pined, as though the cord that tied her to her children was being streched apart and needles pressed slowly into her heart. She tried to soldier on and put these feelings behind her. She had to. The children would return, she was sure of it. Old Man Wood would find them.

But what if he didn't? What if her children were stuck out there?

Tears swam down her cheeks, falling in drops on the wooden surface. Her head pulsed with doubt and sorrow as she cradled it in her hands and wept.

Realisation dawned on her that if this storm continued, and if Old Man Wood failed, she might be alone in the world for the very first time.

FIFTY-SEVEN

GUS' QUIZ

'Oh, *ARK*!' Sue exclaimed. 'As in, "*Joan of Arc*".'

Gus clapped slowly. 'Blimey. At long last. Remind me never to partner you in a pub quiz. Ever.'

'You mean,' Sue said, 'you've actually been to a pub quiz?'

'Of course, every Friday night with my dad.'

'Really? My parents never do that kind of thing. What's it like?'

Gus wondered if he should make it sound exciting. 'Well, it's OKAY. Actually, it's quite nerdy, so you'd probably like it.'

Sue's eyes sparkled. Gus was full of surprises. *Just goes to show*, she thought, *you really can't tell a book by its cover.* 'So, what subjects are you good at?'

Gus made his brainiest face, which made him look pretty stupid. 'Particle physics, geography, English history from 1066, current world affairs and, yeah, modern American history.'

'You're joking me!'

'Try me. Go on,' Gus said, moving even closer.

Sue didn't know what to think. She screwed up her face as though deep in thought and asked: 'Which President of the United States of America wrote the Declaration of Independence?'

Gus scratched his chin and made lots of quite odd-looking faces. 'Abraham Lincoln—'

'Ha, wrong—'

'Won the Civil War,' Gus continued, ignoring her. 'Thomas Jefferson was the main author of the Declaration of Independence.' He tried hard not to smile. But he did raise his eyebrows. And they were huge eyebrows.

Sue couldn't believe it. 'Correct,' she said, trying to think of another question. 'Name the English monarch who came after William Rufus.'

'You can do better than that, sexy Sue.' He pulled a serious face. 'William Rufus, heir to William the Conqueror. Shot by an arrow by a noble who thought he was a knob-end. Succeeded by Henry, as in Henry the first, also a son of the Conqueror, who sat on the throne for a middle-age marathon of thirty-five years.'

Sue shrieked. She couldn't believe it. 'Gus, you're brilliant at this. Why are you such an idiot in class?'

Gus shrugged. 'Low tolerance to teachers.'

A clunking noise stopped them in their tracks. Gus raced up to the bow step. "The Joan of' has hit the roof,' he yelled. 'Here we go.' Gus ducked his head inside the canopy. 'I hope you're ready for this. Pass me that long bit of wood and sit at the end. And Sue...'

'Yes?'

'Whatever you do, don't scream. It won't help.'

Gus had never really expected the water to rise quite so high, nor so fast. In fact, he was pretty sure they'd remain in the boathouse, quite safe from the tempest outside. Now, it was different.

He grappled with the piece of wood, eventually holding its base, and thrust it up towards the corrugated sheeting directly above. *Come on, you little beauty. Move.* Nothing happened. He changed his tack, trying to lever the roofing off. *Move, you little tick*, he murmured, as he pushed the wood with all his might.

As he pushed, he became aware that the entire building had begun to move. Gus stopped hammering on the roof and watched as the shed began to drift off all on its own. He couldn't believe it.

He wondered if, incredibly, the buoyancy of their boat had given buoyancy to the entire building, and now it had gone adrift with them inside it. That, or he was suddenly immensely strong.

The only thing he knew for sure was that the whole unit was moving quickly into the swollen floodwaters. As far as he could tell, they were safe. In fact, he rather suspected they were safer than any place they could otherwise have expected to end up in, so long as 'The Joan of' didn't fall apart.

He ducked down under the canopy to find Sue crying hysterically.

'Everything ship-shape and dandy, Captain,' he said, saluting.

Sue looked confused. 'What's happening, Gus? I'm scared.'

Gus shrugged. 'I pushed the roof and the entire shed came away. Funny thing is, I always suspected I had superpowers.'

'Is it safe?'

Gus looked at her blankly. 'Truthfully?' He shrugged. 'I've no idea, but, so far, so good. Now, how about another brainteaser.' He sat down and put his legs up. 'Can't wait all day.'

Sue peered up at him. She simply couldn't believe his brazen attitude to the disaster unfolding around them. The boat lurched and her eyes widened. But Gus rubbed his eyes and yawned.

'Gus Williams,' she said. 'I don't know how you do it.' She took a couple of deep breaths to settle her nerves. 'We're on the verge of plunging into Armageddon and you want another teaser?'

Gus nodded. 'Yeah. Absolutely.'

'Good Lord. Okay. Physics question—you said you were

good at physics, right?' He nodded. A question popped into her head. 'Where does bad light end up?'

Gus confidently put his feet on the seat. He was grinning like mad, which Sue later discovered was a sign that his brain was working. 'Okay,' he began cagily, 'either it's in an ohm?' Sue giggled but shook her head. 'OR,' and there was quite a long pause. He clicked his fingers, 'In a prism?'

Sue clapped her hands. 'Brilliant! You're a big, bloody genius, aren't you?'

Gus was bursting with pride. Big and genius—in the same sentence—from delicious, sexy Sue. He hardly dared tell her he'd read the answers in a magazine at the dentist. 'One for you,' he said. 'What did the male magnet say to the female magnet?'

Sue burst out laughing. 'I'm seriously attracted to you?' She turned purple on the spot.

Gus caught her eye. 'Not bad. Want another try?'

Sue shook her head. 'Tell me.'

Gus looked quite serious. 'From your backside,' he began, 'I thought you were repulsive. However, from the front I find you rather attractive.'

Sue clapped her hands and laughed as Gus punched the air.

Suddenly, a terrible noise, like the body of a car scraping along a road, stopped both of them in their tracks.

Gus slipped out the front. Then he dived back in, and dashed toward Sue at the rear. 'Move up front,' he ordered.

Sue shuffled up as Gus headed out of the canopy at the bow.

Seconds later, he reappeared and without hesitating sat in the middle of the boat grabbing the oars. He started to row, pushing the oars in the water to go backwards, as fast as he could.

'What's going on?' Sue cried.

'Our time has come. 'The Joan of"s' moment has arrived.'

With a terrible crunching noise, the back end of the shed

levered high into the air, while the nose dived into the water like a sinking boat. Gus took a deep breath and, praying "The Joan of" held together, he rowed with all his might. The little boat plunged backwards, creeping under the raised end, out into the river.

Now, for the first time, rain whammed into the canopy and the boat rocked in the water the sound like a relentless pounding of drums.

After a couple of minutes, Sue put her head out as far as she dared, and tried to survey the scene. The only things she could see were the faint outlines of cars, wood, and sections of plastic, bobbing along beside them.

She ducked under the canopy, her face ashen.

'Everything all right?' Gus yelled, noting the distress in her face.

'Isabella, Daisy, and Archie are in this, with no protection,' she yelled back. 'They haven't got a hope.'

'They'll be fine,' he yelled back. He looked down. 'Sue,' he hollered. 'Get a bucket NOW and start bailing!'

FIFTY-EIGHT

DAISY AND ARCHIE FIND SHELTER

At long last, Daisy recognised a boulder at the bottom of the covered tree track.

A mini triumph, Daisy thought, as a long booming thunder roll drummed gruesomely overhead. She covered her ears, wincing, but after only a few paces she realised there was a far bigger problem. She kept close to Archie. 'Mud!' she yelled at Archie. 'Look! Mud and stone, rushing down.'

The lane was so knitted with branches, brambles, and rocks that every step forward was like walking through barbed wire.

Worse still, the canopy of branches, bushes, and creepers above the lane was bowing to the pressure of rain. Branches were falling in. Not just dead twigs, but stems as thick as a man's wrist. Even though they'd only stepped a few metres in, the canopy was clearly close to breaking point.

Archie slipped as a branch whacked into him, the muddy water dragging him down the hill. He dug his fingers into the bank, grabbed a root, and pulled himself to safety.

Daisy climbed up onto a large stump on the bank and waited. She looked down the track to see Archie struggling. For every two steps forward, he slipped one back.

'COME ON!' she screamed.

Every time Archie tried to grapple with the side of the track, it collapsed in on him. Not only that, but his ankles were being stripped bare by the mud, stones, and wood.

At last, he made it to Daisy's position and climbed up next to her. Gasping for breath, he rubbed his scratched, blood-covered ankles. 'We'll never make it. Not like this.'

'We have to!' Daisy yelled into his ear. 'Do you think it'll be any easier out there?'

'But it's a massive ditch,' Archie complained. 'It's become a gigantic storm drain. All the water's cascading down here. It's about as dangerous a place as you could wish.'

'What's your suggestion?' Daisy fired back.

'Up the bank and crawl along the top,' he yelled.

'But it's a mile of crawling—'

'I know. And one mile of not being swept away. We can use the shelter of the trees, there's no other choice.'

Using the roots of the big oak they were sitting beneath, they climbed up the bank. On hands and knees, they made their way uphill, brushing aside the branches and thorns which willingly ripped into them.

Daisy rubbed her legs, slashed and pricked by blackthorn and dog rose. 'Stunning idea, Archie!' she yelled.

'Look!' he replied, pointing down at the track.

Through the veil of rain, she could just see a moving torrent of mud and branches halfway up the bank. It was flushing downhill at great speed.

'Okay, Okay. Good decision.' Daisy drew in her breath. 'How far along are we?'

'Soon, we'll be at the big oak with the swing rope. We can rest there.' Archie had no idea whether this was true. But he noticed how Daisy's eyes kept closing. Giving her a target was probably a good idea.

Another huge boom clapped overhead.

They crawled on, Archie leading, with Daisy closely behind. But, after a short while, when he turned, Daisy wasn't there.

He backtracked fast. Hanging halfway down the bank, dangling above the rushing waters, and held only by the thick tendrils of a rose, he found Daisy screaming at him to help.

He grabbed the base of the rose and tried to swing it towards him. But the huge old rose was near to breaking point and sank further towards the rushing water, its thorns digging into his hands. He swore.

There had to be a better way. He shuffled to a nearby hedge and noted a small ash tree. He bent down, put his hands around the trunk, and tugged with all his might. The roots slipped their anchors and, with one last tug, the tree broke free.

In a flash, Archie turned the tree round, ripped off some branches, and lowered it to Daisy. She grabbed hold of it and, as the rose tore into her side, Archie heaved her out.

They moved under the relative shelter of a nearby oak tree and gasped for breath.

'So,' Daisy yelled between gasps, 'we've learnt three things from that. The first is that the bank is collapsing. The second is that I'll be plucking out thorns from my skin for the next decade, and the third is that you've been working out without anyone knowing.'

Taking a wider berth away from the track, they continued on all fours, rain pummelling their backs, necks and heads until they were numb.

Eventually, they reached the large oak tree with the rope, which now dangled down from its branch into the running water.

Archie pushed Daisy ahead and upwards, her hands gripping the nodules and hand-holds of slippery bark as though her life depended on it.

Where the branch with the rope met the trunk, a huge bough curved over like a mini cave. For the first time in ages, it offered them almost complete protection from the downpour. Archie sat with his back against the trunk and Daisy sat in front of him, leaning into him.

They shut their eyes and in no time, Daisy fell asleep through sheer exhaustion.

Archie didn't mind. He checked his watch; at least an hour until sundown.

The problem with being stationary was the cold. The wet had soaked, sponge-like, into the marrow of their bones. Body warmth was crucial.

Archie wrapped his arms around his frozen sister, her body rattling like an old engine. A rest was a good idea, but Archie knew they weren't safe. At some point, they were going to have to keep going.

As Daisy dozed, her head resting on Archie's chest, her mind swam. She dreamt fleetingly of the cottage, of Old Man Wood and their parents. She dreamt of scoring a goal with a sensational bicycle kick and Archie making a flying, fingertip save. The storm could have been a million miles away.

A noise clicked in her brain. It was that same crackling sound, like sizzling bacon. She studied the strange fizzling sound with her eyes shut tight. Then she realised what it was.

'MOVE!' she screamed. 'NOW!'

Archie opened his eyes. 'Eh? What?'

'Incoming! I can hear it. MOVE!'

'Where to?' Archie yelled. 'We're on a bloody branch!'

The sizzling increased, the noise building miles above them.

'To the end, Arch. GO!'

Archie did what he was told, and shuffled his bottom as fast as he could down the branch, the rain smashing down once more.

'Further,' she screamed. 'As far as you can.' She was skimming along, almost bouncing, when she stopped and wrapped her arms and legs around the thick branch. She hugged her body into the wood and hoped for the best.

Archie continued on his path, oblivious to Daisy's action.

From out of nowhere, a terrific surge of power smashed into the tree. The branch severed like a beheading and crashed down, bridging the track just above the flowing mud.

Daisy convulsed with electricity and her ears smashed with pain. She uncurled her body from the branch as rain crashed over her back and head.

Archie?

'Archie!' She called out, barely a croak coming from her. Even if she could scream for help, he'd never hear.

Suddenly, a hand flapped out of the water, and momentarily it gripped the end of the branch. Then it fell away, caught in the torrent.

She shrieked and fished pathetically into the water feeling nothing but twigs, leaves, and debris flashing beneath her.

Daisy thumped the branch, tears streaming from her eyes, rain biting into her back. How much more could she take?

Not much, she realised, especially now she was on her own.

FIFTY-NINE

OLD MAN WOOD FINDS A CLUE

Old Man Wood stared around his room and thumped the air.

'What a marvel-blister of a goal!' he roared.

He stared at the ceiling, a big smile on his face, his head sizzling as though a rocket had detonated leaving his entire body tingling.

'What a wonder-apple-tastic dream,' he said to the empty room.

His foot throbbed. 'Ouch!'

He discovered he'd walloped the end of his bed and, looking closer, he noticed a hole in the wooden board that covered the bed-end. He studied it, pulling a few wooden splinters away, chuckling at the absurdity of it all.

Old Man Wood wiggled his toes, grateful that he'd lain on his bed with his shoes on. Leaning forward, he heard the rain pounding down and his heart sank. His earlier worries flew back to him. He kicked at the broken piece of wood, as though recreating the goal might lift his spirits. It wasn't the same.

He climbed off his bed and peered out of the window, but the rain was so heavy he saw only grey vertical lines.

His heart filled with heaviness.

Were the children safely tucked away at school? What if they were outside trying to get home. What could he do?

If something happened, he was responsible.

Old Man Wood lay down.

He looked at the hole in the wooden panel. A tiny flicker of light, like a dim torch whose batteries were running low, leeched out from behind it.

Now, wasn't that strange, he thought. *A trick of the light?*

He tried the light switches. None of the house lights were working.

Maybe he should crank up the generator. At least it would give him something to do. He swung his feet off the bed and, as he did so, the flicker from behind the wooden panel intensified for a second or two.

He inspected the hole a little closer and found that there was indeed a faint glow emanating from behind the wooden screen. He prised it open with his fingers and, feeling more than a little intrigued, began to wrestle with the wood surround that covered the bed-end.

Old Man Wood found a torch, and went to his tool cupboard under the stairs. He selected a crowbar and returned his room.

Old Man Wood wedged the metal in behind the panel. He attempted to lever the wood away by leaning on it gently but firmly, as he thought necessary. But whatever angle he tried, the panel would not budge.

He scratched his head and slipped out of the room, returning moments later with a flat head screwdriver and a hammer. Old Man Wood thrust the flat head into the tiniest of gaps and gave the end a smart whack with the hammer thereby lifting the nails that secured the panel.

Placing the crowbar in the newly created gap, he levered it once more. After a few more hits, the panel popped off.

He rubbed his chin. 'Well, I'll be blowed,' he said, as he ran his fingers over the three panels that now stared back at him. 'What in the apples do we have here?'

In front of him were three beautifully inlaid panels that seemed to glow like three small monitors, rather like the children's computers. The difference was that these were part of the bed, and were surrounded by similar, matching carvings.

He stared at them for a while, his face a picture of confusion and the wrinkles on his forehead deeply etched. Every now and then, images in the panels moved, causing Old Man Wood's heart to race.

Was he seeing things?

Overlying the images he noticed a blurry, streaky haze, as if, somehow, he were looking through water.

Maybe, it was mirroring the weather right now.

As he became more accustomed to the movements, the images on them became a little clearer, until he realised each panel focused on a figure.

'Three panels, three figures,' he said out loud. 'And why do they look so familiar?'

He studied the carvings to the sides of the screens.

He touched an ornate arrow icon that faced away from the first panel. To his astonishment, the image moved out, exactly like a zoom on a camera.

He did the same with the next panel pressing on the arrow that turned in. The picture zoomed closer.

The blurry image showed a person in the panel who appeared to be walking, and tripping, as though trying to negotiate a pathway.

He rubbed his hand over another carved icon adjacent to the arrow, which looked rather like a cloud. He pressed it and magically the picture transformed, the layer of rain disappearing altogether from the image.

Old Man Wood gasped as he stared at the new image. That balance and gait could only belong to one person, and that person was Daisy. He pressed the inward arrow a couple of times and saw her in detail.

The reality of this odd technology was that he was viewing

the children, right now, in real time. And it dawned on him that if he could determine which buttons to press, he'd be able to see exactly where they were. He did the same to the panel on the right, pressing the cloud and zooming out.

He clapped his hands. Archie! It was definitely Archie, with a kind of spiky hat on his head, sitting next to Daisy. But where were they?

He zoomed out. They were by a large tree with a thick rope, or a creeper, hanging from a branch.

The oak tree with the swing, it had to be.

He pressed the away arrow and the image zoomed out even further. Apples alive! Look at the water gushing down the track.

He clenched his fists. Oh deary! No, no!

His heart sank. At least the twins were together. What about Isabella?

He scoured the left panel and picked out her outline. He honed in on the image, pressing first the cloud icon, and then the outward arrow, in order to try and figure out her position.

She was heading towards a large rock-like object with a sheer face, pushing past bushes and through trees. The only sheer rock he could think of was the cliff underneath the ruin. The question was, why had she separated from the others?

Old Man Wood breathed a sigh of relief. At least they were alive. He looked at his clock. How long was it since he'd been out for a walk? Two hours? He trembled.

That long?

Old Man Wood hadn't taken his eyes off the panels. It was impossible. How could children so young survive the tumult out there? *They're only little,* he kept thinking, tears forming again in his eyes. Now the panels changed as a huge flash burst onto the screen.

Old Man Wood fell back. *Lightning, again? Sweet apples!* His skin prickled.

Daisy lay on the tree branch, screaming, hanging on for dear life as the wood crashed into the bank, but had Archie been swept away?

He couldn't take his eyes off the scene. Another flash struck directly at Daisy. Old Man Wood shrieked and felt for his heart. He could hardly bear it. He watched as the entire branch of the tree hurtled down the makeshift drain towards the swollen river, Archie dragged behind beneath the water.

Old Man Wood yelped and clasped his head in his hands. How did the boy have the strength? Daisy lay there, just as she had before. She hadn't moved and her screen flickered, as though faulty.

Old Man Wood leaned forward, and gave it a tap in the hope that that might restore it, but it flickered again. Lines cut through the clear picture as if there was poor reception.

All of a sudden, he figured what this meant.

The colour drained from his face.

'NO, NO, NO!' he yelled out. 'Don't give up, Daisy. Whatever you do, littlun, DO NOT *EVER* GIVE UP!'

His heart thumped as he spurred himself into action. He needed to find them, and fast.

SIXTY

ISABELLA GETS TRAPPED

For every step Isabella took forward, she seemed to slide back two more. When she was out in the open, she found herself pushing blindly through sheets of water with no idea where she was heading.

She extended her hands out in front of her and felt a gentle pull, first one way and then the other. With each step, her feet touched on harder ground. Sometimes, her hands swung her around at right angles, and every so often she had to backtrack. She trusted in this strange form of navigation, though, for it was the only thing she trusted.

The one thing that terrified her was the thunderbolts.

Daisy seemed to be able to hear the thunderbolts forming. She recalled how every time Daisy screamed, they'd run and a thunderbolt had crashed into the spot where, only moments ago, they'd been. Now there was no Daisy, and Isabella had a deathly feeling in her gut that it was only a matter of time before another thunderbolt would shoot out the rain directly at her.

She moved forward, all the while waiting for the crack or the blast. As fast as she went, the trickle of water around her ankles kept up with her. For every surge she made forward out of the water, in no time the water reappeared, sometimes to as high as her knees.

A stomach-wrenching fear filled her and she redoubled her efforts, crawling and scampering over fallen branches and brambles until she bumped into the base of a tree that would offer her decent protection from the rain.

Isabella leaned back and, instinctively, pushed her hands into the air above her head. She forced her palms outwards, her fingers touching.

She channelled every thought, every single ounce of energy she had into protecting herself. She didn't know why, but for some deep, unknown reason, her hands and her spirit were her last hope.

She closed her eyes and waited.

Just as Isabella thought of putting them down, a thunderbolt sliced out of the sky. A fraction after she heard the distinct crack, Isabella slammed her hands towards the space in front of her with everything she had.

An intense burst of heat thumped into her hands, her flesh instantly burning, her body pushed into the ground.

She gritted her teeth and pressed against it harder and harder. The stink of burning skin invaded her nostrils, as if rods of molten iron were being welded in the place of her fingers.

As suddenly as it had arrived, it was over.

Isabella slumped to the ground, her hands smoking, her eyes closed, and with a look of serenity fixed upon her face.

It was the water licking at her lips that brought her back. Isabella opened her eyes, aware that her body was shivering like it did after a swim in the cold North Sea.

The thunderbolt! She'd survived! How long had she been out? Five minutes, or half an hour.

She sat up and inspected her hands. Even in the dim light,

she could see that large, black, circular burn marks radiated on her palms. Her body tingled, the electrical charge still fizzing through her like gas in a bottle of opened soda.

How? She thought. *How had she done it? It didn't make any sense.*

She checked her limbs one by one. By rights, she should be frazzled but they all worked, even her fingers though her body ached like crazy, and her head buzzed as if someone had opened up her skull and given her brain a scrub with wire wool.

'Keep going,' she thought she heard from somewhere. 'Move! Now!'

She looked around.

She heard it again, as if someone was with her, egging her on, boosting her, begging her not to give in.

She forced herself forward and, instantly, fell flat on her face.

Again, she heard the voice, encouraging her, so she crawled, finding a steady rhythm with her knees, elbows, and hands. Soon she was above the waterline, and she kept on going until she doffed her head on a large, sheer rock.

'OUCH!' she cried, rubbing her forehead, conscious that the rain had now ceased pummelling her.

She must have arrived under a rock shelf, she thought, and, for the first time in ages, she felt a thimbleful of comfort.

She sat back and stretched her legs, cradling her head in her hands. Damn, she was hungry.

But where would the next meal come from, if she remained alive long enough to eat again?

Isabella pulled herself together and tried to gather her bearings.

She inspected a split rock and wondered if she could narrow down where she was by working out where this type of stone might typically be found on the river bank.

Moments later, there was a terrible explosion of noise seemingly coming from somewhere above her, as though two trains were colliding, crunching and scraping, the sound getting closer and closer, until, for a ghastly moment, the noise travelled directly through her.

She curled into a ball, shut her eyes, and covered her head.

Out of the sky, a deadly cascade washed past, careering onto the area from which she had only just crawled.

Isabella shook uncontrollably. Even above the shower of water, the cracking, crushing, and splintering sounds told her that everything in its path had been utterly obliterated.

For several seconds, the cascade rattled on until the landslip had done its bidding and the cacophony ceased. Isabella's heart thumped wildly. She wouldn't have stood a chance.

At length, she ventured out into the rain. Only a couple of metres forward and through the veil of water, she encountered a vast pile of boulders, rocks, mud, and splintered wood, that rose up like a slag heap in front of her.

She slunk back to her sheltered position as a terrible thought began to wash over her.

If she'd found refuge underneath a cliff face, the likelihood was that it was either a landslip off the top of a hill, or—and she thought this to be more likely—a section of the cliff face had simply collapsed. That would explain the boulders.

In her mind, she pictured the geography of the area and, especially, the position of the cliffs. If she was correct, behind her probable position was a ledge. Above this, a sheer wall of rock rose up vertically for seventy metres or thereabouts.

Then, like a thought one doesn't want to think about but cannot avoid, she had a terrible realisation that if Archie and Daisy had come after her, they would almost certainly not be alive right now.

Much to her shock, the other thing she realised was that if the water swept all the way around her, she was now completely and utterly trapped.

SIXTY-ONE

CAIN'S HUNGER

What a wonder, Cain thought, rubbing his new eyes. *Sleep. How invigorating—if only for a few moments! But I have a strange feeling of emptiness inside me.*

'Food!' he yelled out. 'Schmerger, I think I require food. Where is my food?'

Lying down, Cain saw the black pointy beard of his servant stopping at a respectable distance. The little creature bowed. 'Your Lordship?' the bent figure of Schmerger said. 'With respect, Sire, you haven't eaten for a thousand years. Are you yourself today?'

Cain rose and marched up to the servant. 'I require food, immediately. A feast.'

The servant recoiled. 'You have become... ASH, Sire.'

'Marvellous, isn't it. I have a human child within me and it requires feeding. Understand?'

'But there is no kitchen,' he replied.

'NO KITCHEN! What kind of palace is this?'

Schmerger shook his head. 'May I be bold, Sire, and say that ever since I was assigned to your Lordship, there has never been a kitchen. Your Lordship banned them.'

Cain thrust out his arm, picked the man up by the throat and threw him at a table which splintered over the floor. 'Is that so?'

The servant rubbed his neck.

Cain walked over and pulled the little man up. 'How and where do you eat, Schmerger? Show me.'

The servant bowed and led the ghost down the wide main staircase, down a corridor and through several doors, before entering a small room.

Cain followed, delighted that for once he could actually see the outline of rooms and his grand bed. Even his dim profile in the mirror was now visible. It was a shame he couldn't see with any detail, but it was a great deal better than nothing at all.

Schmerger picked up a wicker basket. 'From Mrs Schmerger, Sire.'

'Tell me,' Cain quizzed, 'what is in it?'

'It was lunch, Sire,' he said. 'Little remains.'

'Give it to me!' Cain said, thrusting his hand into the basket. He pulled out something black and stodgy and, without hesitation, stuffed it in his mouth. For the first time in ages he chewed. Aside from a tingle, it tasted like soot. But he hoped the boy inside found it favourable.

Schmerger backed out of the room, trembling, leaving the food for Cain.

Cain pulled out another piece and popped it in. This time, it crunched and splintered. Cain spat it out. 'Schmerger,' he yelled, 'what is it?'

'It is the leg of a bird,' the servant said from outside the door. 'One does not ordinarily eat the bones.'

Cain crashed a fist down on the table. 'I need more food. What is there to drink?'

'Nothing but water, Sire,' Schmerger said, bowing. 'Your Majesty has never had a requirement for any.'

'Well, I do now. Bring me some this instant. We have a great thirst.' Cain marched out of the room leaving a trail of dust behind him.

Cain knelt down and brushed a glass-like puddle, seeing a face smile up at him. 'Let me reacquaint myself with my poor frozen people.' He stood up. 'In time, let us banquet. Let there be a glorious feast with wine and song.'

Cain marched through the doors and found himself at the foot of the grand staircase, his mood bordering on euphoric. He wanted to know the situation with the heirs.

'Dreamspinner, dreamspinner, dreamspinner,' he called out.

Moments later Asgard appeared, his maghole tingling with electrical current. 'You called?'

Cain smiled. 'Now, my dear ugly dreamspinner, why don't we pay another short visit to find out how the Heirs of Eden are dying? Earlier I sensed Archie was close, the girl even closer. Perhaps this time I can persuade the boy to join willingly with me, before his poor soul is cast into the wild expanse of space.'

Asgard's maghole opened wide and Cain, seeing it's outline for the first time so clearly, forced the boy within him to bend down. And in one motion, they dived through.

If he could just get Archie, an Heir, to join him, then in one easy step this theatre, this charade that held on to the idea that these puny Heirs of Eden might survive, would cease, and everything would be resolved as he had originally imagined.

SIXTY-TWO

ARCHIE IN THE RIVER

Archie was catapulted into the air and crashed in the middle of the torrent where his body was instantly shipped away by the water. He swam with all his might. When he surfaced, a huge branch straddling the track lay directly in front of him.

His lungs burned.

He reached up, but however hard he tried he couldn't get a hand-hold on the bark. After several attempts, he felt his nails starting to detach.

Before long, Archie let go.

The water took him. He needed to keep his head up, but every time he managed this, the rain battered it down. While he searched for buoyancy—a branch or a tree he could grab hold of that might keep him afloat—he thrashed out like a madman, kicking the water beneath him in a last, massive effort to survive.

Something caught around his left leg, rendering him helpless. A root?

He succumbed, shattered and beaten and smiled as he let himself go, Cain's words coming to him as he floated away: *If it wasn't the thunderbolts and it wasn't the rain, it was the landslides.*

But, to his surprise, he remained bound by the snare around

his leg and found the water pushing him towards the bank. He made a grab for a protruding root, twisting his body round while keeping his head up.

He sucked in a mouthful of air and gave his foot a yank. It did not yield.

He tried again, this time while holding the root on the bank with his other hand. It moved! He did it again, and then again. Now there was enough slack to allow him to bend forward and feel his ankle. He pulled his left leg towards him and touched something coarse and thick. Archie's mind worked overtime. Then it struck him. The swinging rope!

He pulled harder and the rope came away a little more with just enough give for him to try and untie the knot.

It wasn't the trickiest knot he'd ever come across, but the rope was thick and the water pulled him away from his task. The rain beat down, and every time he thought he had untied the knot, the slack tightened and he was back to where he started. He gave the rope an even bigger tug and the whole branch jerked. This time the rope slipped off his foot and, while holding the end, he fixed the rope around his waist.

He heard a scream. Even above the roar of the rain and the torrent, it couldn't be mistaken.

It was Daisy, screaming:

'INCOMING!'

She's still on the branch!

Archie pulled with all his might and felt the wood slip further off the bank. He tugged harder, nudging the branch towards him. He gritted his teeth and jogged it, pulling in rhythm.

Suddenly, the branch twisted and slid just enough to give him encouragement.

There couldn't be much more time. One huge yank was all it needed.

He harnessed the rope around his shoulders and hollered.

The branch broke free and sped forward, just as a thunderbolt crashed into the bank almost exactly where the bough had sat moments before.

Archie wondered if Daisy had managed to get out of the way. But, he had no time to think, for now the branch slipped fast down the slope, joining the torrent, which sped them down the track.

Archie felt the rope go tense and found himself dragged behind it. Trying to keep himself above the water but gaining speed, he hung on for dear life as the branch hurtled into the main body of the river. As the river levelled out, he pulled himself along the rope, closer to the tree-trunk, and gritted his teeth as he dragged himself up and onto the end of the branch.

He dropped his left leg out, using it as a rudder, and the great branch pitched towards what he hoped was the bank on the left-hand side.

Exhausted, Archie collapsed, his head face down on the wood, water bucketing over him.

Hearing a noise, Archie lifted his head. Was someone sitting near him on the branch?

'Daisy… Daisy?,' he groaned.

'Come with me, Archie de Lowe,' the voice said. 'Only I can save you now.'

'Save me,' Archie repeated.

'Say yes, and it will be done.'

Archie's eyelids closed. 'Cain?'

'Archie, just say the word.'

What did he have to lose, why didn't he just agree?

'Do the easy thing, boy,' Cain continued. 'Your life is not over by any means.'

Archie's brain swam but all he could think of was his sisters.

Nothing else. Only Isabella, and Daisy.

The branch jolted.

Right then, he knew there was no other way. Archie had to move Daisy to safety and then he would find Isabella. Better to die together trying to save the world, than not trying at all.

'I'd rather die with my sisters than join with you,' he called out, weakly.

The voice laughed back, 'I will return, Archie, one more time. You may need me yet. Your dear sister is so very close to her death and, when that happens, you will all have failed.'

SIXTY-THREE

CAIN AND KEMP

Back in Havilah, Cain wondered how his relationship with Kemp would work in their combined state should his alliance with Archie fail. Right now, the boy was slowing him down to an alarming degree, and yet there was so much to do.

Would the boy continue to do as he willed?

Cain threw his arms up in the air and clapped his hands as a shower of ash fell over his head.

All of a sudden, a feeling of heaviness overcame him.

Sleep, again? Really!

Cain clenched his fist and found that when his concentration focused on that movement alone, the fingers came together whether the boy liked it or not.

Cain pressed one foot down, followed by the other. He felt a modicum of resistance, like a badly fitting drawer that needs to be forced shut.

He willed his leg to move, but the movement felt sluggish and sleepy. Instead, he pulled his leg back and thrust it forward in a loose kicking motion, ash spraying everywhere.

He flailed his arms about, moving them faster and faster until the boy trapped inside him did exactly as he wished.

'We've places to go, my little friend, and there's not a

moment to lose.' Cain said out loud. He couldn't tell if the boy inside him could hear, though the odd cries he heard told him that the boy wasn't entirely deaf.

'Do my bidding, little friend of Archie de Lowe,' he said, 'and everything will work out just fine. Who knows, we may even get to like one another. But until then, I am going to make you do as I wish.'

But as hard as Cain pushed and cajoled, the boy inside him soon slowed to a standstill.

Where was this child's energy? I mean, wasn't that the point of this entire exercise? Or was the boy being deliberately difficult?

A few minutes of rest should do the trick, and then he'd be off. What was it called, *sleep*?

Perhaps he also needed food and water. He'd try Schmerger and see what the elf might come up with. Anything to get the damn boy moving properly.

'In due course, there will be sustenance and rest for you,' he spoke out. 'But for now, boy, I need your energy. Resist, and I will hurt you.'

If the boy was going to be a deliberate nuisance, then he could play that game too.

SIXTY-FOUR

'THE JOAN OF' MOVES

Gus tried to row with the flow of the water but the current was too strong and, besides, he had no idea where he was going. When he stole a look from under the canopy, he was met by a wall of water sluicing from the sky.

He drew in the oars, inspected the canopy, and drove a couple of nails into the areas where he sniffed a weakness.

Then he returned to the bench to help Sue bail out water. With the amount coming in, it needed both of them to work flat out. Sue felt like she'd scooped out enough water to fill an Olympic-sized swimming pool three times over. Her arms ached so much she thought they might simply drop off.

As 'The Joan of' pitched through the waters, and as the storm smashed down upon their tiny vessel, Sue thought of Isabella, Archie and Daisy. Every time she imagined them trying to soldier on through the storm and getting swept away, her spirit plummeted. And her previous thought of rescuing them could never happen.

Every so often, 'The Joan of' would bash into something hard and solid, like a wall or a car, and they would be thrown forward. It was at these moments that both of them knew the strength of the boat would be tested.

All it took was a crack or a small hole, and that would be the end of it.

At other times, "The Joan of" ground against something, or span around as it diverted off an object, the water pitching the boat one way and then the other.

Several times, Gus levered the boat away with an oar, lurching back into the swell.

Sue kept her head down, sobbing as he went outside. On returning, Gus would hold her, and stare reassuringly into eyes which betrayed nothing less than abject terror.

His eyes, she noticed, were wide. Not so much in fear, she thought, but with excitement. To her, Gus was having the time of his life.

She heard him singing a hearty sea shanty as he tossed the water out with his bucket, his singing grew louder and louder with each movement until it was in direct competition with the rain.

Sue didn't know whether to laugh, cry, or hit him.

For a while, at least, the singing stopped her wallowing about the disaster and about her friends.

After what felt like hours, Gus pointed upwards. 'I think we've moved away from the main rain belt.' She nodded in agreement. 'Problem is—how far do you reckon we've gone?'

'No idea,' she said.

Gus agreed. He knew it was impossible to tell.

SIXTY-FIVE

OLD MAN WOOD TO THE RESCUE

Seeing Isabella's monitor struck by lightning followed by Daisy's monitor crackle spurred the old man into immediate action. What should he take with him?

Old Man Wood switched on the torch and shot off towards the shed.

With his heart and mind racing, he grabbed a section of rope, a small axe, and his hard helmet with a built-in torch on the front. He dashed into his cold room where he stored his huge variety of apples and selected eight rather small ones from the special box he kept near the door.

In the cloakroom, he found his long, waterproof coat, and his walking boots, which he slipped on as fast as he could.

Back in his bedroom he went straight back to the screens.

Archie was cradling Daisy, he could see that, but tears streamed down the boy's face.

'Oh my dears. You poor things,' Old Man Wood cried out. 'Keep her warm. Speak to her, little Archie. Don't let her drift away, whatever you do.'

Now, where was Isabella?

Old Man Wood furrowed his brow. 'Apples-alive,' he

muttered, 'she's in a peculiar place. Bang next to a rock face and surrounded by a heap of boulders.'

He zoomed in.

She's shivering, and no wonder. But how on earth did she get there?

He zoomed out and pressed the cloud button, which removed the rain.

'Apples-alive!' he exclaimed again, kneading his head with his hands. 'They're on opposite sides of the same pile of rocks… and they don't even know it!'

He zoomed out further on Isabella's monitor.

'I know where they are,' he exclaimed, his eyes almost bulging out of his head in excitement. He checked his watch. It was ten minutes before four o'clock, or thereabouts, just over an hour before nightfall. He'd have to hurry.

He darted out of his room, bursting with an energy and purpose he hadn't felt in years, when an idea shot into his head. He turned on his helmet light, and skipped down the cellar stairs.

Now, which door was it?

He headed along a musty brick corridor that smelled of old wet rags and linseed oil. He stopped outside a low, thick wooden door laced with metal studs right at the end. Cut into it were the markings "II". Roman numerals for cellar number two.

Now, he thought, *how did the door open?* There wasn't a key, he was sure of that. It was something smarter; keys could be lost or discovered by nosey children or unwanted guests.

He strained his brain trying to work out what it might be. 'Oh, come on!' he cried out. 'Why does my brain always go blank at times like this?'

He thumped his fist on the wall. One of the bricks shifted. His eyes darted up and he groped about, pushing the bricks to see if anything would happen.

Nothing.

He screwed his eyes up. He couldn't even remember the last

time he'd been down here. From the corner of his eye he spotted a piece of stone protruding from the wall. *Maybe that was it.* He pushed it.

Again, nothing.

He left his hand there as his head tilted forward, and he tapped the wall with his forehead in frustration. The stone moved! He doffed it further and heard a neat 'click'.

'Ah-ha!'

He twisted the metal ring on the door and the latch clicked open. He was in.

Inside, a smell of moss and dust mixed with eucalyptus oil surprised his senses and, as he brushed past the cobwebs that drooped from the ceiling, he shone his helmet torch to see what he could find.

He smiled. Neatly stacked on slate shelves running around the walls were hundreds of small bottles obscured by layers of dust.

Starting at one end, he picked each bottle up and blew the dust off to reveal the writing which was neatly etched into the glass. Names like Spindle Wood, Ogre Blood, Wood Ox, Willow Potion, and Oak Spit. He hurried on, hoping like mad that when he saw it, he'd know.

A flood of memories rushed in, almost overwhelming him.

These were his bottles. HIS potions! From a time... well, from a lost time, a time he'd forgotten.

He continued along the row, reading out the names as he went until he spied three bottles with the words 'Resplendix Mix' in bold writing scratched on each.

He pulled one off the shelf and brushed it down. In the torchlight, the colour was like liquid gold, and, as it moved, little diamonds of light danced within it.

*Resplendix Mix. T*his brilliant potion would help them, he was sure of it.

He shoved a bottle into his pocket and tore out of the room.

Closing the back door, he was instantly set upon by the

water, the weight on his hard hat pushing his head into his body.

What was the best way to the bottom of the cliff?

The lane was acting like a drain, so the road was impassable.

Maybe he could lower a rope from the ruin and let himself down? He fingered the coils strapped around his torso. But he knew the rope wasn't long enough, and what if he was swept off the top?

No, he would have to go across country, through the woods and then somehow up, along and onto the ledge.

He'd need a lot of luck and most of all, he needed to hurry.

SIXTY-SIX

SOLOMON IN THE TOWER

Fifty-seven! Solomon scrolled down the page of names. He rather hoped that perhaps one hundred people had fled by car, and others had gone when the lightning started.

Still, that left an awful lot unaccounted for. He hadn't factored in the opposition players, parents, and supporters.

Half the football team were missing; no Sue Lowden, no Williams, Kemp or Allen. The list went on… five of his teachers out there, somewhere, too.

He only had to look at himself to shake with shame.

He'd found the doorway to the tower as much by luck as by design, and was dragged in by Mrs. Rose who'd reached out into the curtain of water and swept him in. Exhausted, he sat on the step catching his breath and waiting anxiously to see if anyone was close by.

Only one other person came in after him. It was a small girl who had felt her way around the exterior walls, inch by inch. Solomon cried as he helped her up the stairs.

It had made him hope there were more, but no matter how long he stayed, no one else came by. Looking into the sheet of water flashing from the sky, this was no surprise.

In no time, the water level forced him to move up the stairs, as a pool of water quickly formed beneath the first landing. He insisted the door should be left open, just in case.

The children spread themselves out over the two floors of the library in the tower, cowering together. As the storm smashed overhead, the children sobbed, despite teachers doing their best to keep spirits up. Even the teachers, Solomon noticed, had anxious eyes as they flicked nervous glances towards one another.

The chef, along with his assistant, fed the group bread buns from a huge sack they'd pulled across the yard moments before it all happened.

Only when the water reached three quarters of the way up the front door did they shut the door. A realisation that the level might get higher and higher dawned on Solomon and this time he wasn't taking any chances.

Solomon excused himself and headed up to the old library right at the top of the tower, accessible only by ladder. Up there, he removed his jacket and trousers and sank into an old chair.

Placing his hands over his eyes, he sobbed openly.

He couldn't remember the last time he'd cried. When his father died many years ago, he'd shed a small tear, alone.

Now, tears flowed.

When his grief had subsided, he tried to reflect. Of course, with the benefit of hindsight, he realised that he had been nothing short of a fool, no more, and no less. A stubborn fool at that. He hadn't listened.

His brightest pupil had demanded his attention, and he'd refused her.

Worse still, he'd lied to her!

Lied! Dammit!

Solomon felt his stomach knot. He'd lied to a student who had gone out of her way to prove that something major and remarkable was about to happen.

And he'd pushed her warnings straight back in her face.

He banged his fist down on a dusty table. Wasn't that what

headmasters were supposed to be good at, listening, giving people the benefit of the doubt? Encouraging students in their academic and recreational activities?

All he'd been interested in, he realised now, was his banquet, the glory of his school and his moment in the limelight. And now…

Three times Isabella had tried to tell him. Three times he'd denied her.

All along, it was as if she knew, and Sue knew. He recalled her crazy screaming. Was that part of these strange happenings? Perhaps even Archie knew, the way he let the penalty slide past his foot into the goal.

Solomon stood up and moved over to the window. On a good day, the view expanded way across the Vale of York in one direction, marked by a green patchwork quilt of fields and woods. In the other direction, the tree line of the Hambleton Hills wiggled around the North York Moors, intersected by cliff faces and shadows.

This was the exact spot, twenty-five years ago—almost to the day—where he'd fallen in love with the glorious scenery, the light, and the big skies. He remembered how he'd accept the job at Upsall school on the spot.

Now, he stared at death, destruction, and chaos.

He knew that, if and when this rain ceased, the scenery would be a different hue, the land would have a new orientation. A vale filled entirely with water.

'Isabella,' he said. 'Will you ever forgive me for ignoring you? For being such a toady old idiot.'

He sighed and brushed another tear from his eye, knowing that it would be a miracle if the de Lowe trio ever made it home.

All that talent, he thought, *gone to waste. And I could have prevented it.*

'I am so terribly sorry.'

SIXTY-SEVEN

ARCHIE HOLDS ON

Archie stared at his watch. It had gone four. When was sunset; five, half five?

He'd hauled himself onto the log and found his twin. Now he cradled her in his arms.

'Hey, Daisy,' he said, sheltering her face. 'Don't give up on me. There's only a little while to go, you know. And I'm going to keep you alive, if it's the last thing I do.'

He ran his cold hands over her face.

If he was cold, then she was icy.

Softly, he massaged her heart. He didn't know why, but it just seemed the right thing to do. 'Please, Daisy, you've got to come back. Don't you dare back out now. I don't know what I'd do without you. If you go, we've all had it. Everyone, not just us.'

Her eyes flickered and the corners of her lips turned up.

Thank goodness, he thought. *A spark.*

He'd keep talking, and, somehow, he had to keep her listening.

'Right, here's what we're going to do,' he said. 'I'm going to pick you up and start carrying you over these rocks and stuff, okay?'

Very gently, he picked her up and negotiated footholds in the debris. One step followed another, each one swaying, each a desperate act of concentration.

Every so often he studied her face to make sure she was still with him before carrying on. He leapt from one rock to the next, disregarding the rain, disregarding his burden, worrying only about the next step.

As he climbed, he carried on talking. He spoke about what was going to happen and how safe they were going to be in only a little while. He chattered about anything else he could think of.

When he ran out of things to say, he started singing.

The first song that came into his head was a song their mother had taught them when they were young. With chattering teeth, he sang it as best as he could. When he forgot the words, he hummed it, his voice shaking with cold.

After a few minutes, Daisy's eyes flashed open. He looked down at her and smiled, trying to hold back his tears while he continued humming.

He felt her tensing. Her eyes opened wide, telling him something.

What was it?

Her eyes rolled back.

Archie tensed.

NO! NOT ANOTHER ONE!

Instantly, Archie tossed Daisy over his shoulder in a fireman's lift. He reached the top of a boulder and tried to see beyond it, but saw only the steady veil of rain.

'Daisy!' he cried out, 'I've got to jump and I don't know where we'll end up. If this goes badly, just remember that I love you. You're a cool girl, sis.'

He had no more time.

Archie sucked in as much air as he could. He closed his eyes, bent his knees, and jumped as high and as far as he possibly could into the dark unknown.

✳

Archie had no idea where he might end up, but a broken leg was preferable to being flash-fried to death.

They splashed in a pool and sank down to the bottom, at the exact moment two lightning bolts smashed into their previous position. Their brutal force displaced shards, pebbles, and larger stones. Everything shook. Water fizzed, the currents jabbing at every nerve-ending in their bodies.

Archie stayed down, holding Daisy and cradling her head for as long as he dared. Suddenly her eyes opened wide.

Archie thrashed to the surface and winced as a stone hit him on his shoulder. Another whacked him on the head. He let go of Daisy and felt his mind begin to drift away.

The pool and the torrential rain were blurring together.

He saw stars spinning.

Daisy was accelerating away from him.

With one last effort, he pulled himself up but his head spun so fast that in no time he felt himself go, his body slipping away to a place of softness and light.

A feeling of warmth enveloped him, like a comfort blanket brimming with love, holding him tight.

With his last breath of consciousness, Archie had the where-withal to reach up and grasp a hand-hold. And then his mind slid into the darkness of a black and deep abyss.

SIXTY-EIGHT

A LEAP OF FAITH

Shivering, Isabella remembered their last holiday as a family, skiing, high up in the Alps.

Beautifully hot with a bright blue sky, at lunch she had stripped off her jacket, thrown off her hat, and ditched her long johns, giving them all to her mother who crammed them into a rucksack.

They'd jumped on a chairlift and headed up to the top of the mountain. Halfway up, the chair had stopped and swayed in the air. They stayed like that for ages; an hour, maybe more.

Then, the weather changed. First, clouds blew in, followed by an icy, biting wind and horizontal snow.

She sat there, freezing, with nothing but her father's arm around her to protect her. In the seat behind, her mother was holding the bag with her clothes. An hour later, every bone in her body ached, from the top of her head to the tip of her toes.

She remembered how it took two hot chocolates before she could move her jaw open enough to say anything.

What she would give for that hot chocolate now.

What had her father said?

Keep moving, girl. That was it. *And if you can't keep moving, hug someone. Hug them nice and tight.*

A warm feeling filled her as she remembered how Archie thought this was the perfect excuse to go around hugging people. Everyone had thought him rather cute; even, momentarily, Daisy.

Isabella tried to smile. Now out of the rain, the cold had begun to creep into her like roots of frost knitting into soil.

She needed to move. Using her hands as a guide, she felt for a jagged, protruding rock so that she might get a decent foothold. She found one, lifted herself up on it and then fingered another further up. She'd done enough climbing to know that planning a route up and making sure one's feet were stable were the keys to success.

The problem was visibility. Combined with the numbness in her fingers, it meant that she couldn't determine if her grip was true. She slipped back and landed with a wet thud on the ground. Isabella shook her hands vigorously out in front of her, and slowly the blood began to return. She jogged on the spot, the wet remains of her trousers sticking to her legs, and rolled her head on her shoulders.

She needed to search further along.

Once again, she followed the face of the rock, guided by her hands, her legs now knee-deep in the water. A little further on, she found the perfect spot; an outcrop of stone concealed by bushes.

Moving them aside, she found two easy steps. She pulled herself up, placing one foot carefully on the first step, then, hugging the rock, she tested her weight slowly on the next. It felt solid, as if purposely carved out of the rocks.

Her arms searched around trying to find another foothold. She levered herself up and did the same again, noting that the steps curved around. She climbed until she realised she was on a flat ledge.

With the rain driving at her, she had lost her sense of direction. She sat on the ledge trying to fathom the angle of the steps in relation to the rock face. She crawled on her hands and knees in the direction of the cliff face, scanning for any sudden gaps or boulders. Aside from pebbles, it felt smooth.

She edged on further before she realised the rain was subsiding, then it ceased altogether. She wiped water from her face and leaned into a big, round rock. Isabella felt strangely elated, as if she'd solved a tricky equation.

She examined the boulder, and figured that it sat directly under the cliff face, with the incline protecting her from the rain.

But how would she get out? The logical answer was to head high up to the right, towards Eden Cottage. The light was failing fast, though, and the rain still wasn't letting up. Maybe she'd have to stay put until the morning. At least, she'd be out of the rain.

Anyway, hadn't Archie told them the storm would continue until sunset, or some nonsense like that?

Two lightning bolts suddenly blasted out of the sky. They were directed just beyond the landslide, where she'd come from.

She hardly had a chance to react, only to duck down.

What if those were for...?

In a heartbeat, she threw herself off the ledge, just before a huge charge spat out and smashed into the exact spot she'd been standing.

Isabella tumbled into the water.

She sank as low as she could go, amazed at how much the water had risen in such a short time. She stayed underneath as long as her lungs could hold her, hugging the cliff face, as splinters of rock and stone punched the pool like deadly shrapnel.

When Isabella surfaced, she noticed a big difference in her surroundings. The water level had edged close to the surface of the ledge, so that instead of climbing the stairs, she simply pulled herself out and sat down with her feet dangling in the pool.

She shivered in the near-darkness, her heart thumping wildly.

She realised what the difference was. Drizzle! The torrents of rain, the endless pounding, had almost gone.

With the quiet came an enormous sense of relief.

She smiled through her chattering teeth.

The remains of her clothes stuck to her like cold, soggy slime, but she still had to survive through the night. The temperature would drop, as it always did at about this time of year, and there was no hope of a warming fire.

In the next breath, her thoughts turned to Daisy and Archie. There had been three huge thunderbolts; one for each of them. Why—she had no idea, but it felt right—even if it was absurdly illogical and absolutely terrifying.

She shuffled along looking out in the darkness.

'Archie. Daisy!' she yelled *'Are you there?'*

She listened, but heard only the swishing sounds of the running water beyond.

Again and again she called out, trying to hear a response.

No reply was forthcoming.

Deep within her, Isabella sensed they were near, but it was so hard and she was so tired, so cold, so hungry.

Come on, she told herself, no time to be lazy; look for them. A thought kept returning: what if they were a few feet away and died in the night because she couldn't be bothered?

Isabella crawled along the ledge as far as she dared, all the while making sure she kept a firm grip of the surface, calling out for them in turn *'Daisy! Archie!'*.

She shivered, her lips quivering involuntarily as she stared out into the darkness. Occasionally she heard a groan, but it was hard to tell if it was the crunching of metal on metal, like cars or sheds being swept down the river and colliding with each other, or whether it was the desperate cry of people or animals.

Tears built as an overwhelming sense of sadness flowed over her. Her feeling of helplessness was almost complete.

As if in response to her cries, a tiny sliver of light appeared on the lip of the horizon and threw a grey light over the water. Isabella peered at it and, for a short while, thought that she must be dreaming. It looked so beautiful, like a gentle sparkle of light catching the rim of a silver bracelet. She blinked and shook her head.

The moon? *Moonlight.*

Now, she could distinguish the outlines of boulders and a flat ledge. Looking up, the sheer face of the cliff-face above her felt like a prison wall. She scoured the valley, observing a dull, ever-changing watery mirror that gently lapped in front of her.

As the moon rose, its brightness lifted her spirits further.

She noticed how the round boulder she had hidden underneath before the lightning struck had been reduced to rubble. Where it once stood, an unnaturally dark hole beckoned her in.

Isabella approached. With every footstep, she grew more curious.

She edged closer still, testing the cracked sections that might be unstable, until she found herself peering up at the perfectly symmetrical entrance of a dark cave.

Without hesitating, she placed one foot ahead of the other and, leaning against the side, she made her way in.

She caught warmth on her face.

Hot air, here?

She took another step, hoping that her eyes would adjust.

It's like a warm hairdryer.

Thermal rocks, here, in Yorkshire? Never!

Isabella was about to take a further step in when she heard a strange cry coming from behind her. Her heart skipped a beat.

Daisy? Archie?

She rushed out and scanned the area but found that the ledge was now only fractionally higher than the swollen river, and it was hard to tell where one stopped and the other started. She heard it again, a groan followed by a cry and a tiny cough.

Her heart raced as she studied the ledge again. She concentrated and pushed her hands out, trusting them, following them.

She ran to the right, urging her eyes to peer deeper into the night.

Nothing.

She walked cautiously to the left.

Nothing.

She repeated her movements, extending her range.

To her right, all she could discern was a long shape, like a fat, black branch typical of the debris. She walked straight past, but turned when there was a tiny noise.

Isabella was there in a flash.

A body! Face down.

Bending down she noticed dirt intermingled with bloody cuts, angry bruises, and tattered clothing.

They never made it, she thought.

Isabella's hopes sank.

As she turned the frame over, the white arms folded limply and splashed helplessly in a puddle.

The eyes were closed.

Isabella screamed as though someone had ripped her heart out.

In front of her lay Daisy's shattered body.

SIXTY-NINE

KEMP CONTEMPLATES HIS SITUATION

Kemp felt another long burst of heat on his leg. He grimaced. Reluctantly, he moved his limb and the pain faded.

The de Lowes had had to save the world? But they were crazy, nutty kids and never super-heroes.

Even now, the thought would have made him chuckle, if only he wasn't so filled with pain.

Why wouldn't the ghost leave him alone for just one minute?

When he yelled, Cain didn't hear him and didn't react. He needed food, water, and rest. How long had it been? Five or six hours constantly moving, constantly burned in little patches from head to toe.

It felt like a week, or a month even.

He yawned, and felt his body moving off, his legs clumpy as if made with wet sand. Every time he stopped a surge of intense heat smashed into him and he had no choice but to keep going.

He could see, although not well. The sickly vapours of singed hair and fried flesh caught at the back of his throat.

Every sound was muted, like being underwater. Soon, his thoughts turned to death. If he refused to go on, would he simply burn to death within Cain?

SEVENTY

STUCK ON THE CLIFF

Old Man Wood was at the point where he needed to start making his way along the steeper, sharper cliff face. He faced the rock and shuffled along, happier in his step where the mud gave way to stone. As he angled across the cliff face, overhangs gave him welcome relief from the downpour, while other parts showered him with mud and loose rock. He dug his fingers into every tight crevice and small hole. Moving along as quickly and carefully as he dared, he hoped he hadn't started too high.

Presently, he was able to take stock of his position. He rested under a deep overhang where he found a decent foothold. He gulped in huge mouthfuls of air as he leant into the stone.

Should he drive a bolt in to the rock so that he could attach the rope, just in case?

He found a hole, delved into his pocket, and found a quick release bolt. He thrust it in and the metal fastened. He put his weight on it, and the bolt held. Good. He tied the rope to the metal loop and attached the rest around his body.

As he turned to inspect his next footholds, a huge electrical pulse flashed out of the sky to his left. He looked on in shock. A second bright charge rocketed out of the sky from the same place a millisecond later, almost blinding him. His eardrums seared with pain.

The valley lit up, and he saw everything move like a huge grey beast filled with water. 'Apples-alive,' he muttered under his breath as his heart raced.

He was too high above the ledge.

He felt for a footing, making sure his hold was solid. He tested his grip and bent down, but, in the next moment, a huge thunderbolt smashed out of the sky directly into the cliff face beneath him.

For a second Old Man Wood held on for dear life.

There they were!

He could see them all, as clear as day for just one-second.

His heart whooped in his chest. He had to get down there, fast.

Old Man Wood picked his way along as rapidly as he could, letting the rope out behind him. After several metres, he tightened the rope and started to descend.

He sucked in his cheeks and braced himself. Pushing out with his feet, he flew through the air, rain smashing into his face as he readied himself to land.

It was going to hurt, he thought, rather a lot.

The rope swung out again, this time gaining speed, and all too soon he was back to his starting position like a pendulum. He kicked out, and as he reached the limit of his arc, he suddenly noted that the rain had stopped.

The shock forced him to hold on, the moonlight offering a shadow of vision over the ledge below.

He swung out one more time.

As he looked down, he swore he saw Isabella walking away towards a rock.

He swung back, grasping onto the rope for dear life. He was wondering how much lower he ought to be when the bolt disengaged from the rock, and Old Man Wood and the rope plummeted down.

Old Man Wood lay in a heap, his breath knocked clean out of him, pain searing into his ankle and back.

He gritted his teeth and watched Isabella. Then he heard her scream followed by muffled cries.

Had she found one of the others?

Oh! apples alive, he cursed, *how could he be so hopeless?*

He summoned his strength, trying to ignore the pain screaming through his legs.

He urged himself on, but each time he slumped back down.

His eyes watered. He probed the swollen flesh, now juicy like a purple summer-pudding. Was it a tear or a break? He turned his head and his back screamed out as if a knife was stabbing at his vertebrae. Even his hands were hurting, blood pouring from a cut in the middle of his left palm.

What had he been thinking, swinging on ropes at his great age?

His body was beginning to shut down. Shock; Old Man Wood knew the feeling well. Then it struck him. The Resplendix Mix he'd found in the cellar! Of course, he'd self-medicate!

With his swollen hand, he reached into his pocket. He transferred the bottle to his bleeding left hand and attempted to remove the lid.

Did it twist? Did he have to pull out a cork, or was there some kind of stopper?

Nothing happened, apart from his hand slipping around the rim.

He inspected the bottle.

But there was no lid, or stopper.

Maybe it needed a sharp pull. He tried, but there was nothing to pull on.

Old Man Wood shook his head in frustration. No shaking, twisting, pulling, or yelling would make it open.

He felt his eyelids grow heavy. He thought of smashing the top on a rock, but even this idea slipped away as he fell into unconsciousness.

SEVENTY-ONE

GUS WONDERS WHAT WILL HAPPEN

Gus put his head out of the canopy. 'Still can't see a thing,' he reported back, 'apart from muddy water. Fancy some grub?'

Sue was starving. Gus opened a tin of tuna and a bag of salt and vinegar crisps and took a swig of water. When they'd finished, he had an idea.

'Look, Sue,' he began, 'one of us had better have a kip—we're going to need to sleep at some point and there's not much room. If we do it this way, the other can keep look-out.'

Sue hadn't thought of this. 'Good idea, brain-box. On sailing boats, I think they do four hours on and four hours off. Want to give it a try?'

'Sure,' Gus said. 'It's five-fifty now. Have a sleep till half nine—if you can, then I'll look out till one and do the early morning shift at four or five. Sound OK?'

With a bit of a shuffle, Gus pulled the planks he'd stowed from the bottom of the boat and made up a bed—of sorts—where at least one of them could lie down. Gus unfolded a plastic sheet and laid it on top of the boards so they wouldn't lie in the wet. Sue lay down and he spread the dust sheets over her. It wasn't great, but it would have to do.

Sue closed her eyes. She didn't really feel like sleeping, but having a rest now after all that bailing out was welcome. And Gus was right, one of them needed to be on look-out—especially if there was a place they could land—and it would be a disaster if they were to miss out while they slept.

Gus moved out to the bow of the boat and breathed a sigh of relief.

Quite amazingly, it seemed that for the time being they had got over the worst and his makeshift canopy had saved their lives. He laughed. He'd have won the DT prize for that; just goes to show what you can do when the pressure's on.

He wondered if Sue had any idea how close it had been, and then he thought of his mum and dad. Mum would be worried sick, but he reckoned his dad would be chuffed to bits. He hoped they hadn't gone looking for him—there was nothing he could do about it if they had. Anyway, what a surprise it would be when he got home.

At least they had food and water and could keep dry. And so long as the boat held together he reckoned they had every chance. Plus they made a good team. He took a deep breath as the last gasps of daylight started to eke away. Yeah, they made a very good team.

If only they had some way of telling where they were. He thought for a minute if it wouldn't be worth dropping the oars and trying to make it to land by rowing hard to one side. Or maybe he could drop an oar at the back and use it as a rudder. But, then again, what if he didn't have the strength to handle it and spilled an oar into the water. It wasn't worth the risk. He wiped the rain, which was now bearable for more than a minute, off his face. Best keep on and hope the boat might bank somewhere they could make off to safety.

He ducked inside and, as Sue dozed, he slipped past her, grabbed a bucket and started the process of bailing the water out all over again. How long would the rain continue? Perhaps they were over the worst, but what if the deluge came back? He shivered. They had been lucky—astonishingly lucky; he'd never seen anything like it—but he didn't fancy their chances if it happened again.

Staring at her peaceful face, he moved in and planted a small kiss on her cheek. What a curious stroke of luck, he thought, that they'd run into each other.

SEVENTY-TWO

GAIA'S DREAM

It was Asgard had betrayed the dreamspinners; Asgard who had sided with Cain!

It was common knowledge and already many dreamspinners flocked to him.

Gaia poked a leg in her burning maghole.

In which case, she thought, *it was time to add balance to the drama.*

Instantly, Gaia spun a dream into Old Man Wood's mouth, the minuscule, fine powders sucked deep into the old man's lungs.

Let the powders work fast on the old man, for the effect must be sharp and quick.

The dreamspinner hovered, waiting. She needed Old Man Wood to wake up.

Shortly, the old man yawned and stretched his arms out wide, then howled in pain.

Gaia watched as the old man's face contorted in agony then moved to an expression of surprise as he found the Resplendix Mix in his lap. He studied the bottle.

Let us see how he does it this time.

Gaia saw the old man place the top of the bottle to his lips and kissed it. The seal opened.

Excellent, Gaia thought. *It worked. And though the old man will feel great pain as he heals, there is a chance this drama will play out to the bitter end.*

SEVENTY-THREE

A CRY FOR HELP

Old Man Wood gritted his teeth as the Resplendix Mix set to work mending damaged parts. The liquid burned like the white heat of a soldering iron welding him back together.

Shortly, he rolled his head, blinked his eyes, and breathed deeply, the air filling his lungs like bellows. Invigorated, though tingling with shooting heat, he coiled up the rope and scoured the moonlit ledge.

Now, where were they?

He'd seen Isabella below him from the rope, but the other two? Old Man Wood headed out onto the ledge. There she was, kneeling over something. A body?

Old Man Wood hurried over.

As he neared, he heard a terrible wailing noise. He prepared himself for the worst and coughed as he approached.

'Looks like you could do with a hand,' he said, solemnly.

'Old Man Wood!' she said, flinging her arms around him. 'Look! It's Daisy! I think she's, she's...'

Old Man Wood bent down and ran a hand over Daisy's brow. He felt only coldness. He searched for signs of breathing.

'My goodness,' he said softly, 'you've taken a horrible beating, sweet Daisy.'

He withdrew the Resplendix Mix from his pocket noting how her lips were a pale crimson against her white skin.

He felt for a pulse and his heart nearly stopped. He couldn't feel one.

He could sense Isabella staring at him, searching for answers in his face.

'Now, Isabella, there is only one thing I can do,' he said, showing her the bottle. 'She only needs a couple of drops—'

'Anything, Old Man Wood!'

'It's an old remedy of mine for healing—I'll tell you about it another time. Thing is, Bells,' he continued, a deep frown filling his forehead, 'the bottle will only open if the potion within can heal the person whose lips it touches.'

Isabella frowned. 'Do it, please—hurry!'

Old Man Wood lowered the bottle to Daisy's mouth and pressed the top against her lips.

'Why don't you just open it?' Isabella growled, mostly in frustration.

'As I said, I can't. The bottle will open itself if it can heal, otherwise I am afraid we have lost her.'

He shook his head.

'What is it?' Isabella cried.

Old Man Wood's lips trembled. 'I'm so sorry.' A tear rolled out of his eye and landed on Daisy's cheek. He wiped it off and inspected the top of the bottle, which remained closed. 'I fear I am too late,' he said, his eyes glistening. 'I am so sorry, dear little Daisy. So terribly sorry.'

Old Man Wood bent over, his body shaking, tears falling.

Isabella stared numbly at her lifeless sister. An intensity of energy she'd never experienced before rushed into her. She demanded action.

Directing her hands towards her sister, she closed her eyes and screamed.

'Don't be stupid, Daisy de Lowe. You are not going to die. Understand! I will not allow it!'

A strange, pink glow emanated from her hands, cocooning Daisy's body like strands of candy floss.

'Do not give up,' she roared. 'Not yet.'

Daisy's eyes flickered.

It worked! What had she done?

Isabella held the glow as long as she could, then reeled, stumbling and falling, exhausted beyond reason. The pink cocoon floating away like vapour.

Old Man Wood, reacted fast. Placing the bottle to Daisy's lips the spout opened.

'Come on, Daisy, one drop is all you need.'

Moments later, he noticed a blush of pink in Daisy's cheeks and felt the trace of a heartbeat.

The old man carefully scooped up her limp and cold body, and carried her into the darkness of a cave he'd noticed.

Inside, Old Man Wood switched on his torch and found a circular pit, like an empty, buried hot tub. It looked as good place as any to rest. More importantly, as he stepped inside, he felt a soft, sandy, talc-like substance which, to the touch, was smooth as tissue and as soft as thick fur.

He lowered Daisy in, making sure her head was propped up. Clambering outside again, he rushed to Isabella's side and placed the Resplendix Mix to her lips. In no time, he'd done the same to Isabella, placing her sleeping body next to her sister.

Two down, one to go.

At least the girls would be warm and out of danger while he set about finding Archie.

SEVENTY-FOUR

ARCHIE FLIES

Archie's mind was a blur, his head whirling. Before long, he found that his body was turning and heading into a spin too.

He steadied and, as he levelled out, he realised he was flying. He soared like a bird, swooping first one way, then another, before shooting high into the air, twisting as he went, enjoying the sensation of weightlessness. Each gust of wind caressed his body and he cried out at the freedom of flight and the thrill of speed.

Now he was diving, flying fast as an arrow. He screwed left and found himself heading, at breakneck speed, towards a rock face as if he himself was a bolt of lightning.

Maybe he was.

He couldn't stop, he couldn't turn fast enough and there wasn't enough room for him to manoeuvre. But he wasn't afraid. He would wallop it with his head and it wouldn't hurt, it couldn't hurt him.

BANG!

The rock shattered into several pieces.

In place of the boulder was the entrance to a cave. He looked inside. Isabella and Daisy were there with Old Man Wood. They were beckoning, teasing him to come in and join them, laughing and smiling. They wanted to tell him something.

He raised his foot and carried on through the entrance. But as he did he felt the anger of Cain smash into him and he fell, Cain kicking him, first in the ribs, then chest, and finally, his face.

Why would Cain want to hurt him? They were on the same side, right?

He felt air leaking out of him like a balloon with a small hole, shrivelling quickly.

He gasped, struggling to breath.

He gulped, realising he needed air so badly; so badly that it hurt...

Archie surfaced and thrashed the water, desperate to find a hand-hold. His fingers touched on a rock. He pulled himself up and vomited, expelling water from his lungs and gut, retching and hacking until his internal organs threatened to come out as well.

He lay on a flat stone and shivered.

Daisy? Isabella? He couldn't see anyone close by. In fact, he couldn't see anything at all.

He crawled further on and curled up like a baby, shaking uncontrollably.

Cold, so cold.

'Help,' he called out, his voice squeaking like a shrew. 'Help me.'

But with Isabella gone, and Daisy gone, who was left?

He wanted to yell for his parents, for Old Man Wood, for Mrs Pye. But in this cold and inhospitable, broken place, however, he knew there was only one person who could help him.

Cain.

'*Cain!*' he yelled. 'Cain, HELP ME!'

Through the cracks in his eyes, he swore he could see a figure appearing.

'Cain,' he cried. 'You've got to save me.'

SEVENTY-FIVE

SUE ON WATCH

The boat continued to float freely, bumping into driftwood and other debris washed out into the river and then into the North Sea. Occasionally, the vessel spun and pitched from side to side, but not with the same force as earlier.

Gus wondered what they were going to eat for supper, before resisting the temptation to wolf down a chocolate bar. He squeezed past Sue to the front of the boat where, through the drizzle, he imagined he could see a spark of light way off in the distance.

When Sue woke, they tucked into a cold pork pie and shared a few pieces of chocolate. Gus stated that until they had some idea where they were they needed to conserve every single morsel. Sue complained bitterly, but Gus made it quite clear that this was non-negotiable.

By the time they had given each other a few more brain teasers, and told stories about their childhoods, it was midnight. Gus reluctantly lay down on the planks while Sue kept look-out at the front of the boat.

For a while she hummed sad melodies, her thoughts turning to Archie, Daisy and Isabella.

Had they made it? Had any of their friends survived?

Once again, Sue wondered why she—like the de Lowes—had had the premonition of the storm. Gus's comment about her being a twin with Isabella endorsed her earlier observations about the baby photograph of the two of them.

As she thought the situation through, she noted how inseparable and similar they were, in so many ways. *But best friends do that, don't they?*

And anyway, wouldn't one of the parents have said something?

She'd told Gus she would investigate further and when this was all over she'd begin by checking with the Registrars at the Town Hall. To her delight, Gus said he'd accompany her. He told her he liked that kind of thing.

An ache in her body made her wonder if Isabella had understood her mad shouting at the football, and she wondered if earlier, when the torrential rain gave way to spitting, that this 'event' was also something to do with them. A deep well of sadness filled her that she might never see them again.

At one o'clock, her jaw quivered on its own accord and her fingers reminded her of icicles. Staring out into the dark night and spat on by rain as 'The Joan of' bobbed along, her eyelids drooped, and her head fell into her chest.

Sometime later, her chattering teeth woke her up. She knew that trying to stay awake was a hopeless task.

She climbed under the canopy and instinctively lay down next to Gus; nestling up to his warm body, rearranging the dust covers, and inhaling the boyish smell of his clothes.

'Thanks, Gus,' she said sleepily while staring at his sleeping face. She let her head fall down next his and wrapped an arm around him. 'For everything.'

In no time, the gentle rocking of the boat sent her fast asleep.

SEVENTY-SIX

MRS PYE FINDS SOME RUGS

When Old Man Wood slipped out of the door, his hard hat on his head and ropes wrapped around his torso, she'd received a top-up of confidence about seeing her children again. After all, Old Man Wood had once rescued her, so why wouldn't he rescue them?

Energised, Mrs Pye set about keeping busy. She waddled round as fast as her legs would carry her, placing buckets in every grate and under every chimney flue, mopping water out of each fireplace, rolling up the hearthrugs and adjacent carpets and then emptying buckets of water down the sink.

Round and round the house she went, from the children's bedroom in the attic, to Old Man Wood's room, to the parents' room. Downstairs to the kitchen, sitting room and study, then across the courtyard through sheets of rain to her apartment. She repeated this circuit many times, drenched to the bone.

In Old Man Wood's room, she noticed five filthy rectangular rugs that sat on the wet floor, each the size of a hearthrug. She folded them up and took them to the back door, giving them a bit of shake under the wide roof trusses. As she did so, flecks of mud and dust flew in every direction.

How revolting, she thought wondering if he'd ever bothered cleaning them.

As a rule, she never ventured into the old man's room, but on this matter she'd give the old man a good talking to when he returned.

If he returned.

As the rain belted down upon the rugs, a black sludge dribbled from the fabric, like slurry. Immediately, Mrs Pye worried the rugs might get washed away, so instead, she draped them over a wooden clothes-horse under the wide porch.

Then, covering herself in a blanket, quite overwhelmed with tiredness and worry, she nodded off in the rocking chair in the kitchen, next to the warm metal range beneath the thick oak beams.

Later, she woke suddenly wondering where she was.

She yawned and for a brief moment her excitement level rocketed as she thought she could hear tiny, shrill voices like the noises of children playing in the courtyard. She looked around searching in all the obvious spots but there was nothing. Just her imagination wanting them to appear.

In the kitchen, she added a handful of kindling and two dry logs to the range then struck a match, the bright light extending into the large kitchen before dying back. A hot fire just in case they returned.

She felt the familiar stabbing pain in her shoulder.

Where were her little angels? Where were the adorable children she'd grown up loving?

Maybe they were safe at school, playing with their friends.

She'd get Archie a whole new uniform when their parents returned. She'd insist on it. No more patched up clothes for Arch.

Then she thought of Isabella and Daisy. Funny, pretty Daisy with her wavy hair and red cheeks, her keen eyes and her warm smile.

Why, they all had warm smiles, she thought, as a tear rolled down her cheek.

Imagine being stuck out in that tempest all alone. The mere thought made her tremble.

She pulled her woollen blanket tight as she noticed the flames taking.

What would happen to her if no one returned?

SEVENTY-SEVEN

OLD MAN WOOD FINDS A BODY

At first glance, as Old Man Wood hurried towards the body, he could have sworn it was Archie's friend, the one who was always so deeply unpleasant to the girls, the boy Archie liked to go fishing with.

As he approached, Old Man Wood remembered the name. *Kemp.* That was it. The large boy with thick ginger hair, like dear Mrs Pye.

He wondered if the child was alive and just before he made to check, his attention was taken away by a strange groaning noise, followed by a high-pitched screech coming from the flood waters. Old Man Wood gazed over the water, squinting, wondering who, or what, it might be.

When his focus returned to the boy in front of him, he looked down upon the curled up shivering figure of Archie.

Old Man Wood rubbed his chin. Was he seeing things?

Kneeling down, the old man's heart sank. Archie's mouth foamed, and his eyes flickered in different directions. His body was battered and torn.

Then, to his surprise, Archie called out a name, 'Cain!' Then he said it again, his voice urgent, but slurring. 'Cain, Cain,' over and over, as if he was delirious.

Who on earth was Cain? Old Man Wood wondered. And why did this name strike a chord deep within him that made his hairs prickle?

Old Man Wood searched his memory. That name, Cain, seemed to dredge up a confusing mix of love and anger, hope and despair.

Later, Old Man Wood sat on the edge of the pit and studied the three children who lay sleeping in the strange soft substance in the base of the pit. The sound of their gentle breathing was the sweetest music he had ever heard.

He reflected on his fortune; the curious bed panels and the timely rediscovery of his Resplendix Mix potion.

Old Man Wood shook his head and whistled a note of relief. How had they survived the torrential rain, lightning, mud-slides and cold? How, in all the apples in the world, were they alive?

He lowered himself down and examined them in more detail. The sheer volume of bruises and cuts on their bodies was remarkable. Daisy's legs were black and blue, criss-crossed with cuts. Some of these were deep and sharp, like punctures. Other lacerations were longer, where she must have been raked by rocks and thorns. Her fingernails were black, and on her fingers entire nails had become detached leaving red, raw skin. Her shoes had gone and her feet looked as though they had been 'worked on' by a garden strimmer. Her tracksuit bottoms were tattered, and one of her football socks was attached by threads which flapped against her raw shin.

Old Man Wood wondered if he should give her some more Resplendix Mix. But this was powerful stuff; and powerful potions, he suspected, needed careful portioning.

His attention moved to Archie. Like Daisy, the boy had been battered, beaten, and pulped to within a millimetre of death. But there was one significant alteration to his appearance; Archie's hair, though softer than when he'd found him, the folli-cles were gelled together, hard and spiky like brushed strands of metal glued together. He remembered that when he'd seen him on the panels he'd presumed Archie had put on a strange-looking hat.

He inspected Archie's hands, which, like Daisy's bore terrible lacerations and bruises. He suspected a broken finger or two by the way his digits were angled. His head and body was marked with blows, as if he'd been sprayed by a rock gun. Some of his cuts seeped, others had already congealed.

Most extraordinary of all, and perhaps even odder than Archie's hair, were Isabella's hands. The markings on her palms looked symmetrical, as if they had been painted on using a circular template and black paint.

Now that he looked carefully, the flesh inside had been burnt through, as though punctured by a red-hot poker. He could see right through them as though they'd been drilled through.

Old Man Wood sucked in a deep breath and, shaking his head, he started to consider how he would get them home. He wouldn't attempt anything now, not while they needed to sleep. And they'd be safe enough where they were for a while.

In the fresh light of morning, he'd address their wounds and give them another drop of his healing mix, but sleep was their best method of recovery while the potion set to work.

Looking about, he noticed higher ledges; berths he could pop the children on if the waters continued to rise further.

He climbed out of the pit and headed towards the cave entrance, grateful for the moonlight reflecting off the water just below the stone ledge in front of him.

He pulled himself up onto a higher rock, stretched his arms out, and lay back, trying to envisage how far the water must extend. Two hundred, three hundred metres, or perhaps even a mile towards the Dales? It could be further.

And everything in its path destroyed in the space of a few hours.

SEVENTY-EIGHT

SUE WAKES

'The Joan of' felt, to Gus, as if it were climbing up a small hill before skidding down the other side. And the process repeated the rising and falling sensations. Up and down. Up and down.

For a second, Gus dreamt he might be at a funfair. He yawned, and found himself looking into Sue's sleeping face.

What an utterly beautiful way to wake up.

Then he wondered what his breath must be like. Probably gross. *Heck.*

Trying not to disturb her, he shuffled to the end of the boat and pushed his head out of the canopy.

He yawned, closed his eyes, stretched out his arms, and inhaled a lungful of fresh air.

He opened one eye, swiftly followed by the other.

After a few seconds, he whistled.

Okay, interesting.

He could hear Sue stirring.

'Morning, first mate,' he quipped, dipping his head under the canopy.

'Oh! Morning, Gus,' she said, rubbing the sleep out of her eyes. 'Still afloat, still alive?'

'Yep, think so,' he said. 'How was lookout?'

She cringed. 'Thought you needed company. And bodily warmth is very important,' she said, a flicker of naughtiness in the corner of her lips. 'Everything all right out there. Seen any landmarks?'

He ducked inside and sat down. 'Well, it's fine and dandy-ish.'

'Dandy-ish,' she repeated. 'Then I take it you have no idea where we are?'

'Ab-so-lute-ly none,' he said, smiling. 'Take a look for yourself.'

'What's for breakfast?' she yawned, as she crept down to the other end. 'I'm starving.'

She put her head out.

Gus waited, his expectation of a verbal explosion reasonably high.

'Oh!' she said, popping her back down. Her eyes were wide open.

'Oh?' Gus said. 'Is that it?'

'Yes,' she replied, curtly. 'Oh!'

Gus smiled his biggest smile to date. 'We've drifted possibly miles out to sea with no way of knowing where on earth we are and all you can say is "Oh".'

'Yes,' Sue began, her face pale. 'Oh.'

She took a deep breath. 'Right, Gus. Now the thing is, I've never sworn at anything or anyone before in my life. But I've heard my mum do it quite a bit and from looking out there after all we've been through, I think it's the perfect time to finally give it a proper go.'

Gus looked confused. 'Oh?' he said.

'You see, every time she properly swears, she actually begins it with "Oh".'

Gus raised his bushy eyebrows. 'Really?'

And with that, Sue slipped out from under the canopy, took

a deep breath and screamed over the wide expanse of sea at the top of her voice:

'Oh — $*%@!' &^%*W$!'

SEVENTY-NINE

KEMP'S PAIN

Kemp groaned in agony.

He'd had a chance to say no, and he blew it.

For a brief moment, he'd been peeled out of their union and found himself lying naked on the ledge and set upon by rain that pummelled his skin. What a feeling to feel his own skin again.

In front of him lay Archie, battered and broken, his body marked by cuts and bruises, his head bloodied. His body motionless, pale, and deathly.

He'd looked at Archie's strange hair and managed a wry smile. A classic bad hair moment only Archie could pull-off. Thinking of hair, he wasn't sure that he had any left. All singed. Burnt down to his scalp—as bald as a baby.

Cain had tried to force Archie to go with him but Archie was too far gone to make a choice willingly, and Cain knew it. Cain had miscalculated badly.

And then the old man had appeared.

Kemp had given himself back to Cain freely. At the time it didn't feel as if he had an option. But now, he regretted it. He should have refused. If he had the chance again, he'd rather subject himself to the violence of the tempest than the burning hell he was now trapped within.

Cain burned him badly after he went back.

And now, here he was, living in the darkness of a body with no food, no water, and no sleep. Where Cain's energy fried his flesh like hot oil. Kemp imagined it had been less than one whole day. But even now he wondered how long he could keep going.

It was like being trapped in space, he thought, *with no one there to hear his cries.*

EIGHTY

IN THE PIT

Old Man Wood slept fitfully. His mind raced from Archie's shouts about Cain, to the boy with the matted ginger hair, to the terrible injuries of the children. Then his dream flashed to the strange bed panels, his old cellar, the pictures on the cave walls, and scoring goals.

A fizzing, gurgling noise woke him.

Had he been asleep for hours?

The moon had slipped behind a high cloud and rain was falling as a light spray. The old man jumped down, his feet splashing into water over his ankles.

His heart missed a beat. *Water?*

Apples alive! The children!

He sloshed round to the entrance and heard a gurgling sound coming from a strange, billowing steamy cloud.

Cautiously, he peered in, his eyes wide.

Inside, the cave floor was dry, and water flowed along a neat, straight channel that he presumed led directly into the pit.

Old Man Wood's pulse raced and, crouching down, he followed the channel through the thick mist. As he crept closer, the colour of the water changed from blue to pink and he could tell it was gently bubbling. He put his damaged hand in. The water tingled on his cut and a warm buzz ran up his arm.

He leant over the edge of the pit, his heart thumping. Were the children alive?

He pulled his hand out and inspected it: the wound was healing in front of his eyes.

Then he heard a voice. Or was it laughter?

'Old Man Wood, what are you doing?' Daisy said, her face appearing like a ghost in front of him briefly before sinking back into the steam.

Old Man Wood reeled.

Daisy giggled. 'Hey, why don't you get in?'

Old Man Wood felt himself choking up. 'Goodness me!' he cried. 'Daisy! Is that you? Is that really you? I can't see you.'

'Yeah, it's me all right. Come on in. It's gorgeous and warm and fantastic,' she replied. 'And it smells delicious, like an ace blend of lavender, pine needles and lemon.'

'But… are you all in there?'

'Yes! And we're absolutely fine,' she said. 'Come on in—see for yourself.'

Old Man Wood was confused. 'Are ALL of you fine, I mean Isabella and Archie?'

Old Man Wood heard a splashing noise. Archie's head popped out. 'Yeah. Not bad,' he said.

'Apples almighty! It IS you.'

Archie smiled. 'Well, it's good to see you too. How long have you been here?'

'Your head?' Old Man Wood exclaimed.

'Yeah, I know. I think it was a lightning bolt.' He patted his hard hair before drifting back into the steamy water.

Old Man Wood didn't know what to think. Perhaps he was dreaming. 'Isabella?' he called out.

'Uh-huh,' she responded lazily.

Old Man Wood's heart leapt for joy. It was impossible, a miracle. 'Right then, you lot. Watch out, I'm coming in.'

He could hear them laughing.

'There's bags of room,' Daisy said. 'Though watch yourself. Archie might puncture you with his hairdo.'

Old Man Wood removed his coat, socks, and boots, and dipped his foot in the water. Then, ever so slowly, he lowered himself into the hot pool.

The water, like a winning combination of champagne and cream, bubbled up and sparkled around him. He closed his eyes and let himself drift under. Almost immediately, he felt the bubbles caress his aches and pains, targeting each one like mini lasers.

When he resurfaced and opened his eyes, the children were beaming at him.

Old Man Wood laughed out loud. 'You did it! You made it! How in apples' name...? Are you better, truly recovered?'

The twins floated over and hugged him.

Old Man Wood inspected Archie, looking for the cuts and bruises on his head, hands, and ankles. He did the same with Daisy, but the procedure was quick and easy as their skin was smooth and clear, as though the battle through the storm had never happened.

'I can't believe it. I simply can't believe it,' Old Man Wood repeated. 'I thought you were, you know, not alive, you twins! Battered to bits you were, and now look at you...'

Old Man Wood listened attentively to their stories, noting that each one had survived an almost direct strike from a lightning bolt.

But there was an awkwardness in Archie's face, the same expression he'd seen when he'd handed over the strange overcoat? And he was keen to find out more about "Cain" that Archie had called out for?

'You lot must be starving,' he said.

As one they nodded back.

'I took the liberty of bringing you something special. Afterwards, it'd be a good idea to grab some rest. After all, we've still got to find a way out of here.'

'Mmm. A chocolate brownie,' Archie began, 'with a spoonful of ice cream!'

'Or a plate full of Peking duck pancakes with plum sauce, cucumber, and spring onions,' Daisy said.

'Or a huge slice of banoffee pie, with thick cream,' Isabella added, licking her lips.

Old Man Wood got out of the pool and made his way over to his coat.

'Now, before you start complaining,' he said, 'these are my special ones, so make sure you eat the whole thing, understand? Pips and all. They'll fill you right up. Trust me. I don't know how they do it, but they will.'

He tossed an apple at each one, and ravenously the children bit in. They were rewarded with tastes of golden syrup, honey, apple pie, and sweet raspberries.

Before long, the children pulled themselves out of the pit. Their bodies, now devoid of cuts and bruises, dried in the warm air. Old Man Wood pointed them towards the four protruding shelves, like stone benches, built into the walls high above the floor.

Daisy climbed up into the one nearest her and wearily tested it, scrunching her hand in the soft velvety texture, before she lay down.

'This is lovely,' she purred as she sank into it. 'Like amazing memory foam, really comfy...'

Before long, soft snores filled the void above.

The others followed behind, and they too experienced the extraordinary sensation of the warm silky powder, softer than feathers, moulding perfectly around their tired bodies.

EIGHTY-ONE

WAS ANYONE LEFT?

From his bunk high up on the cave wall, Archie peered through bleary eyes through the cave entrance at the night sky above the Vale of York. Rippling waves caught flecks of light that flickered over the moving floodwaters which had already risen higher than the floor of the cave.

A moonbeam radiated soft light over the walls, highlighting lines of curious pictures sketched all around. He smiled. Strange how there was so much beauty and yet so much destruction in the world.

The thought that someone had been here long ago gave him a fresh sense of comfort.

He wondered about Kemp and the ghost. His memory was just a blur, an outline, but he couldn't work out whether Kemp had sent him on his way to save him, or if he'd done it to deliberately to take his place at Cain's side?

In any case, they'd passed the first test. And he remembered how Cain had told him they didn't have a chance. His lips turned up at the thought.

His dreams had been right all along. And wasn't it funny how Sue had also known, and tried to tell them on the football pitch?

But tell them what, exactly? Something about finding clues, something about Eden Cottage?

And what about the visions in his dreams about the Ancient Woman and her murder that he'd seen over and over again?

Perhaps Cain was right about her. Perhaps saving her was the answer to all his woes?

Isabella, he thought, as he breathed in deeply, must have known too. Her frantic efforts to persuade Solomon to abandon the game now looked like sage advice. What would Solomon make of them now... if he was still alive?

And poor Mrs Pye, sitting at home worrying. He could imagine her pacing around, mumbling to herself. Tears running down her cheeks.

And what of their friends? Had they made it? Would there be anyone left? Probably not—unless they'd escaped into the tower at Upsall.

There was nothing he could do about it now. When they discovered a way out of the cave and climbed up through the forest and back home to Eden Cottage, then they might find out.

He touched his hard hair and wondered if they'd been blessed. But strange—if this was the case—how it was them, of all people.

He yawned, his mouth stretching to its widest point. And what of that strange spidery-creature he'd seen over Daisy? Was that also a part of this adventure?

Unwittingly, his eyes closed.

So long as he didn't get any more murderous nightmares... Cain said they'd end. Perhaps Cain could be trusted... and what if he really did have the courage of a horse and the strength of a lion...?

The mists of tiredness swept over every part of his tired body.

He could think no more.

In moments, the Heirs of Eden and Old Man Wood were all fast asleep.

Read Book Two, Spider Web Powder.

YOUR HELP MATTERS...

Dear reader,

Your review would massively help me in my quest to find new readers.

Please spare a moment to give POWER AND FURY your REVIEW from the online version of the store where you found it.

I'm working on several new projects right now. Your words will spur me on to finish my words in the series.

In advance, thank you.
Best wishes,

James

AUDIOBOOKS

Eden Chronicles books are being brought to life by award-nominated voice artist Rory Barnett.

Rory's voices are amazing… check out his extraordinary range by grabbing your copy today.

The Power and The Fury and Spider Web Powder are available at most audio-digital outlets:

The Power and The Fury — audiobook

Spider Web Powder—audiobook

ABOUT THE AUTHOR

Restless after schooling, James traveled and experienced plenty of adventures. He has been shot at, scaled Pyramids, climbed mountains, been through earthquakes, police detained and even swum with beavers.

James specialized in getting lost quite a bit, for example; in the Canadian wilderness in bear season, as well as experiencing hypothermia, dysentery, muggings, altitude sickness, thefts, a broken neck, desert breakdowns, etc.

Inadvertently these experiences set James to tackle a big writing journey. (If only he'd gone into real adventuring like old school-friend, Bear…)

In the 1990s James worked as a journalist for the financial pages of the Yorkshire Post, scooping the infamous Gerald Ratner; 'Crap' story.

James designed and built gardens for several years in London before upping sticks to a small village between the Dales and the Moors of North Yorkshire.

The inspirational landscape of bleak hills, old monasteries, and expansive views were an ideal choice for the setting of the Eden Chronicles series. James commenced writing the series in 2007.

Following a brief and rather embarrassing appearance on ITV's,"Honeymoons from Hell" TV show (fleeing a psychotic African safari operator), James became an extremely minor celebrity. Fortunately, this happened pre-YouTube!

As a youth, James had his sights on playing the game of

cricket for England, but a long list of injuries and a genuine lack of talent forced the issue. However, a notable sporting triumph in 2013 saw James row the English Channel and the 21 tidal miles of the River Thames in aid of MND and Breakthrough Breast cancer.

James is a stay-at-home-Dad, a cub-scout leader and he retains his childhood passion for making dens, pitching fires, and tall stories.

james@jericopress.com

facebook.com/JamesErithAuthor

twitter.com/jameserith

instagram.com/edenchronicles

goodreads.com/jameserith

pinterest.com/jameserith

amazon.com/author/jameserith

ALSO BY JAMES ERITH

Join my Author list to find out what's coming up…

EDEN CHRONICLES series:

TRUTH—Eden Chronicles Prequel—A novella. (ISBN: 978-1910134313)

Power & Fury—Eden Chronicles, Book One (ISBN: 978-1-910134-04-7) The Power and The Fury, narrated by Rory Barnett, is now available in audiobook.

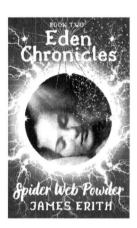

Spider Web Powder—Eden Chronicles, Book Two (ISBN: 978-1-910134-10-8) (Now available on Audiobook)

Blabisterberry Jelly—Eden Chronicles, Book Three
(ISBN: 978-1-910134-11-5)

The Dragon's Game—Eden Chronicles, Book Four
(ISBN: 978-1910134245)

Eyes of Cain—Eden Chronicles, Book Five (ISBN: 978-1910134245)

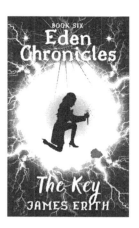

The Key—Eden Chronicles, Book Six (ISBN: 978-1-910134-42-9)

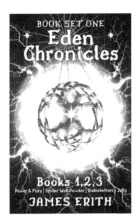

Eden Chronicles Books Set—Books 1, 2 3 (ISBN: 978-1-910134-16-0)

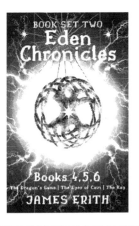

Eden Chronicles Book Set 2—Books 4, 5, 6 (ISBN: 978-1-910134-32-0)

TIME STAMP 2084

Set in 2084, and the world is a very different place; artificial intelligence runs everything; life happens through visual and sensual reality and the world is sanitised, and safe...

But has it gone too far? Are we no longer human?

Have we lost our soul?

When Virtual Reality holiday modeller, Bert Chalmers, discovers the ominous truth of their situation, he must travel back in time to halt the pandemics and the subsequent empowerment of artificial intelligence of the 2020's.

But he's not travelling back to the beginnings of the internet age as he thinks. He's off to the beginning of mass communication...

Welcome to 1840 and the dawn of the Penny Post.

But how will Bert, and his companion, Tor, find a way of immunising the population at the dawn of the Industrial Revolution?

Interested? Find out more.

Go to www.jameserith.com and find the Time Stamp header.

Due for release early-mid 2021.

CONTACT ME

There's a pile of good stuff about Eden Chronicles on my website and please sign up to my author newsletter for updates, observations and freebies.

jameserith.com

..and drop by my Author Facebook page:
James Erith Author - Give it a like,
and follow me on Bookbub.

That would be ace.

Thanks for reading my stories. I look forward to meeting you out there…

James xxx

Printed in Great Britain
by Amazon